SALT BLUE

To Terry & Janet,
love Gill xxx

SALT BLUE

by

Gillian Morgan

HONNO MODERN FICTION

First published by Honno in 2010
'Ailsa Craig',Heol y Cawl, Dinas Powys,
South Glamorgan, Wales, CF64 4AH.
1 2 3 4 5 6 7 8 9 10

The Author would like to stress that this is a work of fiction
and no resemblance to any actual individual or institution
is intended or implied.

A catalogue record for this book is available from
the British Library.

Published with the financial support of the
Welsh Books Council.

ISBN 978-1906784-157
Cover photograph © Tyler Stalman
Cover design: ShedMedia
Text design: Jenks Design
Printed in Wales by Gomer Press

For my mother, Emma and Kate, my husband
and my grandchildren, with my heart and my
soul, with my love and my passion.

Thank you to Honno editor Caroline Oakley
for her advice and guidance.

Colour speaks to the soul in a thousand different ways

Oscar Wilde

SALT BLUE

Chapter One

The morning light is as clean and blank as a frost-bleached linen sheet. Rinsing my cup under the tap I linger over the tingling sting of hot water on my fingers. I smile at my reflection in the fretwork mirror above the sink and say 'Hello', a tip I read in *Woman's Own* magazine. The article was about receiving back what you give out, I think.

When asked, I call myself an 'Accounts Manager'. I file this liberality with the truth, under the heading 'Creative Accounting'. Viewed another way, it is reframing the picture. Illusion I understand, reality requires effort. Actually, I am an accounts clerk for 'Bertie B. Perkins, Timber Merchants, Stanton and Gosford'.

In celebration of the weekend I have chosen an angora cardigan, which I knitted myself, in a sparkling concoction of carmine pink and brandy wine. The colours shimmer, compelling as a pulse of energy. Wearing it back to front gives me 'twice the looks and double the wear', as advised by *Woman and Home*'s fashion editor.

Other ideas for 'ringing the changes' featured a beret and a bunch of woollen pompoms. Fastened with a tiny golden safety pin, this is the way to start the week with a flourish. ('Take care to conceal the pin inside the beret,' the fashion editor cautioned.) Tartan rosettes, velvet bows, a Scottie dog brooch and a bunch of felt flowers in 'glorious' spring colours would brighten both the beret and the day.

I might have knitted a cap to match my cardigan if I had not promised Betsi Sylvester a gift for this morning's raffle at the 'Come and Buy'. I finished the bedjacket last night, half an hour past midnight.

The thirty-six-inch bust size used ten ounces of Emu three-ply Baby Wool in sugar pink. I saw the pattern in *Pretty Gift Knitting* – 20 super money-saving designs – *Women's Illustrated* gift booklet number two, which was free. The lace pattern was intricate and, even for a fast knitter like myself, it took a weekend plus five evenings to complete. Without the crochet shell trimming, which was not included in the pattern, I would have been quicker but I like adding my signature, which is the surprise element. I wrapped the jacket in a cocoon of tissue paper and tied it with silk ribbons. Deciding it was pretty enough for a bride to wear on her honeymoon night, I tucked a velvet pansy into the bow for good luck.

Included in the pattern book was a striped tea cosy, using pretty oddments (scraps of mismatched old wool), a 'cosy hot-water bottle cover' and a pair of 'slipper sox'. The socks needed a pair of leather soles to complete them, which could be 'purchased for only seven and sixpence' (the same price as a pair of slippers in the window of 'Oliver Evans, Boot Shop').

As I pondered the economics of making the slippers, I came across an article on psychology, arguing that the process is more important than the end result. Viewed this way, knitting should be regarded as a means of enjoyment rather than an economical activity. I like the feel of wool playing through my fingers, plastic steel or bamboo needles in my hands, but if I am dissatisfied with the end result I scrap it, however much I enjoyed making it.

One of my other patterns has instructions for a 'winter Parisian coat for a smart dog', (three ounces of double knitting wool to tone or contrast with the colour of the dog's own coat, plus one pair number seven Aero knitting needles for the medium size) but there is no one in this town I can think of right now who owns a poodle.

2

My new rubber Playtex roll-on creeps up my thighs again, so I yank it down. It took a whole tin of talcum powder to dust my stomach and hips before I had any chance of wriggling into it. Mike Price, who ran a fish stall in the market and wore a beret and who is now the area rep for Yardley's Lavender and wears a suit (minus the beret), plus slip-on shoes, gave me a free sample of talc, enabling me to be lavish. *'Mike Price'*, my mind pauses to snarl over the name.

A few weeks after Mike had given me the sample I saw him parking a flashy blue 'Mayfair' saloon car outside the town hall.

'Nice car,' I called, not meaning to stop.

'Can I give you a lift somewhere?'

'No thanks. I'm nearly home now.'

'I'll take you for a spin at the weekend then. We could go to Tafarn Y Sinc or anywhere you like. You say. How's about it?'

I shook my head. Mike did not interest me, new car or not. 'Look.' He'd locked the car and was standing beside me now. 'You and I know each other and I was thinking,' (his voice was barely audible) 'I was thinking, like, I am clean and you are clean and we could, you know,' and he nudged my shoulder and even if I had not heard what he'd said, I would have understood the nudge. I forced myself to look at his face, flushed and almost triumphant. If I had been a good spitter, he would have had a gobbet straight in his left eye. Swift as a dervish, I spun around on my heels, my footsteps pulsating in my ears, like the tattoo from a drumbeat. I could still hear Mike's petulant voice, 'No need to be hoity-toity with me.'

Thankfully, apart from us, the street was empty, the town silent as a glittery morning on a Christmas card.

That was a while ago. Seeing the empty tin of talcum powder now, I aim it at the waste-paper basket. If Mike were here, I might ram it down his throat but the thought vanishes and I think of Connor. The smell of talcum powder gives way to diesel oil and tractor tyres and I feel better immediately.

There's a brooch, china roses, blue forget-me-nots, devilish-sharp, lime-green leaves, that might look good with this cardigan, but if I see Connor and his lips touch mine, ever so lightly, the brooch might scratch his chin, so I leave it in the box.

A quick glance at the back of my legs and the seams appear straight from this angle. I don't always remember to check them, but my mother, Salli, is very fussy about stocking seams. She says the Queen always chooses seams and stockings without seams are 'common'. Mum has decided views on most things and people sometimes say, 'I don't quite remember what she said, but didn't she say it beautifully?'

All that's left to do now is to slip into the red mohair coat, fasten the silk-ribbon buttons and I'm ready to face a cold February morning.

Chapter Two

A sigh eases from the house as I close the heavy front door behind me. My aunt, Oona, with whom I live, is the district nurse in Stanton and Gosford and the local midwife. At six o'clock this morning the telephone rang. Elvira Jones, of 'Pen-y-Bont', a farm about two miles from here, was in labour. After a brief conversation, Oona took the stairs two at a time and was through the front door faster than a fireball.

'The baby's already a week overdue, but once labour starts it will probably be rapid because it's her third baby and she's young,' Oona had mentioned last night.

Oona would probably have liked me to be a nurse like her, but never quite said so. As a child I had a tendency to fussiness, examining my food closely before eating it, always looking for caterpillars in the lettuce leaves, slugs in the cabbage and this fastidiousness reappeared in ideas I had about nursing. My overwhelming fear would have been to give a patient the wrong dose of medicine.

To my mind nursing is a vocation, a burning desire, like the need to be a missionary in Africa or a beautician like Miss Bishop who has a beauty salon in her front parlour, but my needs are different. I could have handled the babies' nappies, emptied bedpans or given enemas to mothers in labour, but it was Carol Bailey's sister, Jeannine, who helped me to make my mind up.

Carol and I were fifteen the year Jeannine qualified as a State Registered Nurse. In Jeannine's bedroom, Carol was twirling around in an impressive nursing cape while I was admiring the sterling-silver buckles on her belt.

'You're thinking of nursing?' enquired Jeannine.

'I'm not really sure,' I replied.

'Your aunt is a midwife, isn't she? I might train in midwifery later on.'

Suddenly Mrs Bailey appeared at the door with a tray of biscuits.

'Would make a nice change from what she has to do.'

Carol's mother had the knack of interrupting every conversation Carol and I had in that house. Personal space was an alien concept to her.

'Bed baths,' she whispered theatrically, her body inclined at an acute angle, leaning towards me as she edged the tray onto the dressing table. 'For men.'

At this, Jeannine's head jerked abruptly and she interjected, 'That's just one of my jobs, Mum, and I always wear rubber gloves for hygienic purposes, so I never have to actually touch anything.'

Anything? The word 'anything' turned around in my mind, acquiring different layers of meaning with each revolution, but I said nothing, not wishing to detract from the SRN qualification.

'She takes a little hammer with her.' Mrs Bailey was nodding enthusiastically.

Three pairs of eyes locking onto my face felt uncomfortable.

'Do you know why?' queried Carol.

'To test knee-jerk reactions?' I answered swiftly. That cup of coffee I drank earlier must have gone straight to my brain. If Mrs Bailey's face had not twisted into a sort of spasm, I would have thought my assumption correct. Carol was looking at me quizzically but Jeannine seemed uncomfortable.

'Thick as broom handles some of them,' nodded Mrs Bailey, pausing for effect and pulling her middle finger and thumb together to create a big circle.

'She has to give a really sharp tap to get them down again.'

'Mother!' Jeannine's face was redder than a roasted beetroot but her mother did not seem to have noticed. In the manner of a costermonger Mrs Bailey called raucously, 'Small, medium or large.'

'Mother!' There was a murderous glint in Jeannine's eyes, but it was too late. Gasping and choking noises started gurgling in Mrs Bailey's throat which, coming from anyone else, would have sounded like a gasp for breath. As Mrs Bailey turned away I saw her dabbing tears of laughter from her eyes. She laughed so much, I thought she was going to collapse and Jeannine would have to demonstrate her resuscitation skills.

Looking like she'd swallowed a whole hornets' nest, Jeannine advanced on her mother and, without more ado, grasped her elbow and steered her out through the door.

'Mother, Stella has not come to hear this. She is considering a nursing career.'

But Jeannine was wrong, SRN or not. I was never to be a nurse now. Never. Ever.

'Yes, all right, I'll go, but let me just say this.' Mrs Bailey stopped, framed in the doorway, her reddish hair wisping around her face, her sparkling grey eyes turned in my direction.

'I never had that problem with their father, the reverse, in fact.'

She peered over Jeannine's shoulder at me.

'He had a little problem, my Harold, but I knew the remedy. There was no need for fancy pills and spending money on swanky consultants. No, I just tickled him up with my feather duster.'

Everyone apart from Mrs Bailey froze. The air was taut with tension, so tight you could have trotted a mouse on it. Jeannine was the first to stir and I still admire the way she manoeuvred her mother out onto the landing and down the narrow stairs of the old house and, as they disappeared, we could hear Mrs Bailey vainly protesting, 'I was only having a little laugh, you know.'

Carol looked uncomfortable but then, like the sound of ice crackling in a frozen pond, we both burst out laughing. Carol, who was sitting on the windowsill, slipped and banged her bottom, hard, on the floor.

'You OK?'

She nodded and we both laughed again, this time less hysterically but in an 'It's OK, don't worry,' way.

Downstairs, Mrs Bailey was singing 'I'll be With You in Apple Blossom Time'.

Carol whispered, 'Did you notice Jeannine's use of the term "Mother"? It's always been "Mammie", but now that she's an SRN she's a lot grander.'

After a while Jeannine returned.

'What's got into her since I've been away, Carol?'

'I think she had a sherry earlier. I saw a sticky mark on the sideboard where she keeps it and I could smell it.'

'Must have drunk a tumbler the way she behaved. Now,' and Jeannine took command of the situation again, 'I'm sorry about that but, with Dad's death she's gone a bit–' and, as she was searching for the right word, Carol obliged with 'cranky'.

Jeannine sighed. 'Grief, neuroticism, repressed sexual desires, all tumbling together.'

Carol and I knew Jeannine's aim was to show that now she was a nurse her understanding of life was vast. Behind her sister's back, Carol put one finger to the side of her head and made a screwing gesture.

'Shall we go to the Trocadero, Stell? There's a new jukebox, we could do a bit of Elvis the Pelvis,' and she wiggled her hips.

Jeannine, ignoring Carol and probably thinking she had a responsibility towards me and the nursing profession, had a few final words to say.

'Nursing can be varied and there are different branches, such as gynaecology.'

I nodded in what I hoped was a grateful way, but Carol got us out of there fast.

'Yeah, all right, Jeannine. Stella will think about nursing but we're off to the "Troc" now.'

Chapter Three

Adjoining the side of our house is a shop with a blistered sign, like a medieval roadside shrine, proclaiming W.H. Sivell, Produce Merchant. In a moment of ancestor worship, I nod to it as I pass. William Halford Sivell was my grandfather and he died a month before I was born. Apart from the blood connection, I am close to him because, in numerology, his name has the number six, like mine, the animal lover's number.

Names appear to have an inordinate importance in my family. Dadda had a saying: 'Sivell by name, civil by nature,' which he repeated like a bon mot.

Oona and Mum were chatting once and my aunt said the name you are born with is a truer reflection of your personality than the one you acquire on marriage. Mum laughed. 'I've been a Sivell, a Randall and now I'm a Marsden. Perhaps I have a multi-faceted personality.'

'Why was I called Stella?' I wonder.

Mum and my aunt look at me, almost in surprise, before Mum explains, 'Because the sky was full of stars the night you were born but you were the brightest star I'd ever seen.'

'We'll have one more log before we go to bed,' Oona smiles contentedly, pushing the wood right to the back of the fire so that the sparks race up the chimney into the cold air outside, losing themselves in the darkness.

I loved those times, the three of us together, just as it had been when I was little.

I'm passing the field where Dadda kept Molly the black pony now.

Brambles scribble away whole chunks of the sky but there is a clear path leading to the stable where Oona garages her green Morris Minor.

As the community hall comes into sight my heart skips a beat. Dewdrops pepper the frosty clumps of snowdrops decorating the verge but it's Connor's battered brown van with the rusty mudguard and the string tying the back doors together that puts a spring in my steps.

Connor and his mother run a smallholding in the Cwm, where chickens peck in the field that runs down to the stream. Although Connor and I have been seeing each other for only a few weeks, I heard Oona say on the phone to Mum the other night, 'I know what you mean. She shouldn't marry the first man she sets eyes on.'

It didn't take an Einstein to know who they were talking about. I was annoyed because marriage hadn't entered my head and I didn't know if we were in love even. What is the test? On the radio a psychologist said that thinking too much can be a substitute for feeling, so I stopped thinking. I still couldn't work out whether we loved each other though.

Through the corrugated tin walls of the community hall, Betsi's voice cuts through the sharp brightness of the morning.

'Put the long table by the wall, Con. And can you salt the path outside? Can't have anyone falling.'

Apart from being Connor's aunt, Betsi is the caretaker of the community hall and is holding a coffee morning to raise money for repairs. As I enter Betsi sees me from somewhere down a dark corridor and waves. Dressed in a navy jersey cardigan and matching skirt, with a red stripe around the hem, she presents a smart image.

The suit has come from Suzi Margaroli's shop. Miss Margaroli dresses her impossibly proportioned plaster mannequin in a different outfit each week. Also in the window, an artificial branch rests horizontally across the floor and it sprouts twists of pink-and-white

11

cherry blossom and acid-green silken leaves in springtime. On the branch, a scarf and strings of pearls are artfully twisted, and sheer stockings, kid gloves and a white handbag, similar to the ones the Queen and Princess Margaret carry, are displayed.

Miss Margaroli sells a complete look, dictating fashion in Stanton, which infuriates Mum, who says people should put their own look together. Each week Betsi pays a pound into an account she has in Suzi's shop and, as a privileged customer, receives an invitation to view the new season's styles. A flute of champagne ensures a jolly evening and explains why Betsi has far more clothes than she needs.

Everyone knows each other's business in Stanton, and hears things they are not meant to, but people are very open here so there are no secrets.

'Glad you could make it, Stella,' smiles Betsi. 'I've had plenty of help this morning. Help of the right kind. Connor's here.' This is said with a smile, because she knows we are seeing each other.

And then Connor appears in a jersey so tattered it might have been dried on a thorn bush, which it probably has.

His thick hair, dark on a dull day but a shade of silvery pewter when a spark of sunlight ignites it, like now, has probably not seen a comb all week. He winks at me, his face still tanned from last summer's sun, and my heart pings.

'Did you find the salt?' queries Betsi.

'I've got it and I'm going right away. First things first, though,' and he comes over to give me a bear hug.

'Are you staying?' I ask hopefully.

'He better had. We need him.' Betsi's voice is firm.

When Connor has gone, I turn to Betsi.

'I've brought the jacket. Where's the table for raffle prizes?'

'I knew I could rely on you. Ooh, you've packed it beautifully. It seems a shame to open it; still, we'll have to display it with the other prizes.'

As we're talking two women appear at the entrance, large and misshapen, like models for a Picasso painting. A wobbly outline of pale, oyster-coloured light filters around them, throwing their silhouettes into deep relief.

In a flurry of animation, Betsi rushes to hug them, her stocking suspenders tracing a faint outline through her skirt.

'Come on in,' she welcomes them and, a little hesitantly, they do. The woman, dressed in a knobbly tweed coat, appears to be in her late forties, and the girl is perhaps fifteen or sixteen.

Although there is something awkward about the woman's demeanour, the girl has a youthful assurance. A waterfall of golden hair frames her face and her complexion, pale except for her cheeks, is warmed to a bright shade of toothpaste pink by the cold morning air.

'Stella, this is Mrs Gibbons and Hillary.'

I pull out chairs. Hillary's whispered 'thank you', is accompanied by a smile, while her mother's 'nice to meet you', does not sound as though it is really meant.

'Stella has been knitting for the raffle. Show us what you've made, Stell.'

I hold the bedjacket up, letting the light filter through.

'Ooh, delicate as paper lace,' declares Betsi.

Mrs Gibbons sits impassively, but Hillary leans forward, animated.

'Do you like it, Hillary?' Betsi takes the jacket from me and passes it to Hillary.

'It's beautiful. It looks really complicated. It must have taken you ages to knit?'

'Anyone can do it,' I say, truthfully. 'All I did was to follow a pattern, but I had to concentrate all the time. The stitches were easy. Plain, purl, slip stitch and increase and decrease here and there.'

Hillary smoothes the shell trimming with her fingertips. 'Is this a crochet trim on the edge?'

13

'Yes, but it's not necessary. You can leave it out.'

'I'd love to make one.' Hillary's voice is wistful.

'I'll lend you the pattern.'

'I can't knit.'

'I'll teach you.'

I look appealingly at Mrs Gibbons, willing her to say something. When she does it is not what I want to hear.

'Anything we need we buy.' Her voice is clipped and she appears to address my left shoulder.

Betsi coughs, a dry rasp; my throat feels tight and I know we are sharing the same discomfort. Then a spark of inspiration arrives.

'If you buy a raffle ticket, you could win the jacket.'

As soon as I've said the words I realise they are not going to buy any tickets.

'If Hillary wants a bedjacket we'll look in the catalogue when we get home,' says Mrs Gibbons firmly.

The sudden hiss of the water urn comes as a benediction and, like the bubbles in ginger beer, Betsi and I rise to our feet and rush to turn it down. Unexpectedly, this provides an escape route for Mrs Gibbons too, the exit she has been waiting for.

'We'll have to be going,' she announces in a relieved way.

'Oh, not yet. Wait for tea.' I can't think why I'm feeling so deflated.

'There'll be goods on the stalls you might like to look at,' Betsi suggests, lamely.

'We haven't time, now. We've got lots of things to do, haven't we, Hilly?' Mrs Gibbons tugs her daughter's arm determinedly and I wonder what interesting things these two will find to do with their day.

Though Hillary's shoulders droop dejectedly, Betsi makes no further attempt to dissuade them.

'Who were they?' I wonder when they are safely out of earshot.

'Moved opposite me about a year ago. Edna, the mother, has some nervous trouble. She doesn't go out very much.'

'What about her husband?'

'He works away, though I can't say I've ever seen him. They don't seem to have any friends popping in.' Betsi glances at her watch. 'At least they've had an outing today.'

At ten-thirty the doors open and a stampede of people rushes in. On the craft table, the peg bags, teacloths, table napkins and babies' bibs soon sell, and the cake stall, which wobbled under the weight of the tray bakes, cornflake tarts, sponges, fruit cakes, chutneys, jams and jellies at the start of the morning, is empty. 'There aren't enough crumbs left to feed a hungry blackbird and I've run out of milk,' Betsi confides. 'Best get on with the raffle now.'

Apart from the bedjacket; a bottle of sherry, an alarm clock and an embroidered tray cloth have been donated. And then, in front of a hushed audience, Betsi asks Connor to draw the first ticket and announce the winner's name.

'Mr F. Littler. Number 159 on the blue ticket. Mr Freddie Littler.' A murmur goes around the hall, as necks crane to see if Mr Littler, the pharmacist, is here.

'Mr Littler isn't here, is he?' says Betsi, 'but I've seen Miss Littler this morning.'

Freda Littler waves a ticket in response.

'The first prize is the bedjacket. Perhaps you'd like to take the sherry for your brother instead?' suggests Betsi.

'I'd love the bedjacket, please. My brother has said I can choose the prize if he wins. The bedjacket will be of more use to me than to him.' A chink of laughter brightens the hall. Miss Littler accepts the prize graciously.

'It's lovely. I'm so glad Freddie's ticket came up.'

'I hope it will keep you warm,' I murmur.

'When I lived in Venice we called fine knitted lace "*punto in aria*" or "stitches in the air",' she whispers too loudly. Miss Littler is well known for weaving Venice into as many conversations as she can.

At the end of the morning Connor, Betsi and I sweep the floor, put away chairs and throw discarded paper cups into the bin.

'All that's left now is to count the money, bag it and we're done.'

Ten minutes later, Betsi pronounces.

'Eighty pounds. We've plenty of money for repairs and a few extras, too. That was a very good morning's work.'

'Now then you two, you're welcome to cold ham and pickles if you come home with me and I've a rice pudding baking slowly in the oven.'

'Sounds delicious, Betsi, but not today, thank you. Anyway, you deserve a rest. Connor's coming home with me for "frimpan".'

'Frimpan? What's that?' Betsi looks mystified.

'That's shorthand for "frying pan" in our house. Eggs, bacon, cheese, cold boiled potato, bacon, tomatoes, if they're in season, or mushrooms; anything that can be fried.'

'Sounds good.'

'There's room in the van, if you'd like a lift,' Connor invites his aunt.

'No, you two go ahead. I've got a few errands to do on my way home.'

Curled on the passenger seat of the van is a long scarf that I knitted before Connor and I became friendly.

One day, Connor called at the timber yard and asked why the scarf was that length.

'It's for a giraffe,' I'd replied.

'Why is it in that bright colour?'

'The wool was on special offer.'

I gave him the scarf as a present and we started seeing each other. Now, Connor picks the scarf up and twists it around his hands, like a golden chain.

'When my uncle saw me in this he said I might start warbling like a canary.'

'It's good for keeping the cold out,' I protest.

'Good for other things, too,' and Connor wraps the scarf around our necks and pulls me so close that his mouth comes down tenderly on mine, his tongue nuzzling my lips. His kisses become more urgent and, instead of sitting there limply, like a rag doll, as I usually do, I kiss him back, properly. In a hot glow, my body responds, my face burns, not with embarrassment but with longing, ardour and desire.

Something like a tidal wave breaks over me, so that I lose my breath and see flashes of blue light. Just when I think I'm passing out the undercurrent releases me and I'm brought to the surface again. I sit, shaken.

Connor stops. His eyes search mine.

'OK?' he asks and I nod. We both know something has made us equal, changed our relationship.

'That was good,' he whispers, his voice deep, pulling me roughly to him. I offer him my lips and I want him as much as he wants me.

'Let's go to my house,' I say softly. He holds my gaze for a long moment, before catching my hand and pulling it down to his pelvis, looking at me enquiringly.

'Do you understand now?' he asks.

A feeling of foolishness engulfs me. My innocence is revealed as a handicap, a form of stupidity, proof that I know nothing about anything.

Connor's eyes are deeply intent.

'Do you understand that's what you do to me, because I fancy you?'

With those words, everything is all right again.

I find the scarf and drape it so it covers my hand on his lap. Connor grins and starts the van. Maybe I haven't split the atom but I have made a discovery: I'm in love and if someone were to offer me a dish of diamonds right now, I couldn't be happier.

In Beauchamp Terrace, Oona has parked the Morris Minor by the kerb and is rummaging in the boot.

'I don't have to wait if it's awkward with your aunt here.'

'It's not awkward. Come in.'

'Need any help?' Connor asks Oona as I unlock the front door of the house.

'You and Stella have arrived at just the right moment. I've got potatoes, swedes and carrots from Pen-y-Bont. Could you take them, Con? Stella will show you where to put them.'

I pause to ask about the baby.

'A beautiful little girl. *Scrapan fach*, a proper *cariad*.'

'*Scrapan fach*' is a term of endearment and although it means a little scrap of a thing, Oona uses it whether the baby weighs five pounds or ten.

When Oona has gone upstairs to change out of her uniform, Connor puts his arms around me. 'To be continued later?'

'You bet,' and I kiss him lightly on the cheek.

While the bacon fries on the gas stove, Connor stirs the Aga into life. His eyes travel around the kitchen, 'This is nice,' he says.

'It's all old. Oona won't throw a thing away, calls it wasteful. Nothing's changed since my grandparents were alive. Everything is kept as a reminder of them. Mamma's rolling pin is in the kitchen drawer, her tapestry cushions on the chair and those are Dadda's riding boots in the corner.'

Connor listens intently. 'It's the same with Mam and me, you could think we were still in the nineteenth century, our stuff is so old.'

While the bacon drains on greaseproof paper I fry the eggs in hot lard, watching them change into daisies, edged with crisp, frilly brown lace. Oona joins us and settles herself at the kitchen table, indicating to Connor to sit by her.

'Make enough of everything, Stell, I'm starving and bring the tomato sauce as well.'

Oona eats like a horse when she's been out on a delivery. She turns to Connor.

'I could see lambs in one of your fields this morning.'

'They're not ours. We're renting out the field, but I may buy some sheep, to diversify a bit.'

'I've seen lambs, catkins and new babies, all in one day,' sighs Oona contentedly.

'What are they calling the baby?' I ask.

'"Megan", and they've asked me to be godmother.'

'How many godchildren do you have?' Connor wonders.

'About fifteen, I think.'

After we've eaten everything on the table and Oona's found some raisin cake for us to finish, Connor offers to cut the brambles in the field.

'I wondered what to do about them,' admits Oona. 'We used to have Eddie Gringridge to see to it, but the family's moved away.'

'I'll have a look now, if Stella shows me what's to be done.'

'Let's go through the wooden gate at the bottom of the garden out into the field.'

'Shouldn't take me more than a morning,' Connor estimates, poking the brambles with a stick.

'Mam is going to her sister's tonight for a few hours. I'm not picking her up until ten. Like to go to the flicks?'

'Anything good on?' though I don't really care. I'd watch a Battle of Britain film just to be with Connor again.

'*The Eddie Duchin Story*. Some contortionist, I think,' he adds.

Touching his lips lightly with mine, I promise to be ready by six o'clock.

Oona is tidying the kitchen when I return to the house.

'Leave those dishes,' I command. 'You've been out since daybreak.'

'I've washed everything, no need to dry them, they can drain,' says my aunt.

I can see she's crackling with energy, as she always is after a delivery.

'Give my hair a brush, Stell?'

'The brush in the hatstand in the hall OK?'

'Any brush.'

Oona likes having her dark hair brushed when she wants to relax.

Thick waves spring back from Oona's low hairline and although forty-five, she has few grey hairs and her skin is good. I want to know about the afterbirth.

'Did Elvira ask you to burn the placenta?'

'Yes, three pops, so no more babbies there.' Although she is a nurse, my aunt believes in old wives' tales just as much as anyone else.

I brush Oona's scalp vigorously until her hair crackles then wrap the brush in a silk scarf and smooth it over her head, letting the hair fall back into shape.

'Connor and I are going to the pictures tonight.'

'The film starring Kim Novak?' My aunt's knowledge surprises me. 'I was passing the cinema and noticed the poster. There was a lovely shot of Kim Novak, blonde hair, shimmery dress.'

'Would you like to see the film? I'll come again with you in the week, if you want to go.'

'You enjoy it and tell me all about it later. I'm going to play bridge tonight with the Littlers. They've asked a few people over.'

Later, I run a bath, contemplating the evening. I want to look special for Connor, glamorous like Kim Novak, even though I am not a blonde.

I was still in school when Carol and I went to see a very gloomy film featuring Juliette Gréco and Jean Seberg. Juliette was all long black hair and she sang sad songs in a dark, smoky place. Jean's hair was a beautiful golden Californian colour, cropped short in an outdoorsy way. They both looked so different from anyone I knew and, after the film, my light brown hair felt dowdy so I decided to change my image.

On the following Saturday I called at the pharmacy to see if Mr Littler sold peroxide.

'I do sell peroxide,' he said slowly, 'but I have none in stock at the moment. Anyway, what do you want it for? Dettol is a very good, all-round disinfectant.'

He looked at me closely, as though I might have an infectious disease and was asking advice.

I explained about the film and how I couldn't decide whether to be a dark, ebony colour or a bright blonde, but if I was going to be Jean I would also need a gem-studded dog collar for my neck.

'I know of no place in Stanton that sells dog collars, let alone studded ones,' he said, scratching his cheek.

'I'll write to my mother. She lives in London, she'll be able to buy one there.'

'Salli. Salli Sivell that was. Your mother.'

'Yes.'

Then he surprised me by saying that the choice had been made for me the moment I walked through the door.

'You have no choice other than to be Juliette, because I am out of peroxide. I believe in fate. There is no point in fighting destiny. My father was a pharmacist and I am a pharmacist, so pharmacy is in our blood. You see, some things are pre-determined.'

'You knew my grandfather, William Sivell the "Produce Stores"?' I didn't wait for him to answer before continuing, 'he always said, "Breeding is breeding and blood always outs".'

Mr Littler nodded gravely.

'Is the film still showing?' He seemed interested in seeing it, but it wasn't on. Then he paused.

'Don't cut your hair like Jean. Short hair is for boys, not young ladies,' before disappearing into the back of the shop and returning with a tube of hair colouring.

21

'This is Raven Black. Follow the instructions carefully and your hair should darken.'

It cost two and sixpence but he lopped sixpence off the price because I was still in school.

'It will fade after a few shampoos but if you change your mind, I will have a supply of peroxide by the end of next week.'

It was fortunate that Mr Littler did not have peroxide because, shortly afterwards, I had a holiday job in The Sampler Café, where my midnight-coloured hair suited the mournfully black uniform. Mrs Stubbs, the owner, gave me a black blouse and skirt that the previous waitress had left behind. I rubbed gravy browning onto my legs to give them colour and bought a pair of ballerina flatties.

The sky is low and dark when Connor and I set out for the pictures, but all over the town, streetlights glow, winding along Beauchamp Terrace, around the square and away up the High Street.

When we're in our seats, upstairs, in the back row, the lights dim and Kim appears on the screen. Her short hair is a golden froth of gleaming curls on the top of her head and her backless dress shows off her supple spine. Turning to face the cameras her soulful eyes are either crème de menthe or absinthe green, but I'm not sure, because Connor puts his arm around me and I'm sitting at an awkward angle and can't see the screen properly.

Then, just as Eddie goes missing and Kim's eyes brim with elegant tears, not the hot, blubbery type that make my nose look like it's been left in a pan of hot water overnight, Connor whispers, 'Let's go. I want to be alone with you.' Awkwardly, we squeeze past the other people in the row, trying hard not to step on their toes, whispering apologies as we shuffle along.

Outside, the cold air grazes my face and I pull the collar of the woollen pea coat up under my chin. Pant Farm is only a mile from town, not remote like some of the farms further up the valley and has electricity and running water. Five minutes more and we're in the lane where rabbits bob up and down in the verge and bats swoop low.

A pool of light spills across the yard and Connor parks the van under a large beech tree before helping me out. Fingers entwined, we walk to the side door, which he unlocks and manages to open only after giving it a hard shove with his shoulder.

Smot, the sheepdog, lies quietly in front of the banked-up fire in the kitchen, thumping a welcome with his tail.

'He's old now, doesn't move unless he has to,' explains Connor, patting the dog.

'Take your coat off,' he invites but before I've had time he kisses me and I feel the hardness of his body next to mine and my breath quickens. Then we're on the settee and I'm in Connor's arms and returning his rough kisses. His face feels familiar, right, as though it's in the place it's meant to be. I hold him tightly, his smell like the first Pearmain apples of the season, fresh water streams and spring meadows.

We are locked together until, suddenly, Smot jumps up on us. Connor tries pushing him down but the dog persists. Disentangling himself from my arms, Connor stands up.

'We'll go upstairs. I'll shut the door on Smot.'

'What if your mother comes?'

'She won't budge till I fetch her. Don't worry about her.'

Somehow Connor manages to keep his arms around me as we climb the steep, narrow stairs. We might be treading virgin snow, for we leave no trace of noise on the linoleum covering.

The door of Connor's room is ajar and he pushes it wide open, revealing a single wardrobe, a small chest of drawers, a chair and a bed. Light filters into the room, mixing the sludgy colours of an old Dutch master, a patina of green, verdigris and velvet brown softens the lines of the room, except for the walls which are papered with a tiny pink and red rosebud pattern. Heat from the kitchen below rises and warms the room, providing a blanketing cosiness.

Connor folds back the white cotton counterpane on the bed and lowers me gently into the softness of the feather mattress. We lie at ease in each other's arms on the narrow bed and we start kissing all over again and, after a while, I notice that, somehow, we have taken our clothes off.

Through the window, moonlight weaves in and out of the bare branches of the tall ash trees but here, wrapped in Connor's thighs, I am secure. His fingers tease my nipples into little peaks, and I hold him, feeling his silkiness, cool and smooth as alabaster.

'Happy?' but he knows the answer.

'We're not going to do anything. We'll just lie here. When you're ready, we'll get up and I'll take you home.'

I smell the warmth of his body, absorb the comfort of his skin, cover his mouth with mine.

Before long, Connor starts snoring softly and I wrap the sheet around him, looking at his face, the thick eyelashes gleaming even in the darkness. We lie like this until a glance at the bedside clock prompts me to shake him gently.

'What time is it?' His voice is sleepy and startled.

'We've got half an hour again but better get our things together.'

He finds my bra but, before awkwardly helping me on with it, he takes my nipples in his mouth and nips and kisses them and my hands make a cradle for his head as he does so. After a lot of stops for kissing and nuzzling, we finally dress.

Chapter Four

Sunshine gilds the town, like syrup trickling over gingerbread houses. I wouldn't mind lingering but there are invoices to be folded into exotic origami shapes and tucked into long envelopes, ready for posting.

'Creative thinking transforms the banal into an art form,' Mum remarked once, when she had done something clever with a scarf. Somehow she fails to appreciate the beauty of routine.

Across the road, in 'Stanton Infants' and Junior School', Blod Jones, merry widow of this parish and kitchen assistant, is trundling an empty metal meals container to the school gate, ready to be picked up by the swill van at twelve-thirty. On the container, in large letters, she has chalked 'too much salt'.

I remember it's lunchtime, but before there's time to eat I notice someone in the yard outside.

'Hillary, isn't it?' I try to make my voice sound warm and welcoming as she pushes open the door.

'Miss,' she blurts out, 'Miss, you know you said you would teach me to knit?'

The question hangs in the air.

I nod. 'Yes, I'll teach your mum, too.'

The girl glances away. 'She doesn't want to learn, Miss.'

'But you do,' and I hope my smile is encouraging.

I reach for the bag of jelly babies which I keep under the counter. 'Have one.'

'Just one, then.'

A sting goes through the tooth with a loose filling when I suck on my sweet.

'Mum's not well, Miss.'

'Call me Stella. You help your mum a lot, I think.'

'She does all the housework and cooking herself.' There is a note of defensiveness in Hillary's voice and she shifts awkwardly. 'It's just shopping she needs help with, because she gets frightened outside by herself.'

'Does your mum mind if you take up knitting?'

'No, but I might not be able to stay for long, because Mum needs company with Dad working away.'

'How about half an hour a week, just to get you started?'

'I do want to learn.'

'When would you like to start?'

'Could I start this week? I've got wool, but no needles.'

This means a lot to Hillary and I don't want to let her down, but where can we meet? I could take her home but I don't want to disturb Oona's evening.

'I'll ask Mrs Sylvester if we can use a room in the community hall,' I suggest. 'Would five-thirty tomorrow evening suit you?'

Excitement lights Hillary's face.

'I'll ring Mrs Sylvester now and see what's available.'

Fortunately Betsi is at home and her voice is sympathetic when she hears my request.

'It will do that poor girl the world of good to learn something that interests her and to get her out of the house. There's plenty of unused space in the hall. If others want to join you then there might be a small charge but you and Hillary can squeeze into one of the back rooms.'

I put the receiver down with a triumphant click.

'We can start tomorrow evening.'

'Thank you, Stella,' Hillary's voice is shy as she uses my name.

26

'Don't worry about wool or needles; I'll bring everything you need to get you started.'

The pleasure I feel about helping Hillary powers me through the afternoon. By five-thirty I am out of the office and pushing open the door of Tommy Eddershaw's jewellery shop, opposite our house in Beauchamp Terrace.

Glass cabinets sparkle with diamanté lizards, snakes, clip-on earrings, brooches and enamelled bugs in emerald green and Pompeiian red. Ropes of Ciro pearls, lustrous as lily petals, are displayed on a black velvet cushion. I explain to the assistant that I have a pearl necklace that needs re-threading.

The necklace was all to do with the little princesses, Lilibet and Margaret Rose.

As a child, my fashion idols were Elizabeth and Margaret or the 'Little princesses' as 'Crawfie' their governess called them in her column in *Woman's Own*. I filled a scrapbook with pictures of them gleaned from *Picture Post*.

Lillibet was four years older than Margaret Rose, but they were dressed identically.

When I was about eight, my mother and I were looking at a picture of the girls in the palace gardens, dressed identically in white blouses and pink skirts and boleros. The caption said that their father, King George VI, gave them a real pearl each on their birthdays and they were saving them to make into necklaces. 'I think the King is a bit mean. It will take ages before they have enough to thread into necklaces,' I decided.

On my next birthday, before I'd even got out of bed, Mum and Auntie Oona brought presents to my room. Having Mum and Oona and the presents made me really happy. They were the two people I loved the most in the world. Mum gave me *Five go Adventuring* by my favourite writer, Enid Blyton. Tucked inside the card were five one pound notes. I hugged and kissed Mum before opening Auntie Oona's present.

In a long slim box, wrapped in white tissue and tied with a satin bow, was a string of perfectly round, shell-pink pearls. I let the string slip from one hand to the other, back and fore, then I twisted the strand around my fingers and wrists, watching the light glowing around each exquisite bead, thinking how lucky I was. I had a pearl necklace that I did not have to make myself when I was grown up.

My aunt fastened the tiny gold clasp at the back of my neck.

'The diamond chips in the clasp are real.'

I ran to the mirror, moving my head this way and that to have a better view of the beads.

'Do you like them?' (My aunt has a habit of asking questions which have an obvious answer.)

'I love them, I love them,' and I hugged my aunt again, and she kissed me, though she tends not to be very demonstrative.

I pirouetted around the room and Mum laughed and my aunt smiled.

'You'd better get dressed,' said Mum.

'Was the necklace very expensive?' I queried.

'Let's just say they were worth every penny,' said my aunt.

'Quality speaks for itself. The world sees what you want to show it,' Mum agreed.

I thought the necklace was my best present ever, even better than the tartan kilt and matching umbrella I'd had the year before. Each pearl revealed a little picture. Sometimes, a sun, a rainbow or a weeping willow, shone through. When I saw a mother holding a baby I imagined it was Mum and me. I told my aunt and she looked at Mum, who said, 'She is very imaginative.'

After arranging to collect the pearls at the end of the week, I cross the road to Number One, Beauchamp Terrace, where a light shining from the hallway means my aunt has arrived.

'I've made cawl and it's ready to eat,' she calls from the kitchen when she hears my key in the lock.

'I had to do something with all those vegetables Elvira's husband gave me. I've put lamb chops in with leeks, parsley, carrots and potatoes and a few parsnips. I hope you're hungry.'

'I am now,' I say, sniffing the air expectantly and Oona hugs me.

In front of the Aga, batteries are laid out in a row, for recharging. Mum says that Oona is extravagant and penny-pinching in equal measure, but her frugality does not extend to food. There is a slab of Caerphilly cheese on the table, bread, salty butter and a flagon of cider.

Oona ladles the cawl into large bowls and forks the chops onto plates.

'I bought an apple tart in the bakery and it's warming in the oven. We'll have it with a cup of tea. Carol Bailey's mother was in the bakery; she thinks Carol may be home any day.'

'Any idea of the date?'

'She wasn't sure.'

'How long's she home for?'

'A few weeks probably, if she's coming over from Italy.'

'I can't wait to see her again.'

'She'll probably be straight around here as soon as she can. You two were always close.'

Then Oona kicks off her shoes, picks up the local paper and buries her head in her favourite section, the 'Births, Marriages and Deaths', or 'Hatches, Matches and Despatches' as she calls them.

'I'm going into the shop, to rootle around for some wool for Hillary.'

'Don't be in there too long, you'll catch a cold. How much wool do you need?'

'Not much, just enough to get Hillary started.'

At the end of the hallway, I slip back the bolt of the shop door, waiting for the smell of scrubbed floorboards, bleached counters and long-gone sacks of flour to spiral into the air. Faded blue-and-white wallpaper peels from the corners of the walls and the corpse of a fly clings stickily to the unshaded light bulb in the middle of the ceiling.

Balls of wool, skeins of yarn, patterns, needles and buttons are piled in wicker baskets, open shelves, drawers from abandoned chests. Happiness dances and a sense of the abundance of life floods through me. Colours ripple, merge, creating a river of blue, indigo, royal, navy, phthalo. Ice blue, peacock and all the cobalts run into the greens, the pistachio, forest, peppermint, sage, peridot, tourmalines, chartreuse, combining to form a kaleidoscopic waterfall.

Chalky blackboard colours like custard yellow, rhubarb crumble pink, plum tart red, damson jam conserve, pea soup green, chartreuse and all the faded calico colours swirl and recede in a dizzying glory. At the bottom of the pile, forming a border, is the Indian ink blackness of the 'Pennine Jiffy Knit'.

I want to reach out, hold the buttermilks, the citrines, Egyptian pyramid yellows and the ones on the bottom shelf, delicate like the rising sun in Spencer's 'Morning Calm', feel their tactile comfort, the promise that they can hold back the cold lurking outside the house.

But it is the reds, more than any other colour, that vibrate. Cochineal, verbena, magenta, carmine, fuchsia, flaunting crocosmia, Chinese lacquer red, Marilyn Monroe lipstick red, and all the geranium combinations that lead to the deep red oxblood, the same shade as our front doorstep.

For Hillary, I want a colour to make her heart leap with joy when she sees it. A skein of wool in a delicate shade of orange, the colour of a Californian poppy waiting to burst into bloom, beckons me. This will be perfect for Hillary's introduction to knitting. Then, before leaving the room, I find some double knitting teal wool, just enough to make a jersey for Connor.

Lying in bed that night, the room transforms into a stretched geometry of moonlit stencils. Window frames, verticals, diagonals, horizontals, divide the walls into grids, light from the street lamp spilling over the flat, planed surface of the dressing table to form a frozen solid, like a deep lake in a dense forest, somewhere in Vienna, perhaps.

Last week, Bamford Furnishers displayed a length of curtain fabric which had a geometric pattern, black on white, broken by ellipses of lime green. I mentioned it to Oona, who was with me, but she did not share my enthusiasm, calling the design 'brutal'.

I love geometry. It provides a certainty that is not to be argued with. *Quad Erat Demonstrandum*. QED, taken as proved, as Miss Harries, Senior Maths Teacher, Stanton High, wrote triumphantly across the blackboard when she had worked out something particularly tricky.

Chapter Five

Chipped chinks of light escape from the windows of the hall and the sound of chairs scraping and young voices signals the end of the weekly 'Junior Quiz' hour. Entering through the kitchen door, I find Hillary and her mother sitting quietly at a table. Hillary stands up, apologetically, 'I hope you don't mind Mum coming along?'

'That's fine.' I hope my extra-bright smile will encourage a response from Mrs Gibbons, but all I receive in return is a curt nod.

'Like to take your coat off, Hillary?' I ask, slipping mine onto the back of the nearest chair. 'You'll find it easier to knit without it.'

Winding the wool around my left thumb I cast on, using one needle. Hillary watches quietly, the only sound coming from the hum of the electric heater on the wall.

'You try. If it doesn't work, I'll show you how to do it using two needles.'

Hillary grasps the wool and needle eagerly, but her mother's hand comes out to restrain her.

'We've brought our own wool.' Mrs Gibbons reaches into a paper bag before placing a lumpy ball of wool that looks as though it's been unravelled from another garment, on the table.

'There's really no need,' I protest, 'I've plenty of wool. You keep that for another time. Let's work on this for now.'

Soon Hillary is casting on by herself and just as I'm wondering where Betsi is, the door opens and she joins us. Edna looks pleased to see her, swivelling slightly in her chair to face her.

'Don't anyone move for me, now. I'm better sitting here in the corner, where I can pop out easily if I'm needed.'

Hillary's head is bent in concentration and she sucks her bottom lip.

'I can see you've made a good start, Hillary,' Betsi comments. Shyly, the girl holds the knitting up for inspection and Betsi praises her again.

'I'm taking the bus into Gosford in the week to choose some wool and a pattern for a matinee jacket and bootees. My niece is expecting in the summer so I promised I'll get busy.'

'Need any help?' I ask.

'I'd love some. I'll bring it along next week,' then she glances in Hillary's direction. 'You are meeting again next week, aren't you?'

'Hillary?' I say, silently begging her mother not to stop her from coming.

'If you don't mind.' Hillary's face is glowing and I feel a stab of pleasure.

'That's settled then. We have a knitting group.'

When I leave the hall a large moon hangs over Stanton, like a magical Chinese lantern.

Oona is sitting at the scrubbed kitchen table when I arrive home.

'I've eaten, Stell. Yours is keeping warm in the oven.'

'I'm hungry. What is it?'

'Fray Bentos steak and kidney pie and frozen peas.'

'My favourite meal.'

When Oona buys peas we eat the pack between us.

'I'll make fresh tea,' my aunt volunteers. 'How did Hillary get on?'

'She was really keen and brought her mum.'

'Good. It might help Mrs Gibbons too, getting out of the house.'

I tell Oona about the moon. 'You've got to go and look at it afterwards. It's huge.'

'You know what I think about full moons. High tides, full moons and pregnant women don't mix.'

'But is it really true that full moons mean premature births?'

Oona's expression is inscrutable. 'Funny things happen at the time of the full moon.'

'Nearly forgot. From Nicky.' Oona passes me a postcard. 'And a parcel came for you lunchtime. Luckily, the postman arrived just as I was pulling up outside.'

'Pretty picture,' I say, looking at a sunny field of lavender, somewhere in Provence.

Nicky's my step-sister, the daughter of Mum's husband Tom, by his first marriage. She lives in Rye with her mother. I read the card silently while Oona watches me.

'Anything interesting?' The card is not in an envelope, so Oona must have glanced at it, but I read it out to her anyway.

Nicky's writes in a large, square hand, which is almost childish.

Trawling French flea markets hunting for old tat with Mum. V boring but met Luc – hot, hot, hot! Mum going home without me – ooh la, la! Kisses, Nicky.

'What do you make of that?' I query.

'How old is she now?'

'Eighteen. She's left school and is working with her mother in their shop.'

'Still in Rye, are they? Can't be selling many antiques in the winter. Now is probably a good time for them to go buying.'

'Nicky always seems so sophisticated, so self-assured. Perhaps it's because her mother's French and they travel all over the Continent so frequently.'

'Some people are born with their boots on.'

'Mmm.'

'Oh, don't forget this.' Oona hands me a scissors and a brown-paper package with 'Liberty' stamped across the top.

'Wool?'

'I think so.' Eagerly, I cut through the thick fibrous paper, discarding

34

the tissue until I reach the soft balls of double knitting wool and feel them squashy in my hands.

'What are you going to knit?'

The wool is a bright Cyanthe blue, the colour of an Alpine sky when the sun shines and everything else is a crystalline white.

'I thought I might make a snowflake jumper. I've plenty of white wool for the flakes but I probably won't start it until next winter.'

'How is Connor's jumper coming on?'

'I've ribbed the welt at the back and I'll work on it later.'

'By the way, I've made an appointment to choose some fabric in Horton next Saturday with Rees Powell. Want to come?'

'You're a dark horse. I'd love to come. You're having a new outfit for the christening, aren't you?'

I'm teasing. Oona does not buy many clothes because she spends her days in uniform.

'I'm thinking of having a costume.' My aunt intends having a skirt and jacket, but she says 'costume' and makes it sound like fancy dress.

'Would you like to look in Suzy Margaroli's to see what she's got for spring?'

'I know, what you're thinking. Rees Powell is not a fashion shop.' She shoots me a quizzical look.

'I just thought you might like something different.'

'I know I'm not stylish like your mum.'

'Mum's look is for London. You're style is "County" and it suits you.'

I omit to say that in Stanton you can wear the same clothes for twenty years and not look outdated. Sometimes Oona sends a postal order to an advertisement she has seen in *The Lady* magazine, for a dress with a couture label, such as Givenchy. The quality of the material and the elegant cut disguise the fact that Oona wears a garment which is slightly dated.

My aunt is still girlish, in a plumply soft fashion, with a bust, a bottom and a waist that goes in and out. I wonder, occasionally, why she hasn't married but assume her job is too important to her. She catches me studying her and laughs.

'You'd like me to dress like your mum.'

After that, I began thinking of Mum; the difference between her and Auntie Oona can best be described by watching them in a sweet shop. Mum always chooses something delicious like sugared almonds or chocolate pralines, but my aunt goes for salt water taffies or mints.

My mother's genius lies in combining simplicity with elegance. A fine woollen lilac skirt and jacket, worn with sheer grey stockings and lilac suede shoes, stands out in my mind. Set off by a long twisted silk scarf, tied at the neck in a pussycat bow cascading down the front of the jacket into a glorious burst of aubergine silk frills, this was the outfit she wore when I last saw her.

I would call my mother's style fashionable but she says she likes to look 'twt', meaning 'just so'.

Mum's muse is Barbara Goalen, a model with an incredible twenty-one-inch waist. I was twelve years old when I last had a twenty-one-inch waist. Perhaps my ribs are too low and get in the way of the measuring tape or maybe it is something to do with my posture. Barbara and I probably have little in common, unless we are the same age. Like other *Vogue* models, Barbara's age is indeterminate. Models have an inscrutable expression and I am never sure whether they are eighteen but look older or twenty-five and look younger.

At fifty years of age, my mother looks good. Her eyebrows are plucked, her nails gleam with carefully applied varnish and her mouth is bright with lipstick. Mum's favourite saying is that 'the correct clothes provide an identity' and she must be right, for she is known for her style. From my mother I have learnt that the only impression that counts is the first one and this philosophy leaves no room for mistakes.

Tom, Mum's second husband, is an antiques dealer and they often travel to the south of France in search of things for their shop. Nicky and I went for a holiday to the south of France with Mum and Tom, soon after they married. We booked into a hotel and Tom wrote in the guest book, *Mr and Mrs Tom Marsden, Nicky Marsden, Stella Randall*. The receptionist scanned the names, before peering over the counter and asking, 'Which one is Stella?' When I replied, she responded by saying, 'Aren't you a lucky little girl? Your friend has taken you on holiday.'

As a child, I wore hand-smocked Liberty 'Tana Lawn' cotton dresses, from a shop called 'Marie Dressler'. Mum chose Siname straw sun bonnets, decorated with white daisies and satin ribbons which tied into lavish bows under the chin, to wear with the dresses on a Sunday. Completing the outfit, I had crocheted knee socks and matching fingerless gloves.

It's a sunny Sunday afternoon again and Mum and I are feeding the ducks on the pond. Oona has diced some slices of bread into small cubes, so the ducks will not choke. Older ladies stroll by, admiring my dress, my long rag-ringlets, my 'Dorothy' bag, tinkling with silver sixpenny pieces. The husbands raise their hats and smile tenderly at my mother, the young widow of a test pilot. Mum's stoicism is presented so discreetly that uncomfortable emotions, like pity, are transformed into admiration, a much easier feeling for everyone. I twist the thin gold bangle on my wrist, tugging until it hurts, pleased that my mother's beauty is appreciated because, for her, appearance is important: everything, really.

Clothes were the first thing my mother thought of when I told her that I had a job in the timber yard. A pale green envelope arrived, lined with fine tissue and I recognised Mum's flowing writing in the cognac-coloured ink she favours.

Her suggestion was a mackintosh in a neutral colour, beige, perhaps, might suit all seasons. A three quarter navy coat, to team with some navy skirts, one straight, one pleated, one check, one plain, with some silk scarves in brilliant colours would make a good basic wardrobe for winter. Court shoes and flat shoes were a necessity, the flat shoes to be worn with trousers or skirts. High heels worn with trousers were very common and to be avoided. Included with the letter was a cheque for twenty pounds and a PS. 'If you change your mind, you might consider St Godrick's Secretarial College. Be careful with nylons. Always keep a spare pair in the office. Never, but never, wear laddered stockings.'

Chapter Six

Spring is gentle this year, dotting the lane with shiny celandines. On Monday evening Hillary shows me a pile of knitted squares she has completed, watching me closely to see my reaction.

'Wow! You've taken to knitting in a big way. Are you going to make a throw?'

She shrugs, looking pleased with herself.

'It's your first piece so it's very special. Whatever else you knit, you'll remember this the most.'

Edna rustles a carrier bag under her chair.

'I wouldn't mind trying some knitting myself.'

Disguising my surprise, I answer, 'That's a good idea.' I pull my chair closer to hers.

'I've made a start.' Apologetically, she places a strip of knitting on the table.

'Did you do this? I thought you couldn't knit.'

'I've learnt by watching Hilly.'

I take a closer look.

'That's a very good start.'

Edna's work has a neat appearance, though her hands are not small and delicate like the hands of a knitter.

'I'm thinking of knitting a sponge bag for the bathroom.' Taking a deep breath before continuing, she goes on, 'I saw an advert in a magazine for a pack to include the cotton, the plastic lining and the cord for the drawstring.'

She fumbles in her pocket.

'I've got the address here, if you want to send for one,' and she pushes a scrap of paper towards me.

'Mrs Margaret Youings, 140 High Street, Ilfracombe, Devon,' I read.

'It costs five and ten pence for the striped pack,' Edna explains. 'I'm not bothering with the Fair Isle version because, at the moment, it is beyond me, far too difficult.'

Then she looks abashed. 'Of course, shopping is no problem for you, but I have to send away for a lot of my things.'

'I've got yarn but perhaps I could borrow the pattern sometime?'

Hillary is bursting to tell me something.

'Mum walked by herself to the box on the corner to post the letter.'

Edna pretends not to notice my surprise, as though it is the most ordinary thing in the world for her to go out by herself.

The door creaks open and Betsi Sylvester joins us.

'I've brought my wool,' and she tips it out onto the table for us to admire.

'I'm starting with a matinee jacket, bonnet and bootees,' and she passes the pattern to me. It is a lacy knit, using Copley's two-ply wool, in white.

'I'll use white ribbon, so it will suit a boy or a girl.'

'I'll check the tension for you when you get started, if you like,' I offer.

'Thanks, Stell. I'm such a tight knitter.'

While Betsi casts on, her lips moving involuntarily as she does so, I show Hillary and Edna how to knit purl stitches, hovering over them until they are confident.

My thoughts turn to the knitted cardigans I longed to have when in I was in school.

Carol's mother knew how to adapt a pattern, shape a cardigan, so that the waist was clinched in snugly. Sometimes Mrs Bailey added a roll-neck collar and even used finer wool to produce covered buttons. Those cardigans were works of art but Carol hated them and wanted ones like mine, bought in Bradford House in the high street.

'I would never call a knitted garment "fashion",' was Mum's comment when I asked for a twinset for weekends. I found a pattern I liked, knitted in Penelope 'Colormatch' four-ply wool, featuring a barn owl sitting impassively on a branch on either side of the cardigan. Buttons were used for eyes but, if Mum sent to Liberty's, Regent Street, London, I could have jewelled eyes. When one of my aunt's patients broke her leg and offered to knit something for me I was able to have my twinset.

A tap on the door and Jane O'Brien from the Senior Pupils' Quiz Team appears.

'My sister's been delayed and we need a scorer.'

Betsi swiftly abandons her knitting, but Jane looks at Hillary.

'Perhaps someone else can do it. All you have to do is keep a tally of the scores of the two teams and add them up afterwards. Would you like to?'

'Go on, Hillary,' Edna's voice is encouraging. 'I'm all right here for a while.'

In an instant, Hillary is on her feet. Jane holds the door open for her and then they're gone.

Betsi's halfway through counting her stitches when a shuffling noise outside the door prompts her to investigate.

'Please, Mrs Sylvester, I left my blue pencil case behind here last week.'

'Let's get the lost property box out then, Dewi,' and we hear two sets of footsteps hurrying down the passage.

Edna's ready to cast off and I show her how to do it by slipping one stitch over the other.

'You are a quick learner,' I comment.

'I've always wanted to knit, but it's tricky learning from a book.'

Just then, Betsi returns with some news.

'I've been speaking to Jenni Baxter, who was collecting her son from table tennis.'

For Edna's benefit, she says, 'Jenni's a staff nurse in the County Hospital in Gosford. She's heard Stanton Cottage Hospital might have to close. The roof needs replacing and the easiest thing would be to transfer patients to Gosford.'

'Anything we can do?' I wonder.

'It's all a question of money, as usual.'

'Could we hold coffee mornings? Bring and Buys?'

Betsi laughs wryly. 'We'd never make it. The roof will cost thousands. It's too much for us. Five hundred pounds, perhaps, but when it comes to thousands, I think we've got to say we're out of our depth.'

Edna's head goes up.

'I could help.'

'Knit something, you mean?' Betsi's voice is gentle.

'I'm willing to set myself a target. I could do a walk and pledge ten pounds to the cause if I make it.'

'That's a big commitment and a lot of money,' I venture.

'Starting these classes has given me a new determination.'

'How will you manage?'

'I'll train in the night, when no one can see me.' Her voice becomes reflective.

'I owe it to Hilly. I expect you think I'll change my mind tomorrow, but I'm serious about it. This is an opportunity for me.'

Later, when Hillary and Edna have gone home, Betsi and I walk down the high street together.

'What do you make of Edna's offer? I don't hold out much hope.' Betsi sounds unconvinced.

'What brought on this nervous trouble?'

'It's all to do with her husband leaving her suddenly. She had an awful shock and didn't want to see people. What she's doing is hiding herself away.'

'She wants a challenge but she's setting her sights too high. With the nights getting lighter she'll have to go out later and later. And as for collecting money to sponsor her, there aren't many people in Stanton who know her, are there?'

'By tomorrow she'll have changed her mind. Tonight, she got carried away. It's not going to come to anything.'

'When did Jenni say the axe was falling on the hospital?'

'It will be a while, but there are meetings before long to find out what everybody thinks.'

Chapter Seven

On Wednesday Connor rings me in the office.

'Can I pick you up about eightish, after the Young Farmers meeting is over?'

'Where are we going?'

'I thought of a shandy in the Ship Aground, if that's suits you.'

'I'll be ready. Don't worry if the meeting overruns. I'll just knit until you arrive.'

When I've put the receiver down, I notice Hattie Moss, or Miss Moss as I called her, walking slowly up the road. I used to go to Miss Moss for piano lessons. One day, after I had played 'Für Elise', she said she had a sweetheart who was 'high up' in the town hall. 'I have been his girlfriend for nine years but he doesn't know it.'

After the lesson, I told Mum what Miss Moss had said and I repeated it to Auntie Oona when we arrived home. My mother and aunt looked at each other while I was speaking. Soon after that I stopped going to Miss Moss for piano, because I was in Stanton High and I preferred hockey practice after school.

That evening, knitting whilst waiting for Connor, I wonder how many boyfriends Nicky has had? I push the needle into the back of the stitches, twisting the wool into a rib. Why do I care? Connor is my first boyfriend, the only one who has kissed and held me and there is pleasure to be had in that knowledge.

Oona twiddles knobs on the radio, tuning into *The Archers*, before turning the volume down very low and asking, 'Are you and Connor getting serious about each other?'

'I don't know. Why?'

'Just wondering. Would you like life as a farmer's wife?'

'I might like to be Connor's wife but I don't know about living on the farm.'

Before I say any more, I'm saved by Connor's knock on the door.

'Ready?' Connor gives me a hug and a kiss.

'I'll just get my coat. Come in and see my aunt.'

'Have a cup of tea before you go?' Oona invites Connor.

'We're going for a drink but we won't be long,' Connor says.

'You'd rather Stella's company than mine,' Oona laughs, making Connor blush deeply.

'Away you go. Don't let me delay you.' Oona likes Connor, I can tell.

Before long, we're climbing the coastal road out of Stanton, with St George's Channel on our left. Lights flash from the breakwater and zigzag across the water and the ferry boat is in the harbour, lit up like a floating palace. I don't want to be anywhere else and I'm glad I chose not to live in London. When we round the steep bend at the top of the road, the land drapes and folds into fields and hills.

Connor's hand rests on my knee. 'I've thought of you all day,' he says, the cats' eye studs in the road ahead bright as platinum chips. I squeeze his hand and keep it there until he has to change gear.

'A drink or the beach?'

'The beach,' I whisper, leaning over to lick his ear.

A few yards down a narrow road and we stop by the dunes. Connor locks the doors and we reach for each other. As his hands find their way under my jumper I kiss his neck. He is mine and I don't want him to belong to anyone else.

After a while, the windows start steaming and Connor wipes them with a rag before slipping his arms around me again.

'We could go a bit further,' he says.

'What do you mean?' but I know that he's not talking about driving somewhere else.

'All the way.'

I hesitate. I do not want to destroy this moment by saying the wrong thing.

'We don't have to, only if you want to.'

I want him but I don't know if I'm ready.

'I'm frightened.' I can hear myself whispering.

'Frightened of me?'

'No, frightened of getting pregnant.'

I'm relieved to have told him. In the darkness, I feel Connor's eyes on mine.

'There's a chap who comes around on a Friday. He works for the chemist in Gosford. He's got a little van and Mam buys soap, hair grips, that sort of thing from him.

'Last week when Mam had her arms deep in dough he called. All she wanted was a hairnet so I went out to the van. We got talking and he asked if I was interested in "Family Protection" and he showed me some little packages. I did a double take and said I wasn't married.

'"Don't have to be," he said. "I sell a lot of these to young farmers who can't get into town to buy things." Next thing was, he gave me a free sample and then I ended up buying some.'

I listen silently. 'What do you think?' and Connor kisses my cheek.

This is what real 'courting' is all about and I'm not sure if I'm ready for it.

'I do want you, you know that.'

'There's no rush,' and he kisses me, though he's disappointed.

On the way back to Stanton, I'm uneasy. Connor wants to and I don't, not yet, anyway, and this might become an issue between us. It's only taken a short time for me to plunge into something I'm finding difficult to handle.

Oona's on the phone when I arrive home. Silently, she slips a letter into my hand and I recognise Carol's writing and feel better. I bound upstairs, wanting the luxury of being alone to enjoy the letter.

My eyes devour Carol's words. *Can't say exactly the date I'll be back, but the Italian job has come to an end.* I realise how much I've missed her and can't wait to see her again.

In bed, thoughts of Carol begin drifting in and out of my mind and, in particular, the year we both had summer holiday jobs.

Mine was in The Sampler café, because I could do mental arithmetic. I was never any good at higher mathematics in school but I understood the four rules of arithmetic, namely addition, subtraction, multiplication and division. This may not sound such a big deal but some of the others never quite got it.

I could calculate the cost of one cup of coffee, one pot of tea, scone and butter, jam and cream in my head, check I had received enough money and give the correct change. This impressed Mrs Perkins (Mattie Jackson that was) who had popped in for a knickerbocker glory, two and sixpence, a milky coffee, nine pence, making a total of three shillings and three pence with change of nine pence from four shillings, so much, that she asked if I was looking for a job, because she needed someone in the timber yard to take over the accounts. Garem Green, who was over seventy and unsteady on his feet and had retired once as a ticket collector in the harbour, had been advised by Dr McTaggart to rest more and so he was leaving.

After the summer holidays I did not go back to school but began work in the timber yard. I don't think it was what Oona wanted for me, though Mum made no objection to my choice. I wanted money, my own money. I wasn't clear why I was so sure about wanting money but I had a vague idea that it was something to do with being able to make a choice.

Carol wanted money, too, but for different reasons.

'I want to buy clothes that don't look like my mother could wear them as well,' she said.

Numbers were Carol's weak spot so that summer she had a job cleaning out caravans in the field behind Dol-y-Dderwen, for Mrs Delaport, who also ran a bed and breakfast. Mrs Delaport rented the caravans, or trailers, as she called them, to people who wanted family holidays by the sea. In the week, Carol washed the breakfast dishes in the guest house and vacuumed the bedrooms. Usually she finished by lunchtime but on a Saturday she had to clean the caravans and change the tea towels.

Each caravan had to be vacated by ten o'clock in the morning to give Carol enough time to get them ready for the next week's guests, who arrived by two o'clock. Mrs Delaport was emphatic that the trailers had to be vacated before Carol began work.

'No good trying to clean before the people have gone. They'll only mess them up again, whatever they say.'

One Saturday, when Carol went to clean the last trailer, it was getting on for one o'clock. She was surprised to see someone inside, because there was no sign of any car outside.

A man in his late teens was making coffee.

Carol was about to say she'd come back later, but the boy said, 'No need. I'll just have some coffee, you have a cup, too, then I'll go.'

According to Carol, the story went like this.

'Is this your permanent job?' asked Stew (short for Stewart, Carol explained).

'Good Lord, no. I'd die if I had to do this every day. It's a holiday job.'

'You a student or something?'

'Kind of.' (She did not want to admit she was not a student.)

After the coffee the boy asked Carol if she'd like to listen to some music, so they sat on the bed.

48

Then Stew had said, 'You're gorgeous,' and started kissing Carol.
'What about Mrs Delaport?'

'Oh, I forgot about her. She usually did some shopping on a Saturday for the guest house anyway.'

Then Stew had said, 'Would you like to, you know?' And Carol said she wasn't sure what he meant, but when he unzipped his trousers she understood. Telling her not to worry he would take care of everything, he got a little package out and Carol had said, 'OK, we'll give it a go then.'

I listened breathlessly and if I'd had stalks in my eye sockets, my eyes would have been standing on them by now.

'What was it like?' I asked and Carol said, 'He seemed to like it and grunted a lot but in a trice it was all done and dusted and put away.'(I knew she was not talking about the cleaning.)

Everything was brought to a conclusion when he said to Carol, 'Thanks. That was great. What did you say your name was? Here's my address. Send me a picture and I'll pin it on my bedroom wall with all the other girls I've done it with.'

So Carol said she'd better get on with the cleaning and Stew said, 'Need a hand?' But Carol said she could clean quickly so Stew went outside and had a cigarette.

When Carol went for her pay Mrs Delaport's face was white as a hard poached egg.

'Carol,' she had said, 'Carol, I don't believe it. Not of you. I came over to the trailers with a message from your mother, asking you to get a loaf on your way home. When I put my head around the door of one of them . . . I rang your mother immediately to tell her. I thought it was my duty. Your mother said to leave the bread and get home quickly.'

'What did you do then?' I asked, awe trembling through my voice.

'After I'd had my wages, I went straight home. Just as well, because

Mum was having a type of heart attack, clutching her chest, moaning, that sort of carry on.'

'Furious was she?'

'No. More like wounded. "What if you get pregnant?" she kept saying. I hadn't thought much about that, up until then. If she'd calmed down, I'd have felt sorry for her, but I just said, "So, what?" though I did feel a bit worried by then. She spent the rest of the day in bed but, in the evening, my period came.'

'You must have been relieved.'

'Yeah, I suppose so.' Carol said it as though the fear of pregnancy was of little consequence to her.

'So you told her.'

'Did I heck! No, I decided she could suffer a bit longer because of all the fuss she had made and I didn't want her ringing that crow-faced Mrs Delaport to say, "It's all right now, Carol has had her period."'

Carol could handle things and she had guts. I decided I could never be her equal.

'Next morning, while Mum was still in bed, I went down to the kitchen, found a tea plate, put a frilly paper doily on it then placed the towel in the middle. By now the blood had gone a dark, treacly brown. I watched Mum coming downstairs, her face the same colour as boiled bones. When she saw me she clutched her heart. "I've boiled the kettle," I said before picking up the plate and saying, "Marmite finger?"

'Mum's face was a picture. She felt her way to the fireside chair and more or less collapsed.'

'After I'd made her a cup of tea I lit the fire with the towel.'

Some days I think I should write a book and call it *All I know I learnt from Carol* because, in a way, this is true. Though Oona is a nurse she is rather delicate about these matters and that means she really does not like talking about them.

When Carol and Jeannine were in school, they often menstruated at the same time. Carol thought they must trigger something off in each other. When it was that time of the month, Mrs Bailey lit a fire early in the morning, even if it was a hot day, to burn all the soiled towels. Carol used to say that once a month she stoked the 'crem'.

This led Carol to talking about the new crematorium that had been built and Jack Jenkins, who had been fitting a new dining room carpet for them, told Carol that the heat in the 'crem' made the bodies rise and do the rumba and then the eyes fell out.

When I mentioned it to Oona she said, 'People exaggerate these things.'

But it was Carol who led the way in Religious Studies as well. Miss Bland was discussing a passage from the Old Testament which referred to circumcision. Sitting in the front, Carol put her hand up and asked, 'Please Miss Bland, what is circumcision?' turning quickly to wink at the rest of the class.

Without missing a beat of her measured tread (she paced back and fore between the window and the door throughout the lesson), Miss Bland began to talk about the foreskin on the penis being cut, pulling the skin on the tip of her forefinger tightly back as she explained.

After that, a spider could be heard walking across the floorboards when Miss Bland gave a lesson and Carol stopped asking so many questions.

Chapter Eight

Oona swooshes into the visitors' car park at the side of Rees Powell's shop, the tyres leaving a large 'O' shape in the gravel. Rees specialises in breeches, jodhpurs (ladies, gents and juveniles), hacking jackets, gentlemen's suits, ladies' costumes. He also sells cravats, stocks, nine-carat pins to hold the stocks in place, cufflinks, tie pins with foxes and horses heads. Top hats for dressage events and bowler hats for the judges at the County Show are wrapped in acid-free tissue and stored in deep drawers to protect them from any stray sunbeams that might be unwise enough to push their way into the shop. In the corner, a glass cabinet displays small suede boxes containing dropper diamond earrings which tremble expensively in the ear lobes of the dressage competitors when they sit astride their mounts.

Riding boots stuffed with wooden trees stand to attention in an immaculate row on a high shelf running around the room. As Rees reminds his customers, appearance is paramount. Presentation is the first thing the judges look for and it can be the deciding factor when allocating the prizes.

Nansi, Rees's flame-haired wife, appears and greets us with hugs and kisses. She welcomes us as though we are family.

'You're looking well,' Oona compliments her.

'Do you think so? I've been to Trimsaran and had my hair done.' She pats her hair. 'It's set in the "Italian" style, very popular at the moment.'

I scrutinise Nansi's hairdo, but fail to see any resemblance to Sophia Loren. Oona tells her it looks 'wonderful' and she beams.

'Rees, Rees, come and see who's here.'

Rees appears, a tape measure around his neck. He and Oona shake hands but he gives me a little bow, saying, 'Mademoiselle', which is one of his affectations, before excusing himself.

To tone with her auburn colouring and freckled complexion, Nansi favours a palette of autumn shades. Her fully-fashioned Pringle jumper might be 'fudge', 'donkey brown' or 'burnt caramel'. A discreetly checked Daks skirt and Portland shoes complete Nansi's ensemble. She fits in perfectly into this shop, almost like a fixture.

'There. Make yourselves comfortable,' Nansi commands, positioning two crumpled leather armchairs directly in front of the counter.

Oona explains she would like a jacket and skirt in time for Easter.

'Lovely!' Nansi exclaims. 'Spring is on the way and a new outfit is as good a tonic as any. We've just had some beautiful new fabrics. You'll love them.'

Deft as a conjurer, Nansi twirls an array of material swatches in the air before placing them on the counter for Oona's inspection.

Guiding us through the suiting and tweeds, Nansi's large, single-stone diamond ring nestles against her rose-gold wedding band, the gold bracelet watch on her left wrist matching the heavy bangle on her other arm, accenting the fine gold chain around her neck, complementing the plain studs in her ears. Vibrant as a flame, Nansi warms us with her glow. Words like 'dog's tooth', 'bird's eye', 'Prince of Wales check', 'gabardine', 'whipcord', 'grey flannel', 'navy pinstripe' and 'herringbone' flow like a joyous love song from her throat.

At one point she pauses.

'Of course, these fabrics are windproof, thorn-proof, and I nearly said waterproof, but that's not strictly true. They are almost indestructible. You can take them to the dry cleaners' time and again and they will always come back like new.'

An occasional soft murmur from Oona prompts Nansi to put a particular sample aside.

Draping fabrics this way and that, Nansi twists Oona towards the mirror, smoothes her shoulders to show where the tiny darts will go, pulls the fabric tightly in at the waist, to display the silhouette to best advantage, because clothes must always follow the line of the body, otherwise they cannot flatter, runs her hand down Oona's spine, tracing the position of intricate seams, mapping Oona's body, wondering how long Oona would like the sleeves, though we know it is Nansi who will make all the decisions.

Nansi pats Oona's hands, touches the turquoise rings she's wearing, smiles into her eyes, looks at the rings again, because she wants Oona to know that she remembers these are Mamma's rings. Skilfully, Nansi weaves us into her family, reminding us we are not customers but members of her family, the 'Family Business' that Rees and Nansi run so very successfully.

Oona chooses the brown-and-beige bird's eye suiting and she could not have made a better choice. Nansi congratulates Oona on her good taste, the suitability of the weight of the material, the properties of the weave and the colour. She will look so good in it, because she has the height and the bearing.

Then Nansi remembers how Dadda liked his riding jackets cut slightly longer, he was a gentleman of the old school, dap on the dot when paying his bills, bringing a bottle of port for them. Once he gave them a Caerphilly cheese, wrapped in muslin and hazelnut leaves.

'Now that was a treat! Caerphilly is the cheese I love the most in the world, and I have travelled a little, you know. Once we went to Italy, tasted Mozzarella and Parmesan Reggiano (the real Parmesan), but there is nothing to compare with a Caerphilly cheese. It is moist and crumbly, beautiful on a cracker biscuit with a glass of cider and a Cox's pippin.'

Nansi beckons us to follow her to the office. On the wall is a picture of Dadda and Dysart, one of his favourite mounts. Across the bottom is written, 'Nansi and Rees, from Dysart and Will'.

Pointing to the photograph, she recalls, 'Dysart was a real character. I saw Harry Llewellyn on Foxhunter in Wembley in 1948. It was our silver anniversary and Rees took me to London for a few days. Foxhunter was a wonderful horse, wonderful. He won in Rome, Toronto, Geneva, New York, but nothing, nothing thrilled me like the sight of your father on Dysart.'

My favourite bedtime story had been about the day Dadda rescued Dysart.

'It was a warm afternoon and Dadda and Molly, who was pulling the governess carriage, had been to the station to collect a parcel.

'They were rounding the corner, where you can see Worm's Head Point on one side and the knacker's yard on the other, when Dadda saw Luther Geary, walking a thin horse around to the back of the yard.'

'To be killed?'

'To be put to sleep.'

'Killed you mean, though.'

'"Looks like that horse was once a fine fellow, Luther," Dadda called out, jingling the loose change in the pocket of his canvas apron.

'Luther stopped and wheeled the horse around. "D'you want to take a look at him, Mr Sivell?"

'Dadda thought Dysart might have been a racehorse from the way he held his head and moved, though he limped slightly. A glance in Dysart's mouth showed he was a young horse. Running his hands down the shoulders, withers and flanks, the horse's legs seemed sound. A nail in the frog of the foot was the reason for the horse's lameness.

'Dadda had a half-crown piece in his pocket that he could spare.

"Take that for the horse," he said, handing Luther the coin.

'Dysart was wormed and groomed, fed good hay, bran mash and a bag of oats now and then. He cropped the field with Molly and he grew strong and beautiful.'

'Did Dadda ride Dysart?'

'Yes. His wind was broken but each morning, before anyone was up, Dadda walked Dysart along the coastal path and in summertime he trotted on the beach, splashing along the water's edge.'

Then Mum's eyes would focus on some place which had gone for ever and the story ended with a goodnight kiss.

Clasping her hands together, Nansi beams and Oona inclines her head slightly trying not to look too delighted. From a drawer Nansi brings out a copy of the *Stanton and Gosford Times*, dated 17 May, 1930. Yellowed, marked and creased, it shows a photograph of Dadda with Emlyn the tame crow, Emlyn's beak deep in a pint pot of beer. The caption reads, 'Emlyn crows over the bitter'. Underneath, a short paragraph tells how the crow with the broken wing found his perch with the Sivells of Beauchamp Terrace.

Oona is one of the Powells' most faithful customers and they have many, for they treat everyone like this. How else could Rees run a powerful V8 Pilot car, the one with the arm rest that comes down in the middle of the back seat that is parked on the gravelled forecourt?

In this car he and Nansi go shopping to Gosford once a week and lunch in The Falcon Hotel on creamed broccoli soup, prime roast beef, garden vegetables and sherry trifle.

Other restaurants in the town provide equally good food but it is to The Falcon they return each week. Maisie the waitress greets them on arrival, takes their coats, ushers them to the best table near to the window but close enough to the fire for them to be warm in wintertime. Giving the menu cards an extra polish before presenting them solicitously, Maisie enquires if they would like to see the wine list before she takes their order. She brings extra pats of butter for their rolls and asks if there is anything else they require then, halfway through the main course Maisie reappears and whispers, 'A little more gravy?' her lips close enough to Rees's ear to annoy Nansi and for him to smell her breath, feel her hair on his cheek, her breast invitingly soft against his shoulder.

Rees looks at his plate, wipes his mouth delicately on the edge of the white linen napkin that has The Falcon Hotel embroidered in red skeins in the corner then, shifting in his chair, he says, 'Thank you. I'll have a little more—' and is it a deliberate hesitation on his part, or is Nansi imagining things, 'gravy.'

When Rees settles the bill his generosity is hampered by Nansi, who hovers, watchful, her eyes on the amount, the money, the change, the tip but, when Nansi goes shopping, Rees settles himself in the wing armchair in the lounge for an hour or so, reading the *Financial Times*.

When he has sipped his cup of coffee, finished his brandy, drunk the second coffee that Maisie has brought him without his even asking, he settles the bill again, this time slipping a one pound note into Maisie's hand. She takes it, squeezing Rees's fingers tightly and Rees looks so deeply into her eyes that Maisie blushes. It is for Maisie, and for the unspoken suggestion of something more, that Rees will return to The Falcon every week.

Suddenly Nansi grasps Oona's hands and asks her which shoes she will wear with her new costume. Oona thinks for a moment before declaring she will buy a pair of Norvic lace-up shoes, which she calls brogues. Oona volunteers that she might just buy a new green crocodile handbag from Mappin and Webb, as she has a copy of their latest catalogue.

A blissful sigh escapes from Nansi's throat. The customer is always right. No Parisian *vendeuse* can equal Nansi for charm and flattery and, just for this afternoon, we are the most important people in the world to her.

This is why Oona cannot say 'no' when Nansi suggests a pure silk lining for the jacket and an extra skirt. If Nansi were to suggest weaving a 22-carat gold thread through the lapels and cuffs, Oona would not disagree. As a finishing touch, Nansi has a suggestion: a scarf would show that this is an exclusive outfit. 'And one last thing. The buttons.'

Nansi takes samples from a drawer. 'There is no need for me to tell you ladies that buttons can make or break an outfit.'

Oona nods.

'I have some beautiful examples here.' Nansi positions her face closer to Oona's and lowers her voice slightly.

'Straight from Switzerland. Exclusive to us and a tailor in Savile Row. Do I have your permission to order these?'

Her whisper is quiet, uniting herself and Oona.

'Yes. They're lovely.' Oona's fingers trace the round edges of the buttons.

Before we leave, on a tiny scrap of paper that in no way diminishes the large sum shown, Nansi gives Oona an estimate of the bill. Oona accepts it serenely and slips it into her handbag without even a glance.

Nansi's final words of the afternoon are meant to be reassuring.

'This is "Investment Dressing". It costs, no two ways about it, but you are buying into quality and quality always shows and that's the only thing that matters.'

Oona's face displays a beatific expression, as though the garments herald a new beginning in her life, an impossible rebirth, which will overshadow the cost, making the bill appear a mere trifle. As a final blessing Nansi kisses us both again and we leave her standing in the doorway, a solar ball of golden energy lighting up the horizon.

Chapter Nine

Beauchamp Terrace is situated in what is known as the West End of town. This is not a social comment, merely a geographical description, though the street retains a handsome facade. The houses are constructed in a local sandstone which gleams and sparkles when the sun shines at an acute angle over the town, but now it is dark and the moon sends a slick of light over the Welsh slate roofs. Built in the late 1890s by well-to-do shopkeepers, retired sea captains, milliners and teachers of pianoforte, these are solid houses with heavy front doors, Minton mosaic-tiled hallways and barometers on the wall. The owners, who have mostly inherited them from their parents, are justly proud of their homes. Like well-loved pets, they have names: The Venture, Fair Winds and The Moorings, for this is a seaside town. Quiet kindnesses take place a hundred times a day here and, if there is money, it is discreet.

I let myself into Number One, the familiar smell of crystal chandeliers, purple and magenta cushions, antimacassars, marble fireplaces, chinoiserie wallpaper, heavy bobbled curtains with pink pheasants strutting across a cream landscape, a burr walnut bureau, a 'grandmother' chair and ormolu clocks marking time and greeting me.

If it weren't for the old wireless batteries recharging in front of the Aga in the kitchen, I might be in the *Petite Trianon* or the *Winter Palace* in Imperial Russia.

Bamford Bros are featuring a beech dining room table and chairs, complete with lime and orange cushions, made by Ercol. A three-legged lamp, standing on a coffee table, illuminates the leaf-patterned linen curtain, draped artistically over a curtain pole. This furniture will never find its way into the dining rooms of Beauchamp Terrace, because these tables and chairs are destined for L-shaped, open-plan rooms in the new estate of houses that overlooks the sea. Teachers in the raw brick Secondary Modern School have taken out large mortgages to buy these houses and their wives work as part-time secretaries to cover the payments. The estate displays a uniformity; the gardens planted with pink tamarisk and blue mop-head hydrangea, that struggle to survive the sea mists.

This evening Oona is in the Bay Hotel, having a meal with some nurses from the County Hospital in Gosford, and Connor has gone to look at a van he is interested in.

Time by myself is rare but I don't know what to do with it now. Knitting does not interest me tonight, neither does reading. I get up, sit down, get up and fill the twin-tub washing machine with hot water, throw in some white towels, add two scoops of Persil powder and programme the machine to 'Boil Wash'.

I water the shuttlecock fern in the scullery, watching wobbly splashes of yellow-and-amber gold shimmer across the distempered walls, patterns changing, coagulating, like a slick of oil floating in a puddle of rainwater. A bottle of wine, the colour of a semi-precious citrine, glistens on the concrete slab and I fill a fluted glass to the brim with the precious liquid and carry it into the sitting room.

The warmth of sun-ripened apricots, raisins, herbs and soft breezes bursts inside my mouth and I roll the sweetness around my tongue. Another sip and then maybe I have drunk too much, or perhaps not enough, but the green gloss paint on the walls begins to swirl around and the autumn leaves in the watercolour that hangs above the chiffonier fall over and over again, in a soft shower of gold dust. Hands and arms polish a walnut table, seek out dusty corners with feather dusters, wipe picture rails, beat rugs, shake cushions. China ornaments are washed and washed again, as though life is eternal and this house will never be clean enough.

I want teak furniture, black leather chairs, lights like globe artichokes, muslins, plain linens, rugs in Mexican orange, sierra gold, volcanic red, not Mamma's needlepoint carpets patterned with cabbage roses and wind anemones.

Sparks of orange, sherbet, lapis lazuli, puff-powder pink, pastis, chromatic yellow, absinthe, burst in the blackness, like potpourri shooting through my head. A monster has entered by stealth of darkness and swallowed the sun. Number One Beauchamp Terrace, my cat's cradle of comfort, a riverbed for my dreams, has vanished, replaced by a shadow house: the keeper of other people's lived lives.

Stairboards creak in the night, curtains swish softly and shadows move easily up and down the stairs. My aunt says it's Dadda, checking that fires are out, doors are locked, that we are safely tucked in bed. I am annoyed with the spirits who make themselves at ease here, treat this house as though it is still theirs and, in a way I don't quite understand but which still makes me angry; this house stops me from showing Connor my true feelings.

If Oona were here she would tell me to lie down or go for a walk. My mother's remedy for everything is to buy a new Yardley lipstick and the latest edition of *Vogue*, but I know that nothing will stop these feelings of rage. My hand reaches for the bottle but is frozen by a knock on the front door. I rush to see who it is and, there, on the step, like a goddess, is Carol. I have made endless plans for this visit and, suddenly, unexpectedly, she's arrived. With a whoop, we are in each other's arms.

This is Carol, who introduced me to Tampax, who held a mirror up close for me to squeeze the blackheads on my chin, Carol who asked to use my nail scissors to clip the hairs inside her nose when she thought they were growing too long. When I said that Mum was marrying and we were moving away, Carol had the solution. I was to come back every holiday and we would be air hostesses when we were ladies. And this is Carol who has escaped from Stanton.

'I was not expecting you so soon.' I fling my arms around her, hardly able to contain my delight.

'Shall I come back next week? Come on, girl, let me in.'

Carol had written, 'Boy, have I got lots to tell you,' and I can't wait to hear her news.

In the hallway I feast on Carol's outfit, her flowered leggings, sap-green velvet coat, leather bag, yellow like fluffy mimosa. Her teeth gleam, her skin glows. Whether she is walking down Stanton High Street or by the Grand Canal in Venice, Carol will not go unnoticed.

Wriggling out of her coat, she breathes in deeply, her eyes sweeping over the hallway.

'I adore this house.' Carol's fingertips brush the white petals of the tulips in the heavy glass vase. 'Everything is just as it was before I went away.'

'Come through. I've got wine.'

Carol settles herself on the settee as I fill her glass.

'Have you eaten?'

'Mum stuffed me. Steak and chips followed by jam roly-poly and custard,' and she pats her middle.

'Let's have some chocolates.'

'You know all my weaknesses.' Deftly, she slips a chocolate ganache into her mouth.

'How's everyone been behaving while I've been toiling in Milan?'

'Having a wonderful time, you mean. I used to imagine you, meeting Sophia Loren and the world's rich in the fashion shows.'

'I didn't actually meet them, but I saw Princess Grace and Farah Diba, the Shah of Iran's wife, sitting on little gilt chairs in the front row. At first, I couldn't believe my luck, but you get used to everything after a while.'

'It sounds absolutely fantastic.'

'In many ways it was and I'm glad I went but, often, I just wanted to be back here. Saturday nights and Sunday afternoons can be quiet, wherever you are.'

Carol takes a sip of wine.

'What I like about your house, this town, you in your cosy job is that I can return and know everything will be the same as when I went away.'

I nod wryly.

'That's just it. Nothing much changes here.'

Carol raises her eyebrows, waiting for an explanation.

'While you have worked abroad, what have I done? Accounts clerk for Bertie B. Perkins might be smart at sixteen, but four years down the line? Sad.'

'Bertie's had a stroke, Mum said in one of her letters. You're running it now, aren't you?'

'Yes, but it's more or less what I did years ago.'

Carol chooses a champagne truffle and eats it delicately.

'You know what to do. If you don't like your life, change it.'

I feel I've had an electric shock. It's one thing to be fed up and grouse but to change things? Scary.

'I had a postcard from Nicky a few days ago.'

'Your mum's step-daughter, right? What's she getting up to nowadays?'

'She's in France.'

'France?'

Sensing the interest in Carol's voice, my stomach flips. I envy Nicky because she is younger than me but is far bolder.

'Studying, or what?'

'She has a boyfriend.'

Then I tell Carol about Connor and I don't keep anything back. Carol listens carefully.

She's already on the second layer of chocolates.

'Let's get Nicky out of the way first. A few lines from Nicky and you're upset.'

Coming from anyone else this observation would have irked me, but not from Carol. I should have remembered I could never fool Carol about my feelings.

'By now she may have broken up with this boy, blubbing over her lonely café crème or, she may even be back in Rye, with her mum. Perhaps she made it all up. We know how inventive teenage girls can be. Yeah?'

'Yeah,' I reply, not totally convinced.

'As for Connor, give it time.'

I have not seen Carol for yonks and now all I have to offer is boring conversation.

'How about coffee?' Carol suggests, when there are only two chocolates left.

'We haven't got ground. The Kardomah, in Swansea, is the nearest place that sells it.'

'Camp will be fine. What's happening with the shop?'

'Nothing. No one wants it.'

'You don't do anything with it?' Her voice is incredulous.

'I keep my wool there.'

'Your wool?'

'I've taken up knitting.'

'Knitting? You always liked crafts. Remember those cardboard daisy looms you were mad on, stitching them into bags and belts?'

We laugh. It's good to have Carol around again.

'You're really creative.'

'That's about all I'm good at.'

'Come on, girl. What's wrong with you tonight? Look, Stell, you could be a designer or, or—'

'Yes?'

'Or you could sell your knitting in one of those chic little shops that are cropping up everywhere now.'

'That's about all I'm good at. Knitting.'

'You could open the shop and sell your handiwork. How's that for an idea?'

'Even if I could sell my stuff, the shop is not in the best position. People come this way for petrol or to have their watches mended. The high street is the place to buy clothes.'

For a moment Carol looks downcast, then brightens. 'Let's see the shop.'

'Mind the step,' I warn, Carol so close behind me I can smell the hairspray on her beehive, as we enter William Halford's shop.

'Gosh, there's enough wool here to go into business right away. How come you've got so much?' Carol looks genuinely bewildered.

'Sheer extravagance,' I quip, 'coupled with the fact it's impossible to buy wool in Stanton.'

'You could knit enough clothes to last you a lifetime and a good bit of eternity as well,' Carol marvels, picking up a ball of chunky knit. Her lips pick out the labels on the front of the shelves, with colours like duck egg blue, plum blossom, azure, pumpkin pie, Parma violet, chromatic green and winberry.

Something like bemusement flickers across her face. 'I can see you've written out these labels,' she says. 'You made the colours up?'

I notice Carol is blinking rapidly, a sign of intense thought.

'Over here are the saturated colours,' I explain.

'Saturated? What does that mean?'

'Colours with depth; that you could sink into. Peony pink, Oriental poppy red, iris siberica blue,' I recite.

'Hold, hold, hold,' Carol entreats. 'Something's not quite right here.'

Carol's eyes are lichen-coloured, with hints of silver birch or, perhaps, a mixture of sage and lime.

'These colours—'

'Don't you like them? Aren't they better than pink, red, blue, brown, khaki, navy and bottle-green?'

Carefully patting her hair, Carol hesitates before pronouncing, 'All these exuberant colours, they're like a huge rainbow, splashing a fluid wash over the room. And, d'you know what? They're telling me something.'

Suddenly she wheels around, spreading her arms wide, doing a 360-degree turn, gesturing at the shelves and the wool.

'You've had too much of these northern skies, grey clouds. Right?'

I shrug.

'I detect a deficiency, Stell. A need.'

'What sort?'

'You are hungering for colour, thirsting for it.' Carol pronounced 'thirsting' as 'thii-rrr-sting'.

'Is there a cure?'

'Tricky. This I know, though. What you need is a vitamin, a colour vitamin. You are starving for colour. It's as simple as that.'

Carol leans against the large draper's chest bought from Bonmarché when it closed in 1930. (I know the exact date because the receipt is glued to the bottom of the top drawer.)

'Everything in the universe is made of sunlight. Sunlight streaming through a prism breaks it into nine colours, radiating from the nine planets. With me? Did you know that?'

I shake my head.

'We're all made up of these colours, but when there's an imbalance, it creates a deficiency.'

Her lips twitch and I can see Carol has an idea pending. I recognise the signs.

'Stell, make me something.'

'What?'

66

Somehow, a woolly cap and scarf seem an inadequate definition of Carol's style.

'No. Full stop. I'm commissioning you. Knit me a blanket.'

'A blanket. What kind of blanket?'

'A reiki blanket.' Carol's tone is defiant in a 'there, I've said it' way.

'Reiki? Is that North American Indian or something?'

'Japanese. I'll explain later. Let's choose some wool first. No. Better idea. Cotton.'

I'll say this for Carol. When she has an idea, she plunges in.

'Now where's the cotton. Bet you've tons of it tucked away somewhere.'

'Over here. How about bone white or is that too dull? There's regency red, desert gold, khasba pink, pomegranate or persimmon red.'

'Easy girl. You're further gone than I thought, Stell. We're going to get real colour into your life, get to the bottom of all this wool, the whole knitting thing.'

After Carol has twisted hanks of cotton around her hands, tried turquoise with lime, a mayonnaise yellow with a hank of Sahara sand that she dubs 'dusty mustardy', a final selection is made.

'It will be striped, with a balance of the nine vibrational colours that we all need.'

'How big is this blanket? I'll need some time.'

'No rush,' says Carol. 'Two weeks?'

Carol's name has the number seven in numerology. Seven has magical properties, transforming in its powers. I love Carol but all I can think of at this moment is how impossible she can be.

Carol perches on the windowsill as I sort out the cotton, staring at a shelf which has an assortment of scarves, baby blankets, fingerless gloves, all things I have knitted in anticipation of Betsi's next raffle.

'Tell me,' and Carol crosses her legs, the flowers on her leggings bursting suddenly into bloom, like cacti in the desert that blossom suddenly before dying back again, 'tell me, what is this knitting all about? Why is a girl like you keeping all this stuff? And the colours. Some people gorge on food when they feel empty but you fill a room with wool.'

I gather up some skeins of yarn that have escaped from the shelves, hiding my blazing cheeks.

'When did all this knitting begin?'

My stomach knots. There's no escaping Carol's probing but, because it's Carol, I can be truthful.

'About three years ago.'

'Go on.'

'I wasn't sleeping so good, bad dreams, that sort of thing, so I went to see Dr McTaggart.'

'And was he any good?'

'Quite thorough. He ran all the tests, anaemia, blood pressure, heart rate, asked about exercise, fresh air, did I smoke, drink, the usual things. Finally, he asked was there anything on my mind.'

By now, Carol's expression is thoughtful.

'And was there?'

'I felt as though there was, but I couldn't put any words to it.'

'So what happened then?'

'He probed a bit about work, asked was there something in the job that was bothering me. In the end, I grew tired of the questions and said perhaps I did get a bit rushed in work sometimes so I'd try to pace myself more.'

'Did he give you anything to take?'

'He just said, "Take up knitting".'

'Told you to take up knitting? Yikes. You're kidding.'

'He called it a portable hobby that engaged the hands and the mind. Intricate patterns like Fair Isle, Arran knits were best, all the difficult stuff.'

'Has it worked?'

'I sleep better now and always have some knitting on the go.'

I seize on Carol's momentary silence.

'Getting back to the blanket. What did you call it?'

'A reiki blanket.'

'But what is it?'

'Reiki is all about channelling energy, the universal energy, from one person to another.'

'Where does the blanket come into it?'

'The blanket is wrapped around the person who is having a reiki treatment, for warmth.'

Carol may not have been away from Stanton for long, but she has become very sophisticated during that time, I decide.

'So, what does reiki do?'

'Try it. I'm reiki trained.'

Walking to the doorway of the shop, Carol beckons me to follow her. This is the Carol I am used to, the Carol who has a quick fix for any problem I may have.

In the sitting room, Carol points to the sofa. 'Lie there. Trust me.'

I hesitate.

'You don't have to do this for me. I'll—' and I'm thinking quickly, 'I'll have a manicure instead. I've got a new bottle of Cutex upstairs.'

I glance at Carol and the expression on her face silences me. Switching off the main light in the room, Carol indicates the velvet sofa. I lie down, my head supported by a cushion, the room lit by the sole lamp in the corner.

Carol kneels behind me. 'Relax now,' she says softly. Her hands cover my eyes and in the darkness I feel pampered and safe, the feeling I had as a young child with my mother and Oona. A garden of colours bursts through my eyes, sky blue, saffron yellow, violet, bright, white, lilac light. Carol's hands move to my temples, my head; her

69

touch so light I hardly feel it, I'm only aware of the deep warmth penetrating my body. I float calmly, as though drifting off to sleep, Carol's hands hover over my shoulders and I rest on soft, downy clouds.

From somewhere the pearl necklace drifts in front of me, the mother and baby pictures I saw in it. Then there is the time I left Stanton, to live with Mum and her new husband Tom. Oona came to the door to wave us off, but quickly disappeared. I felt disappointed because I was crouching on the back seat to look at her. Mum comforted me and said: 'Perhaps Auntie Oona had to go to answer the telephone.'

It was only when I went back to live with Oona that she told me she was so sad when we left she had to go inside and have a little cry.

All the time I was in London I wanted to go back to Stanton. Tom did not get used to me, though he saved buttons for me and scraps of lace to make cards to send to Oona. I remember missing Carol and my old school.

With Carol's hands resting on my middle, warmth spreads down from my waist, through my legs, into the calves, the ankles, the toes. Hot blood surges through my arteries, dislodging memories into life.

That time in France again. Tom writing, 'Mr and Mrs Tom Marsden and Stella Randall' in the hotel guest book. The receptionist had peered at me so intently that Mum took my hand and we walked quickly away.

Carol, scatterbrained Carol, is holding my toes now, spending time on me, when she doesn't have to. With Tom, I learnt to make myself disappear, to take my book under the table or say I was ready for bed when I wasn't. After the first few weeks in London, I returned to Stanton at half-term and suddenly everything was back to normal again and Mum and my aunt said I did not have to live in London any more.

Then something embarrassing happens. One mighty heave of my

chest and tears, huge as October cabbages, run slowly, in a salty trail, down my cheeks. Everything is spoilt. I sit up abruptly, but Carol's arms are around me. She dabs my face with the embroidered crinoline lady arm rest and leans her head on mine. The 40-watt bulb from the table lamp casts only the dimmest glow but I want total darkness, a place to hide, where I can't be seen or found.

'Rest, babe,' Carol murmurs, wiping my face with the other arm rest, while I swallow big globules of mucus and spittle.

'Now, imagine being in the desert. Use your finger to trace the names of those who have hurt you in the sand.'

She allows me a few minutes, before asking 'Done that? Now, here's the hardest part. Look at their names and forgive them.'

While I am attempting this Carol goes in search of the kettle, rattles teacups, looks for the tea caddy.

When I join her I try to apologise, but Carol stops me.

'You have an energy block. Old memories that you can't let go of are draining you.'

'Am I cured now?'

'It's too soon to tell. You might need a few more treatments.'

When Carol's made the tea, she covers the pot with a knitted cosy which has three red cherries and two green leaves dangling incongruously from the top.

'Does reiki really work?'

'It all depends on how open you are to it.' She passes me a teacup, commanding, 'Drink up.'

Carol is like a field of electromagnetic energy. Nothing around her is ever stagnant.

The last couple of chocolates in the box disappear into her mouth, ('OK for me to have them?' when she's already swallowed them) and then she finds her bag and her jacket and I slip the almost empty bottle of wine in a carrier bag for her and she hugs me.

'You'll sleep like a newborn babe tonight, after that,' she assures me,

71

before whispering, 'About Connor. Remember, when you're hungry, you're gonna eat.'

I guess she's right. She usually is.

I tell her the blanket is going to take maybe six weeks. Miracles don't happen overnight, after all.

Chapter Ten

When I come down to breakfast the next morning, Neil Sedaka comes on the radio singing 'Carol, Oh! Carol,' which makes me giggle.

My aunt looks up enquiringly.

'What's making you laugh?'

I tell her about Carol's visit the previous evening, editing out some of the details.

'I expect you'll be seeing Carol in the week?'

'Her mother's insisted she visits some relatives over the next few days, but we will be meeting.'

Oona nods approvingly.

'Has Carol changed while she's been away?'

'No, she's still Carol, but even more so.'

My aunt smiles. I'm frightened I'll say too much, so compliment Oona on her hair.

'I'll say this for Miss Bishop; she gives a good shampoo and her set lasts, at least for a few days.'

Miss Bishop, or 'Miss Harriet Bishop – MRCB' (Member of the Royal College of Beauticians) as the brass plaque fixed to the wall of her house proclaims. It used to puzzle me why, if Miss Bishop was a beautician, she specialised in hairdressing.

'I'm not sure about Miss Bishop's hairdressing qualifications,' mused Oona, 'but she went to London years ago and took a beauty course. I do remember her giving shampoos in Ashley Majewski's hair salon, soon after she left school, though. Not many people in Stanton want their eyebrows plucked or to be shown how to apply make-up, so she's spent her life giving hairdos. Everything in life's a compromise, really, and I think Miss Bishop learnt this when she was young.'

Miss Bishop sees only one client at a time and people get lulled into thinking that this ensures confidentiality. If secrets that should never see daylight do slip out, then Miss Bishop reassures her clients that nothing, but nothing, ever escapes through her four walls.

'The Blois-Brookes's son and daughter-in-law are not buying Slade Cottage after all,' Oona says, helping herself to another slice of toast.

'Really? I thought the deal had gone through.'

'Apparently they failed to raise a large enough mortgage. Simon Blois-Brookes does not earn enough, despite his qualifications. Instead, they've settled on a house in Barlow Street. There are no sea views and it needs a lot of work, but it's cheaper.'

'I expect Miss Bishop was thrilled to give you the bad news?'

Oona's eyes twinkle. 'When Miss Bishop said the house needed "absolutely everything" doing to it, she whinnied with pleasure, like a horse.'

'I wonder if it was Mavis Sandall who told her,' I conjectured.

Mavis works for Rob Pritchard Jones, the estate agent and she is a Friday evening client of Miss Bishop's.

Very little happens in Stanton without Miss Bishop's knowledge. In the Harvest Bun Bakery the other day, Miss Bishop told me that Olive Brightwell, my old French teacher, had called off her engagement to Ivor Deighton (Biol), a widower. They were on the midnight train out of the harbour, heading for Cardiff, to buy the ring, when Ivor refused to sign his house over to her before the wedding.

'How do you know that?' I asked incredulously.

'My cousin is the managing clerk for Adams, Davies and Benson, she said, referring to a firm of solicitors fifty miles away. 'He sent me a letter, telling me everything. It's a small, small world,' and Miss Bishop shook her head happily as she scurried away.

'I wonder sometimes if Miss Bishop suffers from an inferiority complex,' Oona murmurs, thinking aloud.

'How do you mean?'

'It's as though she's uncertain about her hairdressing skills and feels she has to tell you something for nothing, to make the weight up. Perhaps she's lonely.'

'Or she might just like a good gossip.'

Once, when I was in Miss Bishop's for a trim she told me all her professional needs came from 'reps' who called on her. She did not appear to notice that the permanent wave solution on the shelf was in a box marked 'Toni' and had 'reduced' written clearly across the back. In the corner there was a familiar tab reading, 'F. Littler, Pharmacist' so I knew it had not been bought from a rep but came from Mr Littler's bargain bin, which meant it was either out of date or pretty close to being old.

'Doing anything exciting today?' Oona queries.

'This afternoon I'm meeting Edna and in the evening Connor's taking me to a barn dance in Horton. He's bought that van he was keen on.'

'Stonecrow Farm?'

'Yes. I'm wearing one of my black office jumpers and the cerise full skirt I wore to school Christmas parties. I've sewn some pompoms on the edges of the skirt.'

'I like the sound of it,' says my aunt. 'There are some white ankle socks at the back of the airing cupboard. You could wear them with flatties.'

Upper Slade is powdered with May blossom when I walk to the fort later in the day. Hillary and Edna are there before me, gazing out to sea.

'All set for the walk?' I ask.

Hillary is a bubble of excitement.

'Mum's going out every day by herself and Stella,' (this is said in a rush) 'she's got a job.'

Edna looks slightly embarrassed.

Mother and daughter register the astonishment in my eyes.

'I'm starting next week, a cleaning job,' says Edna.

'I didn't know you were looking for a job.'

'I didn't think I'd be able to cope with anything outside the house yet, but Miss Littler needed help and Mrs Sylvester recommended me.'

'You've another reason to leave the house now.'

'I can walk to the pharmacy in five minutes. It's only for a few hours each day but I can't wait to start.'

'You'll enjoy it.'

Edna's happy and it shows.

'How far do you want to walk today?'

'Up the hill to Pencnwc. Is that all right with you?'

'That's about two miles there and two miles back. Sure you want to go that far?'

'I'll manage that. You follow me at your own pace,' and Edna strides off ahead of us.

'I didn't know your mum could walk this fast.'

'Mum used to be good at sports. There's photos of her in the album when she was *victrix ludorum* in her school.'

Until now, nothing about Edna has given any indication that there is anything athletic about her. Today she is wearing a three-quarter-length coat, tweed skirt and flat shoes. If she had a shopping bag on her arm anyone would think she was going shopping.

When we approach the convent, Edna's well ahead of us.

'We'll have to let her go. I can't keep up,' I admit.

'She's hoping to finish the real walk by one-thirty on the day,' Hillary volunteers.

'She could do, at this rate.'

Twenty minutes later and we can see Pencnwc and Edna, a dot right at the top of the hill. When she reaches the cottage with the blackberry-coloured tin hut at the side, she stops.

'Let's sit on this bench to wait till your mum comes back.'

Hillary squints into the sun. 'Mum is really putting everything into this walk. She can't wait to do it.'

'She's looking better already.'

Edna retraces her steps and joins us on the bench, patting her face with a handkerchief.

'I used to belong to a ramblers' club once and did a lot of hill walking.'

'Sorry I couldn't keep up with you. We can sit here for a while, if you like,' I suggest.

'I'd rather keep going and really push myself. I'll meet you back at the Fort.'

'I was going to tempt your mum with a short cut on the way back but she's not having it.' Hillary laughs delightedly at this.

'How did Edna get on, Stell?' Oona is halfway up the stairs when I arrive home.

'Fine. Edna was sporty when she was in school, apparently.'

'It's marvellous they're getting out and mixing with people.'

'And what do you know? She's got a job cleaning for Miss Littler.'

'Oh, Edna's got the job. Freda's rheumatism's been bothering her and she needed help, but I didn't realise she'd advertised.'

'Betsi suggested Edna.'

'Keeping busy is the best medicine often. By the way, I've come across a blouse which might suit you for this evening. Come and see it.'

My aunt shows me a gingham blouse in a tiny red-and-white check.

'You could wear it under the jumper for a bit of warmth. I'll leave it on the banister for you to decide about later.'

I want to look as good tonight as any girl who's spent the whole day, or maybe the week, preening herself. I set the scene by running a hot bath but then hit a snag. Indira Gandhi, Nehru's daughter, floats orange rind, rose petals and oil of neroli in her bathwater. I've no rose petals or oil but I'm willing to compromise. Bathing in scented waters might transform me into a princess, straight out of a *Thousand and One Arabian Nights*. It's all going to hinge on what I can find in the kitchen. Greta Garbo was known to perform miracles with a bag of porridge oats and a handful of salt. What she did with them was anyone's guess, but *Picture Post* called her 'One of the screen's greatest beauties'.

A quick raid of the kitchen produces one lemon, an eggcup of Epsom Salts, some sprigs of mint and a bunch of lemon balm from the bush outside the back door. Before long I'm lying in the bath, lemon peel, pips and assorted leaves floating around me, the salts dissolving, looking like Hamlet's Ophelia, or someone slightly crazed. After a broiling I'm ready to step out of the bath. A glance in the mirror confirms I resemble a lobster more than anything else. The only cure is to splash my face and neck over and over with cold water before slipping into a dressing gown, ready to start the serious work on my face.

Max Factor has a whole window to itself in the pharmacy this week. I asked for my usual foundation, Cyclax, the one the Queen uses but Mr Littler mentioned that panstick, as worn by Elizabeth Taylor, was all the rage in Hollywood.

'A very professional finish can be obtained by using a wet sponge to apply it,' he remarked. I declined, preferring not to take risks but, not wanting to hurt Mr Littler's feelings, I bought a Max Factor copper-bronze lipstick.

After applying the foundation with my fingertips, I dust my cheeks lightly with 'Bourgeoise' rouge in *lilas d'or*, a lovely golden lilac and finish with a slick of brown mascara on my lashes and a shimmer of lipstick on my mouth.

'You look lovely.' Oona glances up from *The Times* crossword puzzle when she sees me.

'Sure you won't be lonely without me?'

'You go and enjoy yourself.'

When Connor arrives in his new van, Oona comes out to admire it.

'There's no point in buying a car,' Connor explains to Oona. 'I need the van for the farm.'

'A practical man. That's what I like.'

I climb in and Oona shuts the door. 'Don't forget, enjoy yourselves,' she waves and soon we're heading out of Stanton.

'You're looking special,' Connor says as we drive past the old fishing cottages by the harbour.

'I could say the same about you.' He has rolled the sleeves of his shirt up and is wearing new boots.

'Like the van?'

I nod. 'Comfy.'

'Comfier than you think.'

'How come?'

'The back is carpeted.'

'Carpeted? What for?'

'It used to belong to an antiques dealer. He had to be very careful moving furniture about so he carpeted the inside.'

'Is that why you bought it?'

He laughs and slaps my knee lightly.

Stonecrow Farm is an austere building. Over the centuries, various additions have displayed an astounding disregard for the style of the original dwelling. The surrounding land, scarred by thorn trees on one side and a jagged coastline on the other, offers little relief.

Strains of music escape from one of the barns. Leaving the van around the back, Connor slips his arm around my waist. His eyes sweep over me and a feeling of pleasure nibbles my stomach. 'I'm glad you're with me,' he whispers.

Connor hands our tickets to two girls who are sitting at a table. Wearing American-style prom dresses, one in dark taffeta and the other in pink satin, they are buffed and polished, as though this is a high school event. A McCall's pattern in Sew Like You, the fabric shop in Main Street, featured similar designs. I have a moment of panic, wondering if I've chosen the wrong outfit but some other girls arrive wearing jeans and I relax.

A gramophone plays and we whirl and twirl and Connor tosses me this way and that until we're breathless, but he's not interested in the dance. We find a bale of hay and I help myself to some fried chicken; Connor has a glass of cider.

'Aren't you eating?' I offer Connor a chicken drumstick.

'I'm not hungry.'

'Let's go for a spin in the van. It's hot in here.'

'You're pleased with that van, aren't you?'

Connor pulls me to my feet.

'See what you think of it.'

Outside, sugar-grain stars sprinkle the sky and Connor murmurs, 'I wanted to be alone with you.'

The powerful arcs of the van's lights illuminate drystone walls and lonely farmhouses. It's only a mile before we reach Pentip, a small village with old stone buildings, a Norman castle and a church. At the end of a narrow road we stop by a patch of moorland, above a small cove surrounded by rocks.

Tonight the bay brims with dark, prune-coloured water and seagulls float gently up and down. This is the first time I have been to Pentip Bay with Connor. Is this the reason that dreams I have hidden under my tongue stir into life?

'I love this place,' I say, as Connor turns to me.

'I camped here with the boy scouts. Mam used to cram my rucksack with crisps and biscuits in case I starved.'

'She needn't have worried about you starving,' and I snuggle closer to his six-foot frame. 'Let's give the back of the van a try. That's why you bought it, isn't it? You liked the carpets,' I tease.

'It's handy for us courting, right?'

'We'll see.' I slip my shoes off and scramble over the bench seat, tumbling onto the floor in the back.

'What do you think? D'you like it?'

'Comfy.'

Lying side by side, I rub my cheeks against Connor's skin.

'I've waited for you all week,' he whispers, 'longed to be with you like this. That's all I've thought of.'

'I've missed you, too.'

He slips off my ankle socks and rubs my heels, calves: the back of my knees. I luxuriate in his touch, the feel of his rough calloused hands, his clean scent.

'Hold me.' His words vibrate in the darkness as I reach for his zip and pull it down.

'I love you, really love you,' and his voice is husky. His hands move over my thighs until they come to rest on hidden soft protuberances and fleshy mounds.

I begin to understand the theory of quantum physics, the ability to be in two different places at the same time, here and in heaven.

Connor strokes me and rubs my belly, his hand under my jumper and bra until he finds my breasts, his body insistent by mine.

'Is it the right time?'

'We won't know until we try.'

Outside, a lively breeze blows up, but we pay it no heed, cocooned in the darkness of the van.

Chapter Eleven

Small flashes of colour, the polished blue of a pigeon's feather, crackled red from a crushed bottle top and leaves like twists of lime glass, glitter in the lane behind Beauchamp Terrace, putting a zing into my steps as I walk to the timber yard.

Pink and yellow primulas border the tiled path leading to the front of a boxy Victorian house called Myrtle Villa. Dorothy Battersby, or Dolly Butterbean as we called her in school for some forgotten reason, lived here with her parents and assorted lodgers.

Mrs Battersby, Dolly's mother, appears from a side entrance as I approach. I'm hoping she's not going to make me late for work.

'Stella,' she squints into the sunlight. 'I came out to look for the milkman, but I'm glad I've seen you. I've been hearing about the hospital from Mrs Sylvester. You and she are hoping to raise money for a new roof. Is that right?'

'It's more Mrs Sylvester than me. It'll be a miracle if we manage it.'

'As hard as hatching a live chick out of a hardboiled egg, eh? I'll look in the house to see what I can find, there's sure to be something here you can sell.'

On the inside windowsill, jars of chutney are standing in a pulchritudinous ooze of brown, khaki, sludge green and yellow, speckled with red tomato skins.

'How's Dolly?'

'She's a "Bluebell" in the Folies Bergère, Paris. Dancing is her whole life, now. I'd like to see her more often, but she's where she wants to be and I'm pleased about that.'

Mrs Battersby brushes a stray lock of hair away from her eyes. 'I'm hoping Dolly will come over in the summer for a week or two.'

When I've disentangled myself from Mrs Battersby, my mind flicks back to that December night when *Cinderella* came to Stanton.

We were settling in our seats when Dolly and Mrs Battersby spotted us and came over. Dolly and I sat next to each other, holding hands. Dolly's eyes were like twin stars, never leaving the stage all evening. At the end of the performance, the Prince and Cinderella sang 'For Ever and Ever, My Heart will be True, For Ever and Ever, Sweetheart to You'. The word 'you' was held for so long I thought their voices were sure to crack. Cinderella had stuck sparkly sequins on her cheeks and the Prince, who was lovely, too, and really a girl, wore high heels and stockings and held her hand, while looking deeply into her eyes.

There were tears in Dolly's eyes, because she thought it was real and she wanted the lovers to be happy for 'ever and ever'. I did, too, but Dolly took a decision that night. With her mouth to my ear, she whispered, 'I'm going on the stage when I'm big.'

After the show, Dolly asked if I could go to their house to see the kittens.

Auntie Oona said, 'I think it's a little late now. We'll come another time.'

'Oh, please, can we go,' I begged and Dolly said, 'Please,' in a very pleading way to Oona and so we went.

The house, usually a cacophony of noise, was strangely muted, as though holding its own breath. 'Jack, Jack. We're back,' called Mrs Battersby into the silence.

'That's strange. Where is he?' We watched her walking into the kitchen and stopping abruptly.

'What is it, Mum?' Dolly's voice had a panicky note in it.

'Where's Charlie?' Mrs Battersby's voice hit a high note. There, on the kitchen table, was Charlie's empty bird cage and a few fluffy feathers. In the old brown coat that had been dyed black to 'freshen it', Mrs Battersby gave the appearance of being a night watchman, repeating, 'Where's Charlie? Where's Charlie?'

Then, from the gloom of the scullery, the blobby shape of Mr Battersby emerged.

Turning to Dolly, he said, 'Sorry, Dolly. Ginger' (the senior cat) 'got Charlie while I was cleaning the cage.'

'Got Charlie? What do you mean "Got Charlie"?' demanded Mrs Battersby, but we all knew what he meant and she did, too.

Dolly started crying, big, hollow sobs, quite different from the tears she had shed in the pantomime. Snottle ran down her nose to her lips and she put her tongue out to lick it away.

Pulling Dolly's head close to her bosom, which was somewhere near her waist, on a level with Dolly's head, Mrs Battersby whispered, 'Let's have a cup of tea.'

Oona asked if she could help, which seemed to cheer Mrs Battersby up. Dolly and I went to see the kittens, custard cream biscuits came out of the cupboard and, suddenly, the evening sprang back to life.

As I unlock the office door the telephone rings. The lorry bound for Trimsaran has had a puncture on the top road out of Stanton. 'Sam here. The tyre's picked up a nail. I've got a flat. It's lucky I hadn't got further than the Bush Inn, so I could use the phone. Can you get someone from the garage?'

Sam Pritchard, the driver, is in his forties and has driven the timber yard lorries for more than ten years.

'Don't worry, Sam. I'll send someone right away.'

Bertie B. Perkins' reputation rests on reliability. 'We're on time so you're ahead,' is printed on every page of the complimentary calendar the Perkins send out each Christmas to their best customers. Mattie Perkins makes a proper clack-wack if one of the lorries is off the road for any length of time, so I ask the garage to send a mechanic immediately to see to the tyre.

This is the morning I work on the payroll, checking the clock cards, absences, unpaid leave, then I add overtime where it's due. There's sick pay to remember and the absences must be entered on a record card and book, but I'm helped by the thought of the evening's knitting class, which speeds the day along and if it weren't for the clock I wouldn't have known it was lunchtime.

Halfway through a cheese and Branston pickle sandwich, an advertisement in the *Stanton and Gosford Times* catches my eye.

'Penelope Wyn-Probert Interiors.' Then in smaller print it reads, 'Specialising in soft furnishings, wallpaper, paint. Castle or cottage, ask our advice.' I look at the telephone number, check my watch, dial the number and instantly regret it.

'Dinas 680453, Penelope speaking.' The voice on the other end of the line is warm and young, like fruity wine from a cask.

'I saw your advert in the *Stanton and Gosford Times*.'

'You have a project in mind?'

Imagining Oona's face if she knew what I was doing makes me hesitate before saying, 'Just some small changes to my bedroom, perhaps.'

'I can arrange a consultation to discuss your ideas.'

'I was thinking of something simple, modern.'

And not too expensive, I omit to say.

'I can show you wallpaper samples, fabric swatches, paint cards and you can tell me what you want. It would help if I could see the room you have in mind. Where do you live?'

'Do you know Stanton? I live in Beauchamp Terrace.'

'That's not far from here. I'm just looking in my diary and the only time I have free for the next fortnight is tonight. Tomorrow, I am in Cardiff. Would tonight be rushing you?'

'I take a knitting class until six-thirty.' Then I pause and say, rashly, 'How about seven-thirty?'

'That suits me. We can put a few ideas together and we can get together again when I come back.'

Afterwards a saying plays in my mind, something about there being 'magic in the moment'. I hope I will not be forced to say, 'Rash actions lead to great expense'.

That afternoon the window cleaner comes, I pay him; ask how his dog is; take some orders; write cheques, then my thoughts swivel back to my bedroom. Should it be painted in white, making a feature of the bed by papering the wall behind in a swirling pattern? Alternatively, I could paper the whole bedroom in hessian, but that might be too heavy (and smelly) for a bedroom. The bedroom floor is boring and the ottoman looks stale. New curtains and cushions are a must and so it goes on until I leave the timber yard.

Edna has a brought a brown paper carrier bag to class and is revealing the contents to Betsi when I arrive.

'What have you got there? Looks as though you've been busy.'

'I've sent for more yarn and I've made a few things which might come in handy to sell at a coffee morning.'

She places two sponge bags, one in lime green one and the other knitted in a blue and red stripe, on the table.

'They'll go down well. Oh, and a tea cosy and bedsocks. They're always popular.'

The socks are knitted in a soft grey wool, with little ties and pompoms in violet.

'You and Hillary will be knitting a bedjacket each before long.'

'I'm not sure I'm that good, yet,' Edna replies modestly.

Delving in the bag, Hillary brings out some belts she has made, plus matching cuffs, and decorated with narrow ribbons.

'That's inventive. Any idea what you'd like to knit next?'

Hillary shrugs. 'I don't really know.'

'Would you like to work on some cotton squares for me?'

Hillary nods.

'Choose whichever colour you like,' I invite, tossing balls of yarn onto the table.

Hillary riffles through the cotton. She studies yarns dark as lustrous black olives marinated in oil, rusty-nail browns, pinks that are sweet as Turkish delight, before deciding on a chromatic yellow.

'Start by casting on fifty stitches.' I've chosen needles the colour of tender young spinach leaves.

Edna looks interested. 'I'll knit some, if you like.'

'I'd be glad of the help.'

'How about an indigo, Edna?' I pass her a ball of cotton, a liquid blue dripping with colour, as though it has just been pulled from a vat of dye.

Then Betsi shows me a pattern for a lacy shawl.

'It's beautiful but it looks complicated,' I comment, studying the instructions.

'The finished shawl is supposed to be fine enough to pull through a wedding ring,' Betsi remarks.

Later, with Betsi busily casting on, I finish the last sleeve of Connor's teal jumper.

'Any news of the hospital?' I wonder.

'Jenni says the *Stanton and Gosford Times* had a spy in one of the meetings. The authorities are determined to close our hospital from what she gleaned.'

When I arrive home, my aunt's disembodied voice reaches me from somewhere upstairs.

'There's a baked potato in the oven. Have some beetroot and corned beef to go with it.'

I'm hungry but I've got to switch the electric fire on in the sitting room before Penelope arrives.

I hardly have time to enjoy the food properly and the chunks of beetroot are eye- poppingly hard. I'm wondering how to explain about Penelope when Oona comes downstairs.

'Gosh. You look special.'

Tonight, my aunt, who likes to boast that she doesn't give a monkey's chuff about her appearance, is wearing a forest-green grosgrain coat with matching dress. On her feet are gunmetal shoes and if Mum were here she'd applaud.

'Where are you going?' Secretly, I'm relieved she won't be here when Penelope arrives.

'Miss Littler has asked me to go to *The Mikado* in Gosford with her. Freddie had intended going, but he's caught a cold and I'm taking his place.'

'I expect you noticed the light in the sitting room?'

'Connor coming over?' Oona dabs on some lipstick without looking in a mirror.

'No. I saw an advert in the paper about an interior design service in Dinas.'

Oona slips the lipstick into her bag.

'Interior design?'

'It's someone called Penelope Wyn-Probert. I was thinking of having my bedroom redecorated. She's going to show me wallpaper patterns, paint, fabrics, that sort of thing.'

Oona's expression doesn't change, as though we're used to interior designers, not Maggie Co-op's mother (she worked in the local Co-operative store) who papers the pantry each spring, charges no more than ten and sixpence and brings her own lunch. Luckily Oona's in a rush so there's no time for tricky questions.

'Don't agree to anything until we've seen the prices,' she calls, heading swiftly for the door.

'I won't.'

I give my aunt an extra hard hug, hoping it will speed her out of the house.

As the tail lights of Oona's Morris Minor disappear up the road, a white bubble car with a gold coronet stencilled on the passenger door, draws up.

Dressed in a leopard-print coat, palest pink lipstick and Audrey Hepburn hairdo, and looking more like a starlet than a decorator, a young woman emerges, carrying a large zipper folder.

'I'm Penelope,' she smiles. 'Stella?'

'That's me. Come in,' and I hold the door open, as wide as I can, because her bag is so large.

Inside, Penelope casts huge, doe-like eyes over the chinoiserie wallpaper in the hallway, the carved cornices and deep skirting boards.

'What a beautiful house. Yours?'

'I live with my aunt.'

We go into the sitting room and Penelope gazes at the brass door furniture, the embroidered fire screen that Oona made when she was in Stanton High, Mamma's needlepoint rug, and the bronze sculpture of a horseman leading a fine muscled steed.

'Do you want to sit at the table to spread your things?'

'The sofa is fine. I'll show you some of my work.' Unzipping her case, she produces a coloured photograph.

'This was for a client in Mayfair. As you can see, the influence is Italian which is very "in" now.'

I study the white table and moulded plastic chairs, the low settee, the coloured glass chandelier, the rug, the stylish simplicity of the room, where everything is carefully thought out.

'I've designed interiors for 1930s Art Deco homes, Cotswold cottages, a country hotel.'

Penelope glows with ideas and seems to have enough energy to boil a kettle on.

'I was only thinking of having the bedroom done.'

'Tell me about your lifestyle and I'll have a clearer picture of what we're aiming for.'

Taking a notepad and slim silver pencil from her bag, Penelope writes 'STELLA' across the top of the page in capitals. Although hardly more than twenty-five, her manner is decisive.

'Do you have a colour preference? Most people veer towards one particular colour.'

'I just love colour. Any colour.'

'You have an open mind. A point to remember is that you may look good in a certain colour but it might not be right for your bedroom. Mistakes can be expensive so they're best avoided.' Penelope smiles encouragingly before asking, 'Is it a big room?'

'Let's go and see it.' I jump to my feet.

'Here we are, turn right.' We've reached the top landing and I fling open a bedroom door to reveal the pink taffeta curtains at the window, the pink bedspread, the Ready Cut rug on the floor, the kidney-shaped dressing table with the white muslin skirt and the French armoire. I watch closely for Penelope's reaction.

'This was your bedroom when you were a little girl? It's like something out of a Ladybird storybook.'

'I'd like your help to change it.'

'There's nothing wrong with it. It's charming, but it's not reflecting who you are now, an independent young woman.'

I agree. 'I want something different, modern.'

'Improving our surroundings can have knock-on effects. Looking at tired things can be draining and even small changes, like new lampshades or cushions, can be energising. Let's go back downstairs.'

Penelope has a plan. White is going to be the key colour.

'White is a good basic to introduce into any room, it's sophisticated, neutral and it's fresh.'

'I like white.'

'We'll strip the floorboards, paint them white; hang new linen curtains. How's that for a start?'

Then Penelope darts me a sly look.

'Everyone can benefit from some passion in their life. Red. Know what I mean?'

'I love red.'

'Plumed poppy, calla lily, cardinal red, cochineal beetle red, ruby lips red, there's loads of choice.'

'How will you work the red in?' I wonder.

'We'll have a velvet throw lined with red raw silk, which will warm the room. The blanket box can be re-covered in wide corduroy with a red suede cushion to soften the lines. The overall look must be one of opulence.'

Penelope pauses, but only for a second. 'Think sensuous textures and you will be inviting luxury into your life.

'I'll remove that dingy lampshade hanging in the middle of the room and replace it with a tinkling glass pendant in red.'

'Sounds expensive.'

Penelope promptly dismisses this suggestion.

'I have friends in the trade, everything will be cost. Besides, you need bright, sparkling things around you, giving off vibes that you will absorb.

'Have a vase of fresh flowers, lilacs, peonies, roses and perfumed blossoms in your room, never artificial flowers, they are dead. A beautiful bowl of clean water, in which you've placed a crystal, will add zest to the room. Change the water each day.'

'I adore flowers, especially garden flowers.'

'Flowers lift your mood,' Penelope agrees, 'but once they wilt, out they go. Looking at tired things is draining. Small changes can bring big rewards.'

The next hour is spent discussing fabrics, suppliers, workmen and I realise how eager I am to believe in what Penelope is offering.

'One other thing. Any hobbies?'

I tell her about the knitting, ashamed I cannot offer something more exciting.

'Why not use some glittery yarn to knit a small square? Framed and displayed in your room, it'll be a reminder that you are a creative person.'

When she's left, I remember something Penelope said earlier: '"Interior design" can refer to our hidden selves.'

Chapter Twelve

Last week Mum sent me a silk blouse patterned in cream, black and smoky reds.

'I could not resist it, darling,' she had written, 'and though it's meant to be worn loose, you might cinch it in at the waist with a big soft belt.'

The blouse feels silky and luxurious next to my skin and I've teamed it with a black woollen pencil skirt and a loose coat.

'Your mum's so good at shopping,' my aunt says, admiring the blouse as I leave for work. 'She must have bought it in John Lewis; it's one of her favourite stores.'

The office smells hot, as though it might combust, or explode like an overblown tomato, and splatter the room with seeds, juice and paper clips.

I push open a window then pick through the day's post. An envelope, in Mattie Perkins's handwriting, eclipses the others. As I'm opening it, a lorry with a consignment of wood draws up in the yard and I drop the letter, snatching the invoice book and a pen.

The driver has unloaded the wood and I've checked and signed for the delivery when Will and Maggie Hibbert's MG Magnette car pulls up in the visitors' car park. Stepping out of the car, they are dressed in their best market-day clothes, Will in a brown whipcord jacket and beige trousers and Maggie in a grey, two-piece outfit that she made in night school and is very proud of.

The Hibberts are 'big farmers' in Stanton. Their farm, Pant Glas, is over a hundred acres in size and supports a large herd of milking cows. The highlight of the summer for them is when Will judges

Friesian cattle at the Royal Welsh agricultural show. Despite their wealth, the Hibberts are known as 'tight' and would skin a mouse before parting with their money.

Maggie settles herself comfortably into a bentwood chair while Will places an order for fencing posts. There is a quiet joviality about them, for they are in town to shop and to gauge whether their neighbours are prospering or not.

'Is it right what they're saying about the hospital?' asks Maggie. 'There's a lot of *clebran* going on and I don't know what to believe.'

'There are plans to close it and join with Gosford County Hospital, but nothing's been finalised yet,' I say.

'Such a shame if the hospital closes,' sighs Maggie.

'Betsi Sylvester is going to try to raise money for the new roof, but it might all be a waste of time. The final estimate's not in yet, but we're hoping that when the county councillors see we've got support, they'll think twice before closing the hospital.'

'Money, money, as usual.' Maggie's tone is bland. She has the complacent air of someone who is not going to involve herself.

'Could you help?'

'In what way?' Maggie's flustered, giving being an alien concept to her.

Her eyes fly to Will, hoping he'll think of a way to say 'no' that will absolve her conscience but, to the surprise of the both of us, he ponders the question.

'Give something? How about a side or two of bacon to put up for a raffle?'

Looking from one to the other, I remember that Will broke his thumb not long ago and had to attend the hospital and Maggie's leg ulcer was treated there.

'Can I tell Betsi that you've promised the bacon?'

Will looks at Maggie, who looks back at him and says, 'Yes, put us down.' And, for once, Maggie seems pleased to be giving.

Maggie bakes her own bread but stores it for a few days, because Will eats too much when it's fresh. On Saturday nights, Maggie soaks the crusts she's saved during the week in boiling water and when the bread is soggy, she beats in a spoonful of black molasses, a knob of butter, one egg, a speck of milk and a handful of raisins, some mixed spice. This is baked to a firm texture. Will eats it in slices and, if he finds it too dry, he pours a cup of tea over it, so his false teeth don't crack.

'No point being fussy when you're a farmer,' is Maggie's justification for most things. At haymaking time, Will hires extra men to help and Maggie thickens the mincemeat she cooks for them with porridge oats. 'This was a tip in *Woman's Weekly*,' Maggie told Betsi when she met her in the market. Later Betsi remarked, 'That woman wouldn't give you an egg unless you promised not to break the shell.'

But when Maggie enters the fruitcake competition at the annual County Show, expense is never a consideration. Home-churned butter, double-sieved flour, muscovado sugar, golden-yolked eggs, nutmeg, ginger, mixed spices, twisted curls of candied peel, glacé cherries large like gobstoppers and raisins plump as prunes are lined up on the table, weighed, double checked, waiting for Maggie to cream, beat, whisk and fold them into a greaseproof-lined cake tin and bake in a slow oven.

Maggie's eyes dart to my blouse.

'I'm not one to pass comment but that's a nice blouse you're wearing. Unusual.'

'It's a present from my mother,' I reply.

'I thought it wasn't the type of thing you could buy locally. It suits you,' she says patting my hand as she heaves herself up from the chair, preparing to leave.

'Let me know when you want the bacon,' says Will.

I walk to the door with them and, as the car departs, I'm surprised by the unexpected glow of warmth I feel towards them.

I remember Mrs Perkins's letter. Slipping the paper knife under the envelope's flap, a cheque falls out. A sum of five hundred pounds has been made payable to 'Miss Stella Randall'. The cheque revolves in my hands. I do not understand it. Five hundred pounds is a year's salary.

The letter is brief but concise, her usual style.

Dear Stella,

We are retiring to the Bahamas, on medical advice. Mr Perkins's health, as you know, is not good, so we are seeking the sun.

The business known as "Bertie B. Perkins, Stanton and Gosford" has been sold. I apologise for this turn of events. Due to the delicacy of the negotiations concerning the sale I have been unable to say anything sooner.

The new owners have agreed to employ existing staff and are anxious to meet you.

Please accept this cheque, with the grateful thanks and best wishes of Mr Perkins and myself.

The handwritten letter is Mattie Perkins's favoured form of communication, possessing the advantage of being both personal and distant at the same time.

I zip the letter inside my bag and begin work, smelling the heat and dryness in the fibrous cardboard covers of the ledger book, hearing the paint on the windowsills prickling and crackling.

I can't settle. The fern sitting on a shelf in the corner is wilting and needs a tumbler of tepid water to stir the delicate fronds back to life again. *Adiantum cupillus-veneris* is an adaptable plant, a native of Europe or North America. It has grown so rapidly there's a danger it will burst through the container. As I look at the delicate tracery of fronds, the leaves grow enormous, till they reach the ceiling.

One dry early summer, alexanders, giant hemlock and a buttermilk froth of cow parsley sprouted randomly between the large stones and pebbles in the *Cwm*. Cows with mucus hanging from their mouths plashed the stream, flicking flies from their eyes. In a lush abundance of tumbleweed, bluebells and buttercups, a maidenhair fern grew luxuriously from a log, contributing to the serenity of the grey-green colour palette.

I concentrate on the scene, breathing deeply in and slowly out, allowing a feeling of calmness to wash through me until the plant in front of me shrinks back to its normal size. On my desk the telephone is positioned to the right-hand side and a little to the left is a diary and a leather-bound blotting pad, on which I sometimes place my mug of tea. A typewriter occupies the middle area, directly in front of which is my chair. For four years of days and weeks I have sat in this position, as though it was preordained at my birth.

The top drawer of the desk houses the telephone directory but, in the bottom drawer, I keep personal things.

Freud said, and I am not inclined to deny it, that there are no impulsive actions. What is taken for impetuousness is merely the manifestation of a long-held belief that has, until a particular moment activates it, been concealed.

I drop half a packet of mints, a tea caddy decorated with clipper ships racing across wide oceans and a packet of nylons, office nylons, into the waste bin, wipe the drawer clean and slam it shut.

The words 'I am leaving' resonate in the air. It's my voice. I've spoken them and I know I mean them.

Chapter Thirteen

At precisely one minute past five o'clock I leave the timber yard and the smell of wood, wood splinters, wood shavings and the sound of lorries in low gear, reversing, backing up, unloading a cacophony of wood.

I don't notice Miss Bishop until she waves.

'Stella, Stella.' Skipping across the road, like a bottle-fed Molly lamb let out to play, she comes straight to the point, 'I'm ever so sorry.'

'Sorry?'

'About the timber yard. My cousin, the managing clerk,' (she pronounces 'clerk' in a way that makes it sounds like 'clack') 'has let slip about the Perkins. They're selling the business. You do know, don't you?'

Her eyes scan my face, hoping that this is the first I've heard about it. I hold my silence long enough for her to continue.

'Oh, dear, I haven't let the cat out of the bag have I, said something I shouldn't?'

'No. I know.'

'What will happen to you, Stella?'

Miss Bishop emphasises the 'you', jerking her head like a puppet.

'I do hope the Perkins will see that you are all right.'

Clutching my hand she whispers hopefully, 'It doesn't mean that you'll lose your job, does it?'

'My job is safe.'

'Really? I'm pleased about that, very pleased.' Her sentiments are at odds with the disappointment etching every word she utters.

Turning to go, she decides to come back again. 'You could always take a modelling course in London, at the Lucy Clayton Agency, if things don't work out, that is.'

Her words pulse like a tin can band in my head. She possesses the annoying habit of making suggestions that appear helpful but carry the silent reproach that the other person should have thought of it ages ago.

'It's always best to have a second string to one's bow, in a manner of speaking.'

She stood so close to me I could have choked on the smell of 'Evening in Paris'.

Then, after rubbing my arm in a pretence of comfort, she scurried away, searching for someone to tell that the Perkins had sold the timber yard and, although Stella Randall said her job was safe, you never know, things can change, things can change.

Oona was writing up her notes when I reached home.

'Hello, darling. Did you notice there's a letter for you on the hall table?'

'This seems to be my day for post. Any idea who it's from?'

Oona laughs. 'I'm not a psychic. Go and open it.'

Written on blue Basildon Bond paper, the letter is headed 'Penelope Wyn-Probert Interiors'. I read it out loud.

Dear Stella,

I very much enjoyed meeting you and seeing your lovely home.

I do hope you found my suggestions helpful. Please contact me if there is anything you are unsure about. Enclosed is an estimate of the cost, which I hope you will agree is very competitive.

I look forward to hearing from you when you are ready to proceed.
Kind regards, Penelope.

A glance at the estimate reveals a figure of one hundred and fifty pounds. I pass the correspondence to Oona.

'If this is what you want, have it. The room hasn't been changed since you were a little girl.'

'I've lost interest in having it done, for the moment, anyway.'

'Why is that? You were keen last week.'

'I had a letter this morning, from Mattie Perkins. They've sold the timber yard.'

'Sold the timber yard?' My aunt enunciates each word slowly as though I'm speaking a foreign language and she's having difficulty translating.

'They're retiring abroad.'

'Is this the first you've heard of it?'

'Yes.'

'How do you feel about it?'

I sit, facing my aunt.

'Once the new owners arrive I'm going. Everything seems to have gone stale there, now. I don't want to wait.'

'That might not be a bad thing. Too much balance can result in staleness.'

'I want something more. I don't know what, though.' I bite my lip.

'Twenty is a good age to branch out, find what options you have.'

'Miss Bishop knows, so it will be all over town.'

'She's a proper "*cyw bach melyn*", cheeping everything she hears, like a little yellow chick. Ignore her.' Oona frowns.

'Don't worry about me,' I plead, wrapping my arms around her.

She brightens. 'I know. Speak to Mum when she's back from Rye. She's brilliant in situations like this. Ask her what she thinks. In the meantime, have something to eat.'

I'm biting into a pastie filled with diced potato (this means it's made to a genuine Cornish recipe, so Greg at the Harvest Bun bakery informed me) when the telephone rings.

'Stella, it's Carol. Are you free for an hour?'

'Tonight you mean?'

'Yeah. If you can. I've got news. Don't want to talk on the phone. Mum's away for the evening, so we'll have peace from her.'

I glance at my watch.

'I'll be with you in half an hour.'

I slip into jeans and a sweatshirt, throwing the silk blouse and woollen skirt onto the back of a chair.

Carol lives in Fronhaul, a house resembling a giant sandcastle. Small crenellated towers adorn each corner and the garden walls are embedded with cockle shells. Five hundred yards away, as the spray blows, is the sea.

'Come on in, Stell.'

Tonight, Carol's in Capri pants and a blouse that grazes her ribs, revealing a golden midriff. I sigh with envy. Pink velvet flatties and gold hoop earrings complete the look.

'Carol, I'm a frump. Don't let me out in daylight.'

'Steady on,' she giggles. 'I didn't know you were into dramatics.'

'Help me. I'm zinc and copper, you're platinum and gold. How d'you do it? You'd think you'd never heard of Stanton.' I sound more light-hearted than I feel. 'I'm dumping all my clothes under a bush in the Cwm.'

'When the moon is high?'

We laugh, but I'm serious.

'You're always in nice things, Stell, matching tones.'

'Tidy, like someone's grannie. I want to look as good as you.'

'You've got your own style and I like it.'

She beckons me to follow her into the sitting room.

'Pull your chair up to the fire. It's still chilly out there, spring or not.'

'Looks like the news is good,' I say noticing the Bristol Cream sherry on the sideboard.

'We'll have some in a minute.'

Blue sparks shoot up the chimney and 'Lullaby of Broadway' is coming from the gramophone.

'What's happening? I practically ran here.'

'I've had a job offer, Stell.'

Her smile is wide as a parish oven. She's really excited.

'It's a good one. I can tell. Abroad again?' Secretly, I'm hoping she won't go overseas for a while.

'London.' Her tone is triumphant. 'I have a friend working on *She* magazine and they need a stylist for the fashion pages. Linda, the girl I worked with in Italy, recommended me and I'm starting next week, on a three-month trial period.'

Carol's alive. She's got a new horizon, fresh hopes. There's an aura of zingy colours protecting her from ever having to say words like, 'If only' or 'I could have, but—'

'That's wonderful. Oh, you're so clever. Come on, open the bottle,' I command. 'Let's toast your success.'

Carol fills our glasses to the brim.

'I'd started to worry about finding work. Everything's a bit precarious in the fashion world. You can be hired and fired all in the same day. Luck comes into it somewhere, but it's a risky game and scary when you're out of work.'

'You'll be the fashion editor in no time.'

Carol throws her head back and laughs. 'I'm really looking forward to getting started. I've brought the latest ideas from Milan, luxury silks, kitten-soft leather handbags, jewellery from Murano. Also, I need lots of new clothes, to keep up with the latest fashions.'

'That's not going to be hard for you, you always look fab. You're exactly right for the job. I'm placing a regular order for the magazine and I'll save every article that has your name on it.'

'Stella, you're my biggest fan.'

We top up our drinks again and eat a handful of nuts.

'Where will you live?'

'I'm lodging with Linda until I can find some exorbitantly priced cupboard that's marketed as a flat.'

'You'll be in the middle of everything, shops, cafés, theatres. I'm envious.'

'Got to admit it, I'm a bright-lights girl at heart.'

'Jeannine's in Queen Charlotte's, isn't she? Oona said she's a qualified midwife now.'

'That's right, but I'm not staying with Jeannine, if that's the way your mind's going. Much rather have my own place, even though it's going to cost.'

'You'll do really well.'

'As long as I don't get the sack. Hey, I've not asked how things are with you, Stell, in particular with Connor?'

'You said, "When you're hungry you will eat." I'll tell you something else, "When you're ready, you're ready."'

'And you were?' Carol whoops. 'Good on you, girl. You are my alter ego, Stell, everything I might have been.'

It's my turn to look surprised.

'I just wish I was more like you, Carol.'

'In what way?'

This may not be the right time to tell her about my job. I don't want to spoil the evening, but go ahead anyway.

'New owners are taking over but I can stay on.'

'And you're going to?'

Carol's eyes are large as harvest moons.

'No. I've had a cheque for five hundred pounds from the Perkins' so I'm not desperate for a job immediately.'

Carol draws her breath in sharply.

'I'm finished with the place. I can't wait to get out of there. I'm just done with it all. Suddenly, I hate everything about it. How I was contented there for so long, beats me.'

'What are going you do?' The shock vibes in Carol's voice resonate, which worries me slightly, but not a great deal. I'm positive I want to leave.

'I've no idea.'

Carol listens silently.

'I feel caged in that place now, though I didn't used to.'

'You've changed, Stell, you want more.'

'There are no opportunities in Stanton.'

'The five hundred pounds will give you space to look around.'

'And then there's Connor.'

'Connor? You're serious about him?'

I know what's going to happen now. She's already asked two questions, following on from each other.

I should explain that Carol's connection with literature is slight, (though she did read Marie Stopes's *Married Love* and my copy of *Schoolfriend* comic in the fourth form) but despite this deficiency she has adopted a dilution of the Socratic method of getting at the truth and is about to employ it now.

'Are you sure that Connor is right for you? How many other boys have you been out with? What means of comparison do you have?'

(Were Carol to be questioned in this way, she would call it 'twisting the truth' because, for her, truth is not an absolute, merely relative to a given moment.)

'Don't you want time to find a different job? Shouldn't you discover who you are before getting hitched to someone?'

Then Carol's voice softens. 'Sorry, Stell. I just don't want you to make the wrong move.'

'There's no need to explain. You're right,' and she was.

When it gets late, Carol walks me to the corner of the road.

'This time round, Stell, take a risk. Find something creative to do. If it doesn't work out, so what? Have another go.'

'It might mean moving away.'

'But you can always come back, because nothing lasts forever.'

Carol slips her arm through mine. 'If one dream doesn't work out, try another.'

She pauses, and looks hard at me, 'Now, about my reiki blanket. How's it coming on?'

We've reach the end of the road.

'I'm giving it my all, but it's not quite ready,' I laugh.

'In that case, you've got to deliver it to me in London, and I'll hold you to it.'

Chapter Fourteen

Oona has been invited to lecture one day a week to student nurses at the County Hospital, Gosford.

'I'm looking forward to it. Doing something different gives you a boost.'

'When will you start?'

'I'm having a week's induction in the hospital at the beginning of June and then I'll do one day a week in the hospital and four days on District. Initially, it's for a year only.'

My aunt brings out a packet of Huntley and Palmers' digestive biscuits and a Jamaica ginger cake from her bag.

'Could you do me a favour, Stell?' Oona looks at me with a pleading smile. 'Could you take these to Miss Lilly and Miss Rose? Lilly was sweeping the front step when I passed this morning, on my way to see a patient. I couldn't stop, so give them these with my apologies.'

'I'll go now, if you like.'

Miss Lilly and Miss Rose taught piano in Academy House, which is situated in a road of tall Georgian houses. The families who once occupied these houses have vanished and solicitors and accountants have taken up residence, converting the elegantly proportioned rooms into offices. Directly opposite Academy House is an estate agents' office and further along the road is the College Guest House, a bed and breakfast which also serves Friday night suppers and Sunday lunches to non-residents.

Mum took me along this road when I had a tricycle. Melodies floated in glorious glissandos through the open windows of Academy

House, away over the rooftops, down to the quay and out to the open sea. Window boxes billowed with massive scarlet geraniums and a ginger cat basked on the windowsill.

Ringing the bell, I prepare myself for a long wait, but almost immediately Miss Lilly opens the door, a watering can in her hands. She peers at me, unsure who I am.

I say, 'It's Stella Randall, Oona Sivell's niece.'

'I thought it was someone coming to ask me if we still teach piano.' She puts the watering can down.

'Stella is it? Come in, *cariad*,' and she puts her arm around me. I explain about the biscuits and cake and Lilly propels me into the living room.

'Oh, you shouldn't have bothered. Thank your aunt. That's very kind of her.' She looks delightedly at what I've brought. 'I'll call Rose.'

Lilly disappears for a while and then she and Rose both appear together.

'I was just having a little nap,' Rose apologises.

She looks at me quizzically. 'How is your mother? I haven't seen her in years. Still in London?'

I nod and she seems satisfied. 'Biscuits and cake. Let's have a cup of tea!' she exclaims, pleased with her own suggestion.

Rose walks to the sink in her floral housecoat and fills a whistling kettle, placing it on a gas ring to boil.

'You will stay, won't you?' Rose asks.

I thank them and Rose finds three cups and saucers patterned with primroses, placing them shakily on a lace cloth on the table.

Lilly draws her chair closer, taking my hand.

'Do you know where in Stanton I can buy some wide, white elastic?'

'There are no haberdashery shops in Stanton. I'll get you some when I go to Gosford next. Are you in a hurry?'

'I bought a corset in Oxendales catalogue last year but, when I tried it on the other day, it was too tight for me.'

107

'The fuss she's making over that corset,' smiles Rose affectionately at her sister.

'Anyone would think she had a man pulling at her underwear all the time.'

Lilly and Rose laugh and laugh, hardly making a sound.

'Poor Lilly and Rose, I don't think they've ever had boyfriends or even looked a man in the eye, they've led such sheltered lives,' remarked Oona once.

The kettle whistles and Rose makes a pot of tea slowly, so slowly. She pours the milk then rummages for sugar.

'I'll pour the tea,' I suggest to Rose. 'You sit down.'

'Oh, this is a treat for us, having you here,' and Rose sits in the window seat. 'We've heard a rumour that the hospital might close. Is it true?'

Two pairs of bright blue eyes watch me closely as I place their cups on a side table and open the biscuits.

'I think it's likely. We are trying to raise money to keep it going a while longer.'

They both nod approvingly.

'Are you collecting money?' Lilly enquires.

I explain that money or donations for the raffle would be welcomed.

Rose thinks about this, fingering the little diamond-clip earrings she's wearing.

Looking at the sisters, bright spots of rouge warming their cheeks, they represent a solidity, custodians of the past, yet they are fragile too.

Lilly dunks her biscuit in the tea then has another one. She takes sugar, but never milk.

'Donations, you said, Stella, for the hospital fundraising?'

'Whatever anyone feels they want to give. Of course, you don't have to give anything, only if you'd like to.'

'I'd like to,' Lilly says.

I'd like to, as well,' Rose agrees.

'What could we give?' Lilly muses.

'There's no need to decide now. Have a chat about it,' I suggest.

'No. I've decided.'

Rose looks at her expectantly.

'We have a bowl we no longer use.'

'The one on the slab in the scullery?' enquires Rose.

Lilly nods. 'It's quite a large bowl and if you'd like it, you can have it.'

'Are you sure? Perhaps you'd like to think about it?'

'I think we're in agreement, Rose, aren't we?'

'It's for a good cause and we don't need it. Take it with you when you go, if you don't mind carrying it.'

'How large is it?' I wonder.

'Come and see,' Lilly invites. Painfully, she rises to her feet and Rose and I follow her to a small room beyond the kitchen, bare except for a porcelain butler's sink and a large cream-painted cupboard.

Lilly prises open the door of the cupboard, revealing a tin of peas, a bottle of vinegar and a tin of Birds custard powder, clustered together on the top shelf. In a colander, three potatoes are sprouting little tufts of growth and alongside the potatoes, is a blue-and-white bowl.

'Here we are. This is the bowl.'

Even in the dim light the blue glaze is vibrant. Plants and foliage circle a fierce-looking creature, who gives a defiant stare.

'Can you take it now?'

Lilly wraps her hands around it, holding it out to me.

The bowl is not heavy.

'Or call back another time, if you prefer,' Rose suggests.

'I'll manage this easily. It's a beautiful bowl. Did it belong to your parents?'

'No. When we were young we ran errands for an old lady who lived next door. When I was sixteen she gave me this bowl. Her grandfather had worked for the East India Company and often came home with china from across the seas.'

'Lilly didn't like it at the time,' interjects Rose.

'I'd have liked something for myself,' Lilly agrees, 'but I became used to the bowl.'

'Don't part with it, it's a reminder of when you were young.'

'Oh, I've had my enjoyment from it. The money it raises will be useful and someone else can enjoy it now.'

Rose brings a newspaper, three years out of date, to wrap the dish in. Lilly remembers they have brown wrapping paper in a drawer somewhere, then Rose produces a string bag from another drawer, saying, 'Keep the bag. We don't need it.'

I thank the sisters profusely.

'I'll wash the cups before I go,' I say, but they won't hear of it. 'Tomorrow, I'll take the bowl to Betsi Sylvester and she'll want to thank you.'

'We don't need thanks. Just get what you can for it,' says Lilly.

'I'll let you know what we sell it for. We'll get a good price, I'm sure.'

I leave them waving from the doorstep, poised to fly away at a moment's notice, perhaps even before a quick goodbye.

The Chinese bowl looks different when I place it on the kitchen table for Oona to see.

'I've seen bowls like that in antique shops in Gosford,' I remark, 'but I've not noticed what was on the price tags.'

'It looks old, but I'm no judge,' is Oona's opinion. 'Did Lilly and Rose give any clue as to what it might be worth?'

'Well it's at least sixty years old if it was a sixteenth-birthday present, though I don't suppose that's much help.'

Oona takes the bowl to the window, turning it over.

'I love blue-and-white china but Oriental pottery is not to everyone's taste.'

'D'you think you'll bid for it?' I enquire.

'Depends what price the bidding starts at. It might make ten pounds or a little more because it's for the hospital. I'll think about it. Put it somewhere safe for now, like the chiffonier in the sitting room. For all we know it could be quite valuable.'

Chapter Fifteen

'How about a walk on the beach this evening?'

'What time?'

'It's lighter now, but let's not leave it too late.'

'I've been mending fences in the top field all afternoon. Give me twenty minutes and I'll be with you.'

I'm anxious for Connor to hear about the timber yard from me, not Miss Bishop.

'Shall we go across the dunes?' Connor suggests later, when we're in Pentip.

'Let's go down by the water's edge.' Empty cockle shells litter the beach and sandworms leave their casts in the wet sand.

Connor slips his arm around me, 'This is nice.'

There's a ripple of white water in the bay. I know she's near.

'The timber yard's been sold.'

'Closing down?'

'No. It's changed hands. It's been bought by a firm from the Midlands.'

'All a bit sudden, isn't it?'

'Suppose so. I can keep my job, if I want it.'

'You don't need a job.' I've seen her now.

'Why not?'

'You can be my wife,' and he looks at me, expectantly.

'Is that a job?'

'Yeah. It's a good one, too. What do you say?'

'We're not even engaged, yet.'

'Do you have to be engaged before you can marry?'

'You're clueless, utterly clueless,' I say ruefully, 'but you've a kind heart.'

'Never mind my kind heart, let's get married, is it?'

She's combing the spangles in her hair.

Connor's offering marriage, himself, a share of his life. He wants me, but there's a snag. I'm going to refuse.

Last week, I would have leapt into his arms, perfumed his home with fragrant spices, rose petal jam, the first pickings of the sugar snap peas, bulbs of wild fennel, aniseed, mint humbugs, cinder-crunch toffees, tomatoes big as pumpkins, fed him buttermilk scones, gooseberry and sorrel tartlets, smoothed his aching limbs with balm of comfrey, washed his jeans, brewed hot sweet tea in a white china pot, suckled him with bugloss, dewdrops and the seven colours of the rainbow, laid my scented body bare between aired sheets, surprising him with my nakedness, my passion, my pure, unvarnished lust. But it is too late. I've seen the mermaid, Connor hasn't and never will and that's the difference between us and I can't explain it.

'I've been thinking about us.' His eyes are intense, blue-grey as the blooms of *Eryngium maritimum*, the sea holly growing in the dunes.

His mouth comes over my tongue, rendering me mute. I'm unable to say I won't talk of silage, crop rotation, acreage, tillage, the price of young lambs, when the tractor will need new tyres.

'Was that a "yes" kiss?'

'That's a "we'll think about it" kiss.'

'And then we'll marry? Stell, I love you, really love you.'

'I love you, too,' I reply and I do, but not enough to marry him. It's not lying, but it's worse than a lie, because it's a half truth.

A lie has a simplicity: its own integrity. But half a truth is a double wrong, deceiving and confusing, harming twice. Mum says, 'Lie only to those who want to be deceived, then you can share a fiction. Don't lie to those who know the truth.' I think she's right.

'Why are you hesitant, then?'

'You want us to marry because of what's happening in the timber yard. You're sorry for me.'

'I love you and was going to ask you soon, anyway.'

'But if I hadn't mentioned the job you might not have asked yet, so you've been pushed into asking.'

'Honestly, Stell, your job has nothing to do with it. I want us to be together, always. I mean it, job or no job.' His eagerness, though weakening my resolve, does not destroy it.

'We're going too fast.'

'The farm is not bringing in much money, but I've got ideas. You could do the accounts and the egg money is the farmer's wife's perk.'

'We've got to switch the dial to "slow bake" for the moment.'

'Whatever you want, we'll do.'

He snuggles up and we're warm again, but he's never going to understand that everything's changed.

I hear Carol: 'Reiki will change your life. You will speak your truth.'

Coming from someone else, I would have said 'bonkers'. Mr Iorwerth Lloyd, Minister of Rehoboth, would have gone further and railed against it from the pulpit. Now, just a few weeks later, I'm leaving the timber yard and I don't want Connor either.

Turning away from the sea, we tread on the dried-out strands of bladderwrack, broken urchin shells, the smashed claws of crabs, leaving a pattern of cracked lacquer in the sand. Recycled rays of sunlight float in the rock pools and a crow watches us closely. Connor's face, in silhouette, looks contented, even happy.

Marram grass brushes the sides of the van and the words *amo amas amat*, twist like irrelevancies through the silken leaves. I love, you love, he, she or it loves, declensions from a dead past, the recorded *incunabula* of what has gone. The words are caught on a stray slipstream and tossed to the open sea, the fish and the ravenous craw of seagulls.

Her task completed, the mermaid leaves, carrying my thanks with her.

The smell of engine oil mingles with long-gone seaside picnics, a memory of red-and-white gingham napkins, dandelion and burdock pop, plastic beakers, egg and lettuce sandwiches, crisps, chocolate biscuits, jam tarts, the wicker baskets and Thermos flasks of sunlit days.

I'm not sure what's happened to the stars tonight, though I've rummaged around for them. As a kind of compensation, I pull Connor close and kiss him, kiss him as though I mean it, kiss him as though our love will last, always and ever.

If I truly loved Connor, I'd step off the crust of the earth with him, without even looking. I'd plaster a thousand night skies with stars and still have enough over to take home in my pocket handkerchief. But I don't and I can't say why I know it, but I do.

Chapter Sixteen

Edna is bursting with news.

'Mr Littler has two thousand names on the "Save our Hospital" petition. Everyone wants to sign it. Miss Bishop stopped me to say it was just like the war, when everyone pulled together.'

Betsi listens, her grey pearl earrings bouncing like soap bubbles on the tips of her earlobes as she nods her head. 'Stanton Chamber of Trade has offered to organise an auction for us. I wish we could make a difference but I've heard that a figure of ten thousand pounds is needed to patch up the hospital. We're never going to make it.'

'But we're not giving up, are we? The Young Farmers are holding a pig roast to support us.' Connor had told me.

'We can't stop now,' Betsi agrees. 'We'll keep going and perhaps the planners will have a change of heart, even if we don't get enough money in.'

'Where's Hillary this evening?' I've been so busy talking I'd not noticed her absence.

'Hope you don't mind, Stella, she'll be along as soon as she can. She's having an extra swimming lesson in the school pool.'

'So you came by yourself, that's wonderful.'

'Edna's out and about all the time now,' Betsi beams.

'I've got a pattern. What do you think?' Edna hands me a pattern.

'"A raglan-sleeved jacket, using Penelope Kurlassan yarn",' I read.

'Is it too difficult for me?'

'It shouldn't be. Stocking stitch is used on the main parts and then the borders are in double rib, plain sailing, really.'

116

'Perhaps I'll catch the bus into Gosford to buy the wool. I've brought the squares Hilly and I finished for your friend's blanket. I'll get on with some more now if you like.'

I move the squares into a mosaic of colour, putting the bleached-bone white square in the centre, flanked by milk whites, creams, sorbet yellows, saffron, popcorn yellow, Madagascar yellow, bitter oranges, burnt oranges, Caribbean spices, cinnamons, gingers, nutmeg, ochre.

'Let's have a look at the china, Stell,' Betsi indicates my bag. Carefully, I unwrap Miss Lilly's bowl.

'It's sure to create a lot of interest. Anything from Academy House is bound to be worth a bob or two. That house is stuffed to the gills with curios and whatnots and they're quality pieces, too.'

'Oona thinks it will be hard to value.'

Betsi strokes the sides. 'It's got a lovely feel, just the sort of thing I'd like on my sideboard, piled high with oranges or tangerines to give the blue a bit of contrast. What do you think, Edna?'

'I don't know much about porcelain but the white background has a greyish tinge which you often see in old pieces.'

She puts her knitting to one side, to consider the item more carefully. 'I love all the fat fish and fierce dragons they paint on Chinese pieces. I bought a vase, long ago, from a market stall, showing a small boy holding a fish much larger than himself. It cost seven and sixpence.'

'Blue-and-white is a favourite combination of mine,' Betsi muses. 'It's so fresh, always looks good. The dish might fetch twenty pounds, even twenty-five if someone is feeling generous.'

'There's a little chip on the rim. You can hardly see it, but it's bound to affect the value,' I mention.

Betsi turns the bowl over. 'Mmm. You're right.' She scratches her head with the end of a red, number twelve knitting needle.

'Maybe we could ask Mr Littler for his opinion. His father collected porcelain, Wedgwood and Spode, that type of thing.'

'That's a good idea,' I agree. 'I wouldn't like Miss Lilly and her sister to think we sold it without knowing its value.'

'Tell you what,' says Betsi, 'I've got to call in the pharmacy tomorrow for cotton wool and I'll ask Mr Littler then.'

When Hillary arrives, I'm surprised to notice that Edna has managed to complete two squares as well as contributing to the discussion.

'How did your swimming lesson go?' I want to know.

'I'm down for the school swimming gala.'

Hillary's pleasure is infectious.

'Well done,' Betsi says.

'I didn't know you were good at swimming. Only the best are picked for the team,' I say.

'Hillary's missed out on a lot, because she's spent her time keeping me company in the house.' There's a catch in Edna's voice.

'Those days are over now,' Betsi says firmly.

'Perhaps I might not be able to come to knitting class every week, because of swimming,' Hillary apologises.

'You just get on with your swimming. You can come back to the knitting at any time.'

'My,' remarks Betsi as we walk home, 'there's a change in Edna. It's these classes, Stell; they've made a world of difference to her and to Hillary.'

'And the job you found her with Mr Littler.'

'Stell, Mum's sent a postcard,' my aunt says, when I arrive home.

Mum doesn't know about the sale of the timber yard, because she's been away for a few days. I look at the postcard she's sent from Rye.

Darling,

I'm in Rye and it's oh, so wet! Nicky wanted to speak to Tom (boyfriend trouble), so we're here.

When are you coming to London? You must be due some leave.

(Mum calls holidays 'leave' because she was in the ATS*). We'll shop.
This season's styles are so delicious!*

Lots and lots of love to you and Auntie Oona,

Mum xxx

'Better give her a ring. She doesn't know about the timber yard,' my aunt urges.

I leap to the phone and call Mum's number. I miss her a lot sometimes, but Oona is a second mother to me really.

'Stella, I'm longing to see you. You must come for a few days,' Mum says when she hears my voice. 'London will do you good.'

'I might come up for more than a few days before long.'

'What do you mean? Taking your annual break? That's in July, isn't it, when the yard closes for a fortnight.'

'Usually, yes, but the yard's changed hands, it's been sold.'

There is silence for a moment as Mum takes this in.

'Sold. Why's that?'

I tell her all about the Perkins' retirement, my job, the cheque, the new owners.

'Perhaps I'd better come down,' she suggests. 'What are you going to do? Wait on?'

'No. I've outgrown the yard.'

'What's decided you?'

'Nothing in particular. When I read Mrs Perkins's letter, I realised I had to do something different.'

'Look, darling, there's lots of other things you could do. You just need to take time over this.'

'I'm working until June. Perhaps after that I'll have some ideas.'

'I'm always here if you want a chat. Anyway, what's the latest on the fundraising?'

I tell her about the auction and the Chinese porcelain from Academy House.

'You see, we're not sure what the reserve price on it should be.'

'Who is the auctioneer?'

'Rob Pritchard Jones.'

'I think you need someone who is a porcelain expert to look at it. Rob Pritchard Jones can't be expected to value it. He's an estate agent and arable land, farms and auctioning cattle in the mart are his speciality. If you could send a photo of the dish, Tom will have a look at it. He's not a specialist but he's spent most of his life in and out of auctions. Send the picture soon because there's only a short time left.'

Then Mum finishes by saying, 'Don't worry about your job. Come to London to stay and, darling, put me on to Auntie Oona.'

So I did and left them to an animated conversation which seemed to go on for ever plus a few hours more.

Chapter Seventeen

'I just wanted to check through the day's events for the fundraising with you, Stell.' Betsi looks up from her notebook.

'There's only three weeks to go and the *Stanton and Gosford Times* want details. They're supporting us all the way. If we can give them a run down of all the events they will publish the timetable. Let's hope there'll be no hitches.'

'Not with you organising things, there won't.'

I pull up a chair and sit by her.

'Thanks for coming, Stell. I don't want to take up all your evening.'

'You're already doing the lion's share of the work.'

'Get away with you. You work full time and I've plenty of spare moments. Besides, I'm not courting,' and Betsi gives me a wide smile. 'Meant to tell you, Mr Littler would like to see the Chinese porcelain, but says we need an expert to value it.'

'I've sent Mum a photo for Tom to look at. He might be able to give us a clue as to its worth; he's an antiques dealer.'

'An opinion from a London dealer would be a help,' Betsi says thoughtfully. 'Mind you, it could be a fake, but somehow, I don't think it is.'

'Mr Littler knows about the auction?'

'He thinks an auction will attract a lot of people. We've been given loads of things. Sometimes you get a bargain, other times you pay too much but that's part of the fun. It's all open, there's nothing secret going on. Everyone present will know what we're able to achieve and people can't complain afterwards that we let things go too cheaply: all that sort of botheration.'

'That's true.'

'Mrs Battersby brought a velvet heart studded with steel pins that used to belong to her great aunt. Her sweetheart bought it in Valletta, Malta, during the First World War and she says it's been in a trunk in the attic for years, so we might as well sell it.'

'So, when is the auction?'

'Rob Pritchard Jones says any Saturday afternoon in June should be all right. We can put the items on view the day before to give people a chance to see what takes their fancy.'

'Oona's giving a brass coal scuttle. She was on the phone to Mum the other evening and Mum agreed: one thing less to Brasso.'

'A nice scuttle always comes in handy.'

'Any idea what we might make?'

'Who knows. Things are coming in every day, but if we got to a thousand, I'd say we'd done well. What's the first event on the programme, Stell?'

'That's Thursday night, seven-thirty, the Young Farmers' pig roast on the quay. Help has been promised from yacht club members, who'll see to the drinks, take the money and clear up afterwards.'

'Let's hope the tide is out and the drinks aren't too strong. Someone always falls in at these events,' Betsi clucks. 'Next?'

'Friday evening, six-thirty, the playgroup has a plastic duck race in the Cwm, with a pop and crisps stall.'

'This is beginning to sound good. Even if we don't make enough money to save the hospital, we'll attract attention and show we're making a fight of things.'

'Now we come to Saturday, the Big Day. Nine o'clock and Edna sets out on the walk.'

'Edna Gibbons walks the Coastal Path,' Betsi writes in a firm hand.

'I'm not sure what time she'll finish the walk but we'll have to get the bus back from Pontantwn: her furthest point.'

'Ten o'clock, coffee morning and raffle. Miss Margaroli has donated a ten pound voucher, which is generous of her.'

'Have you decided on a time for the auction?'

'Three o'clock. It shouldn't take more than an hour, according to Rob.'

'Supper?' I wonder.

'Six o'clock. It's best to get it over early, because there's all the clearing up afterwards.

There,' says Betsi contentedly, drawing a line under the list. 'All I have to do now is phone this item through to the paper.'

'Have you finalised the menu?'

'I've jotted a few ideas down. It's much the same as the choir supper.'

Betsi turns to the back of the book until she comes to the page she's looking for.

'Here we are. Salad: just enough to make the plates look pretty, salad cream and tomato ketchup, out of a bottle. Then cold hams, tongue and beef, bread rolls and butter and potatoes, lots of them. Cider and squash to drink with the main course then tea and Victoria sandwich. Connor's mam said she'd see to the baking. How does that sound?'

'Sounds delicious. How long's the meal going to take?'

'We'll allow an hour and a half to eat, giving us plenty of time to clear up afterwards.'

'So, everything's sorted?'

'Could you sell some tickets? We've got seating for two hundred, but I need to be sure of the numbers beforehand.'

'The tickets will go in no time.'

A knock on the door breaks into our conversation and the door opens slowly. It's my aunt.

'I've got news.'

Oona has the ability to remain calm in most situations but she's buzzing with excitement now.

'It's about Miss Lilly's china.'

Betsi and I watch her intently.

'Stell, Mum has been on the line. Tom thinks it might be valuable.'

Oona's got Betsi's full attention now.

'It could fetch fifty thousand pounds.'

'Fifteen thousand pounds?' I stare at Oona.

'Fifty-y-y thousand pounds.'

'That can't be right,' but I can tell by my aunt's face it could be right.

'Tom's shown the photo you sent to a Sotheby's expert. He says there's an outside chance it could be Ming pottery and if so, it's valuable.'

'Ming?' echoes Betsi. 'I don't know what that means but it sounds special.'

Oona continues. 'Charlie Berkeley is a leading expert in Oriental ceramics and he's so excited about it he wants to come to Stanton to see it.'

'We could build a whole new hospital here in Stanton with money like that,' Betsi gasps. 'We'd better keep all this quiet for now. Only tell those who need to know.'

Oona looks thoughtful. 'I'm wondering about Miss Lilly and Miss Rose.'

'That we should tell them their china might be very valuable?' I can follow Oona's thoughts sometimes.

'Would they have given it if they'd known it could bring in thousand of pounds? What if they'd like the money themselves?'

Betsi's eyebrows join in consternation and she looks worried. 'That's a good point. They might ask for it back, in which case we'd have to return it.'

I can hear my aunt's mind turning things over. 'We'll discuss it with them when it's been valued. It might not be worth anything very much, just the few pounds we thought in the beginning, but we'll need to tread very carefully.'

'When is the expert coming?' I wonder.

'Tomorrow,' Oona says.

'Tomorrow?' Betsi echoes. 'It's got to be valuable if he's coming at such short notice.'

Chapter Eighteen

Charles Berkeley's train is due to arrive at four-thirty this afternoon. A room with a sea view has been booked for him at the Bay Hotel.

The ring of the telephone jars through my thoughts. It's Betsi.

'Mr Littler's offered to pick Mr Berkeley up at the Bay.'

'I can't wait to hear what he has to say.'

'Me too. Is your aunt still coming?'

'Nothing's going to keep her away.'

Blanche Harries is trimming the box tree outside her front door when I walk home at the end of the afternoon. A pretty woman with fine skin and silver flashes in her hair, she is about ten years older than Oona. Blanche was modelling hats in one of Miss Margaroli's fashion shows, when Mum said, 'Blanche takes care of her appearance. You can call on her any time of the day or night and she's always elegant.'

Today she is clad in a silky dress, patterned with the sweet pea colours of summer.

She straightens up when she sees me.

'How's the fundraising coming on? I've told Betsi she can rely on me for the full day.'

'But you're doing the coffee morning aren't you?'

'I can do a bit more as well. Betsi's got her hands full.'

'She's worked really hard and she's got a lot of support,' I say, apologising for dashing off.

An hour later and Oona and I join Betsi in the Hall, where she is talking to Mr Littler and a man who we guess is Charles Berkeley, the ceramics expert.

'Ah, here's Oona and Stella,' Betsi says, breaking into the conversation.

A handsome man with eyes blue as a jay's feather turns towards us, his wide smile embracing us both.

'I know Salli and Tom well,' he says, 'and now I'm meeting the rest of the family.'

'Thank you for coming down so promptly. Did you have a good journey?' Oona wants to know.

'Excellent. Lovely countryside and coastline. Salli always gives Stanton a tremendous review so when I heard you had some Oriental porcelain that you wanted valued, I had no excuse for not coming.'

'You've seen the photograph?'

'Ah, yes. Stella, you're the photographer, I believe, and I've studied your picture closely. Tom and your mum are excited about the bowl and I've rather caught their vibe.'

'We're all on pins,' I confess.

Mr Berkeley flashes a megawatt smile, saying, 'I won't pass judgement until I've seen the actual bowl,' then laughs heartily.

'Perhaps I'd better get it so you can put us out of our misery,' Betsi decides.

Spreading a thick Welsh blanket, a *carthen*, over the table, Betsi unlocks a cupboard door and brings out a parcel.

'It's in here. Just a second.' Wrapped in as many layers of newspaper as an onion has skins, is a cardboard box. When all the paper has been discarded, the lid is opened to reveal Miss Lilly's dish, cocooned in a bed of cotton wool.

All eyes focus on Mr Berkeley's face, the bowl; back again to Mr Berkeley's face and then we look at each other. Betsi's lips are pursed, Mr Littler polishes his glasses, Oona runs her fingers through the back of her hair and I swallow unnecessarily.

Placing his fingers together, until the tips turn white, Mr Berkeley's face goes through colour changes, white to bright red and back to the sallow shade he had when he arrived. We all sit motionlessly, the only movement coming from Mr Berkeley's spotted bow tie, which quivers by itself beneath his chin. A silence falls softly, like a shower of pink cherry blossom in springtime.

After a long pause, probably just a few seconds that stretch like elastic to seem like a part of eternity, Charlie Berkeley reaches into the box, his movements slow, as though deliberately teasing, keeping us suspended, like characters in a film noir I once saw in Gosford.

Cradling Miss Lilly's bowl in his soft hands, with the beautifully manicured nails, and the Omega watch on his wrist ticking discreetly, he opens his mouth but the only sound that comes out is a faint click from his jaw. Finally, he addresses us.

'My task is to decide whether this Oriental bowl is of value, or merely an ornament of relatively little worth.'

Betsi nods vigorously.

'I understand that Salli picked up on something I said about the bowl being, possibly, of the Ming period, which would make it very, very valuable.'

Mr Littler watches Mr Berkeley very closely.

'My considered conclusion is that this artefact cannot, in all honesty, be attributed to that period in history which is commonly known as the Ming dynasty.'

A small gasp goes around the table as though the oxygen has been sucked from the room.

Betsi recovers first and her voice sounds like a shriek. 'You mean it's not valuable?' She glances at Oona, Freddie and myself as though we possessed the power to reverse the decision or at least turn clay into gold.

'I did not say it was not valuable.' Mr Berkeley's voice is mellifluous, with the assurance of someone who has sold unconsidered trinkets for not inconsiderable sums. 'I'm sure it will fetch a very respectable price, but not the price that a Ming bowl might have.'

(Big smile to help us get used to the idea.) We're allowed a few moments to ponder this before Mr Berkeley explains, 'Seven hundred years ago, the Chinese were amongst the first to use the cobalt blue glaze, similar to this shade,' and he tilts the bowl towards us. 'They called it the colour of the sky seen through clouds after rain, which, though fanciful, is rather apt, I think. Cobalt came from Persia but, during the Ming dynasty, the Silk Road and other trade routes were closed, making cobalt scarce.'

I can tell by Betsi's face that she is somewhere else now, her mind on the money the bowl might raise. Mr Berkeley continues.

'The decoration shows a rather splendid beast surrounded by lush foliage, flora, jungly plants. There is a lavishness about the design. What might that tell us?'

'It isn't Ming porcelain?' Oona ventures.

Charles Berkeley gives her his full attention, flashing his teeth in her direction. ''Fraid so. Due to the scarcity of cobalt, the designs were restrained, of necessity. It would be fabulous to identify this as a piece of ceramic from the Ming dynasty, but it's just not possible.'

'Ming china fetches the highest prices?' Mr Littler queries.

'Absolutely. During the reign of Kublai Khan, embracing the Ming dynasty, artisan skills reached a peak of perfection, the porcelain so fine that Marco Polo himself declared it almost translucent as glass. Even a tiny wine cup from the Ming period fetches a fortune.'

'If it's not Ming, what is it?' I ask, hesitantly.

'Excellent question.' His teeth flash but his eyes return quickly to the bowl, lest it vanish into past centuries if he takes his eyes off it.

'I believe this bowl can be dated to the Yuan period.'

'Yuan period? What's that? Never heard of it. Ming vaguely, yes, Yuan, no.' Betsi's voice is flat.

'The Ming dynasty began somewhere in 1386. The hundred years or so before that became known as the Yuan period, one of its rulers being Genghis Khan.

'What you do have is a fine example of robust Mongolian art. The artists painted with passion and love, from their souls and you can rather see it in this example here. Compared to Ming porcelain, the clay used to create this bowl is thick and the background colour is a dull white, so we can safely rule out the possibility that it might be a Ming bowl.'

'Older than Ming, yet less valuable,' Oona reasons.

'Less technically adroit, too. But let's not underestimate this very remarkable and collectable piece.'

'So what sort of price can we hope for?' Betsi's brightened up a bit.

'All things considered, I'm quite sure this piece of Oriental art will achieve a price of three thousand pounds at auction, a handsome return.'

'Same price they're asking for houses in Park Road.' Betsi's mood has improved considerably. 'It's not enough to save the hospital, but it's giving us some clout now.'

'Not long ago we would have been very pleased to sell the bowl for twenty-five pounds. We were blown off course by the notion that it might be Ming but three thousand pounds would be very welcome,' Oona sums up.

Charlie Berkeley laughs a slow, contented laugh.

'I'm sorry to have disappointed you, initially. In my work, there are many highs and lows. I would love to be able to say this is a Ming bowl, but what we must focus on now is the three thousand pounds it could achieve. Remember, it's not gone to auction yet and there's some way to go before we're putting any money in the bank.'

Oona has a further point to make. 'And the other thing is; we must make Miss Lilly and Miss Rose aware of what their gift could be worth.'

Mr Littler has been quiet for a while but he has a proposition now.

'I suggest we allow Mr Berkeley to guide us through the sale, providing there are no objections from the donors.'

'I think that's a good idea,' Betsi says, and Oona and I murmur our agreement.

'The next sale of Oriental ceramics will be in a month's time and a reserve of three thousand pounds will be put on it. A true Orientalist would prefer the green Celadon ware but the blue-and-white glazes have their admirers, who are fierce in their loyalty.'

Then Mr Berkeley throws himself into a discussion about receipts witnessed by solicitors, talks about insurances, bank vaults, sellers premiums, auctioneers, bidders, till Betsi feels the weight of the sale of one small bowl growing into a huge burden, sending a flush creeping up her neck till it burns her cheeks, makes her eyes water and forces her to fan her face with her hands. She begins to talk about the tickets she has to sell, the food that must be ordered, the publicity; all the people depending on her until Mr Littler steps forward and rescues her.

'If there are no objections, Mrs Sylvester, I'd be happy to see to the paperwork and liaise with Mr Berkeley.'

Relief floods over Betsi's face like a neap tide, and she beams.

'And if you could take the bowl with you? It might be safer in the pharmacy overnight.'

Then we shake hands with Mr Berkeley, before Mr Littler drives him away in the Triumph Herald, Oona leaves for Academy House and Betsi and I are alone.

'Well what do you make of that? We've been on a roller coaster this evening, but we might still land with our bums in the butter.'

'Amen,' I replied.

Chapter Nineteen

Today is Edna's day. I wake on Saturday morning, anticipation crackling through me. Oona has spoken to Miss Lilly and Miss Rose who insist the vase goes to Sotheby's, with their blessing. The money it raises must go to the hospital fund, as they intended when they gave it.

By eight-thirty I've tucked the ham sandwiches, the plastic beakers and a bottle of Lucozade into my leather bucket bag, together with the plasters and sunglasses I bought in the pharmacy and the free tube of antihistamine cream Mr Littler slipped in for Edna to carry in her pocket.

'Such a shame if an insect bite puts paid to the attempt,' he remarked.

Officially the office was closed yesterday. I took the ledger books to 'Arnold P. Enoch, Accountants' in the morning then dropped the keys in with them after I had locked up for the last time.

Pausing on the steps before walking away from the timber yard was a surreal moment, as though I was looking back on something that had occurred a long time ago. That's how the mind plays tricks, I suppose, but I didn't have time to ponder, because I had to go to the Cwm and cheer on the plastic ducks.

Before leaving the house I check my reflection one last time. Mum always warns that even careful dressers make mistakes with casual clothes.

I'm Audrey Hepburn today. Black Capri pants, black ballerina shoes with little bows and a polka-dot, scoop-neck sweater with a black button-through cardigan and a red cotton square to tie around my head in case of breezes.

With a nine o'clock start Edna should make the Sloop Inn by ten-thirty and Hillary and I will meet her there, catching the ten o'clock bus from the square.

Freddie Littler is opening the shop as I approach.

'What time's the "Off?"'

'Nine o'clock, from the Fort.'

'I'm hoping to come along at some point to lend support.'

A low mist crawls in over the Irish Sea but the six a.m. forecast this morning has predicted fine weather by lunchtime.

A Hillman Husky swishes by with Roy Brown, the town mayor, at the wheel. Edna is in the passenger seat and Hillary is waving from the back. When I catch up with them at the Fort, Edna, clad in a thick jumper and slacks, is running on the spot.

'Warming up?' I call, noticing the canvas daps on her feet and the paisley scarf keeping her hair in place.

'Yes and as long as it stays dry, I'll manage,' Edna responds.

'I'm here to give her a proper send off,' Roy chips in. 'I had the details from Betsi.'

As I'm talking to Roy, Mr Littler's grey-and-white car, registration number 490 JDE, pulls up beside us.

Freddie springs out of the car, a Panama hat on his head.

He turns to Edna, shaking her hand, 'Good luck. Remember it's all about the journey, not the destination.' He sniffs the air. 'You'll have the breeze behind you. That will help. We're all with you, all the way.'

Roy's wearing his mayoral chain and the sun, which has just come out from behind a bush, fractures the gold into twinkling triangles. I remember Connor showing me how to set light to grass by holding a magnifying glass over it until the rays ignite it.

Edna rearranges the scarf on her head, knotting it tightly at the nape of her neck.

My watch shows it is nine o'clock, the time of trial and torment. In school, examinations began at nine o'clock, the moment when we were told to pick up our pens, turn the paper over, read it carefully, choose our first question and begin. Nine o'clock was also the hour when they hanged people.

With a vividness I would prefer to forget, my mind flashes back four years, to when I was sixteen.

My aunt and I were going to Cardigan for some shopping, but there was something troubling me. The previous day I'd read in the paper that Ruth Ellis was to be executed this particular morning at nine o'clock. As we set off in the car, a glance at Oona's cocktail watch showed the time. A speck of dust twisted and twirled slowly back and fore in a narrow shaft of sunlight coming through the windscreen in the car. I kept my thoughts quiet, but I did not want to be distracted from what I was imagining.

Oona was wearing slingback shoes, a red skirt with a drawn thread and a white Swiss cotton blouse. (Red-and-white was Miss Margaroli's theme that season.) I thought my aunt resembled Ava Gardner that day, dark and sleek with eyes like emeralds but I could not forgot poor Ruth Ellis.

The night before, in bed, I'd whispered my way through Keats's 'St Agnes Eve', imagining the convent roofs glittering with snow and Keats's yearning for heaven. I thought of Ruth then and it was unbearable.

I decide Carol is wrong. No one can live in the present alone. Memory is like a shadow weave in a fabric, always there if you look for it and I tend to.

134

I catch Edna's eye. 'Say when you're ready,' I call, fearful in case she panics.

'Whenever you like,' she answers.

Roy is a rugby referee. Now he sprints forward, saying, 'I've come prepared. Makes it all sort of official when you have a proper start.'

Edna crouches down, like an athlete. Just beyond the breakwater the Irish ferry is leaving harbour, nosing into the open sea.

Roy rubs the whistle in his hands, bends over, starts counting down, blows the whistle and Edna springs forward like a greyhound released from a pen.

She breaks into a trot and I turn to Hillary, my eyes round with surprise, but Hillary is bouncing up and down, waving a handkerchief at Edna's disappearing back view.

'I thought she was walking?'

Hillary laughs delightedly. 'It's Mum's surprise. She's going to run. She's been practising secretly.'

'She's off to a good start.' Freddie Littler is standing near me, looking through a telescope.

'She won't take long if she keeps this speed up,' I comment, noticing that Edna has lost a few pounds in weight.

The Royal Mail van is climbing the hill out of the old part of the town, followed by the Davies Bros bus and I don't see Edna taking a tumble until Hillary's gasp of 'Oh, no!' cuts through the air. Freddie lets out a long sigh, barely audible. Hillary is biting her knuckles, her face a network of pink and red blotches. Roy puts his hand on her shoulder.

'Never mind, she tried. Showed a bit of spirit. You've got to give her that. Never going to make it, was she? Stands to reason, doesn't it? Hardly left the house. How was she going to run the Coastal Path?' He gestures to Hillary, 'Go and get her.'

But no one moves and, as I'm holding my breath, Edna pulls herself up, looks around, turns and starts running again.

Putting two fingers to his lips, Roy gives a piercing whistle of encouragement, Freddie repeats, 'Bravo, bravo,' and Hillary tugs my arm.

'She's off, Stella, Mum is off again. Go. Go, Mum,' shouts Hillary.

Edna runs until she is just a small dot in the distance, runs and runs until she's disappeared around the bend.

Freddie murmurs, 'Oh, well done, well done. We all have our setbacks, that's what life's all about y'know, overcoming setbacks.'

'She's going to make it. She will,' Hillary asserts. 'Nothing's going to stop her now.'

'There's five miles to cover,' I agree, 'but she will make it.'

'Where are you meeting her?' wonders Mr Littler. 'I've got the car. We can drive down.'

'How will you manage about the shop?'

'I have a locum in for the day. No point standing around here now: let's get in the car in case she beats us,' he smiles. 'We'll go through Manorowen. It's a roundabout route, but we'll enjoy the ride.'

Slowly the morning unfolds, glittering through hedgerows heavy with sorrel, wild garlic and milkmaids. The seam of damp earth left in the middle of the road by a tractor tyre steams dry in front of our eyes.

'Marvellous what your mother's achieved,' Mr Littler remarks to Hillary. 'She's able to walk down the street now, even if she doesn't complete the whole length of the path.'

In twenty minutes we're at The Sloop which rests on a bank overlooking the sea. Mr Littler consults his watch. 'We've a while, yet,' he decides.

'Let's have coffee in the garden so we don't miss her.'

The coffee, when it comes, is sweet and milky, the cup warm in my hands, the fragrance satisfying. I admire Freddie's silk tie, patterned with gaudy butterflies. I share Hillary's happiness. The sun and the breeze are perfect. This is a sky-blue morning. Everything tells me I've taken the right decision about my job. I should be enjoying a moment of complete happiness but an image of Connor comes into my mind.

I know with absolute certainty I do not want to marry him. Soon, I will have to be brave enough to tell him.

We've drained our coffee cups and I try to shake off the unsettled feeling that has descended on me, when Hillary calls, 'Here she is and she's still running.'

Edna appears, silhouetted against the cliffs like someone moving in another dimension, out of our reach, beyond humankind. Illuminated in a golden shaft of light, she might be a figure from a medieval manuscript, a saint who has endured great suffering, a goddess in an earthly reincarnation.

Her hair, escaping from the confines of the scarf, streams out behind her, shining like gold metallic thread couched in a fine linen cloth. Sea and sky fuse to an enamel blue and, if this were a painting, clamshells, fresh water pearls and clusters of daisies would adorn Edna's feet.

As she gets closer, Edna relaxes the pace and she has a glow. This is not our lady of sorrows, dowdy Edna Gibbons, the woman who didn't go out until darkness fell. Gone is the woman who could not look anyone in the eye, because she was ashamed of herself, replaced by someone who would run over hot coals to reach her goal.

'Have I made good time?' is Edna's first question.

'Excellent. I wasn't expecting you so soon. You've taken us all by surprise with your speed.'

Edna pulls her dap off and examines it.

'I've worn a hole in the toe but, you know what?'

She throws the plimsoll in the air, whooping, 'I don't care.'

Then in front of Freddie, Hillary and me, Edna does a crazy dance, while the three of us clap.

Mr Littler picks the shoe up and examines it. 'I could try patching it up with some Elastoplast,' he suggests.

'There's no need. I'll run the rest of the way barefoot, if I have to. The next few miles will be a breeze. Nothing's going to stop me now.'

'Well said. Have some more water,' Mr Littler offers.

Draining the last drops of water from the glass, Edna stands up, slips the shoe onto her foot, bends over, before stretching her arms high into the sky, a salutation to her own achievement.

'I'm off. Next stop, Pontantwn,' Edna calls over her shoulder.

As she leaves, Mr Littler comments, 'I never thought she'd get this far. Just goes to show appearances can be very deceptive.'

There's a telephone kiosk on the corner and I ring Betsi and Connor to let them know Edna's on the last lap.

'It's wonderful. She's made such good progress,' Betsi enthuses.

Connor remembers I've asked him to do a small job for me. 'I won't forget,' he promises.

An hour later and we're sitting on a cliff, scanning the horizon and I'm beginning to feel anxious about Edna when a limping figure comes into view.

'It's Edna,' I shout excitedly. 'Hillary, it's your mum, she's made it.'

Hillary dashes up the path to meet her mother, whooping and cheering.

'You've made it,' shouts Freddie. 'Well done.'

With one last push, Edna sprints down to join us, throwing the damaged dap in the air until it soars, like a seagull, before plummeting down again. And then, from nowhere, a dog appears, jumps up and catches the shoe and runs away with it.

'That will make a superb picture.'

None of us had noticed the photographer from the local paper.

'Marvellous. So spontaneous. You'll make the front page of the *Stanton and Gosford Times* next week.'

Edna pours the last drops of water from the bottle she's carrying over her head, letting it trickle down her face.

'May I ask a few questions?' The photographer's name is Ken Goderby.

'Sit down to answer them,' Freddie advises, as Edna mops herself with a handkerchief and I pass her a drink of Lucozade.

Edna talks quietly about agoraphobia, being confined to the house, setting herself the target of walking the Coastal Path and donating a sum of money to the hospital cause.

'And it worked. Congratulations. Marvellous story.' Then Ken Goderby takes another photo of Edna but this time Mr Littler, Hillary and I are included.

'Can't leave the back-up team out,' he declares.

When the newspaperman has gone Edna examines her heel.

'I'd have been quicker, but I think I've got a blister. Nettles stung my ankles, but I don't care. I made it. I'm someone else now.'

I hug Edna hard, Hillary kisses her and Freddie asks how her calf muscles are.

'Tender, very tender,' Edna replies.

'We'll drive back to Stanton and I'll stop in the shop to let you have some wintergreen cream to rub into them.'

When we reach town our arrival is greeted by a banner draped across the railings on the square. In large lettering are the words 'Edna did it! Yes she did!'

This was my idea and Connor put the banner up after I'd rung him.

I read the words out loud, looking at Edna, rubbing her shoulder as I do so.

'This morning, before setting out, I felt I was walking the plank, not the path,' she says as I rub.

Freddie drops me at the square. 'You're coming for the auction?' he asks.

'I'll be there.'

'Excuse us if we don't make it this afternoon,' Edna apologises, 'but I think I'll have a long soak.'

'You deserve it. Take as long as you like but be there for six this evening, for the supper.'

When I've left them I rush home to Oona.

'How did it go?' she wants to know.

'Fantastic! And she seemed a different person when she came to the end of the walk.'

'She probably is,' Oona observed.

Oona has already changed into a silk dress, patterned with rectangles in blue, grey and white. It has a boat collar and a nipped-in waist and, with it, she wears peep-toe shoes in soft kid.

'You're ready and changed. That dress suits you.'

'Thanks, Stell. What will you wear?'

Through a mouthful of cheese on toast, I reply, 'The navy-and-white gingham and I've stiffened one of my net petticoats with sugar and water, which should puff it out. It's bound to be packed in the auction and I don't want to be hot.'

'Where are you meeting Connor?'

'At the hall.'

It's only two o'clock when Oona and I reach the hall but the car park is already full. Rob Pritchard Jones's Land Rover is parked in the shade, under a chestnut tree. Inside, Rob is testing the acoustics and Betsi seems to be everywhere at once.

'Sorry I couldn't make it sooner.'

'Edna needed you. I'm really pleased about her.'

'This is a big day. Yours as much as Edna's,' I remind her.

Betsi's wearing a linen dress from Miss Margaroli's summer range, splashed with a large, red daisy pattern and she has a gold chain around her neck.

'That dress is good on you,' Oona compliments her.

'I'll say this for Suzi, she doesn't descend into horrible patterns like cacti and sombreros, something I saw in a magazine,' Betsi says caustically. 'You two look nice yourselves.'

Oona gives Betsi an envelope.

'What've you got there?' she wonders.

'There's twenty-five pounds from Stella and myself to put with Edna's money. That's our contribution.'

'Are you sure? That's very kind of you both. Money is pouring in from everywhere. Everyone is being more than generous. Whether we'll get anywhere near our target, I just don't know.'

'What would you like us to do now?' I wonder.

'We're all sorted. Just keep an eye on the older folk, if you like. See that they have somewhere to sit, that type of thing. My job is handing Rob the goods during the auction. Blanche and Miss Littler are jotting everything down and taking the money afterwards and Freddie shouldn't be long.'

Connor appears with some gramophone records.

'Thanks for fixing the banner,' I say and I touch his cheek with my lips.

I'm stringing him along. It's not a good feeling. Next week, I'll tell him.

I've tried out a few sentences already. 'Connor, I'm sorry. I think we need a break from each other.' That sounds phoney. Why should we need a break when he wants to marry me? 'Connor, you're too good for me.' That's the coward's charter, doing it with a kiss.

Ok, I'll tell it straight. 'Connor I can't spend the rest of my life with you, getting excited about pig manure in an isolated farm in the Cwm. You're kind and thoughtful, but that's not the life I want.' That's halfway there.

Perhaps I could try, 'I'm not ready to marry. I want to earn my own living away from Stanton. My own money means freedom to do what I want, not be tied to you. I've got to go.' That's better, because it's the whole truth, but it's harsh.

There's something else and this is the hard one.

'I didn't understand about sex and love till I met you.' I don't know how he'll take that one.

I could remember wild harebells in a damp wood, shredded slivers of moonlight gliding across the sea, the way we discovered and shared the ley lines of our bodies. But even if I dipped a silver ladle into honey and drenched each word in sweetness, I've got to follow it with the words, 'But I'm still leaving you,' and that's the bitterest part.

'Stella, can you take some pictures during the auction?' Betsi interrupts my reverie, passing me a camera.

'I thought it would be nice to have some photos of the day.' She glances at her watch. 'Ten minutes to go and the hall is full, standing room only. I'm going to take my place on the stage.'

A few latecomers arrive, pushing their way down to the front, stepping on people's toes as they go. Then Betsi picks up the microphone, welcomes everyone, reminds them what the auction is for, thanks them for their donations and support and then hands over to Rob.

Mrs Battersby's steel-pin heart is the first item up for sale and it fetches what Rob calls 'A very respectable two pounds'. The auction proceeds at a brisk pace. Maggie and Will's hams go for three pounds a side. ('Rich people here today,' Rob quips.) Nothing sticks and it's obvious this is a popular cause.

Mamma's brass scuttle fetches four pounds.

'I had to stop myself from bidding for it,' Oona confides, a tinge of regret in her voice.

'Look on it as Mamma and Dadda's contribution to the hospital,' I suggest and Oona squeezes my hand.

After an hour or so, when we've had to open some windows, the auction comes to an end and Blanche and Miss Littler pass Betsi a note which she scrutinises quickly.

Holding the note up, Betsi declares,

'I've been given a conservative estimate of the proceeds of the auction and it is in excess of nine hundred pounds.' Clapping breaks out. 'The Young Farmers raised over four hundred pounds with the pig roast' (massive clapping), 'the nursery group and the plastic ducks have raised one hundred and five pounds'(large round of applause), 'the coffee morning's made eighty pounds' (someone whistles and cheers) 'and Edna Gibbons (whistles, claps) has run the Coastal Path, amount to be revealed later.'

Outside, a dog barks and Betsi waits a moment for it to stop, before continuing, 'I'd like to mention the generosity of two ladies, well known to most of us here, Miss Lilly and Miss Rose, of Academy House, Quay Street. A bowl they've given is listed for auction at Sotheby's, London.'

The words 'Sotheby's, London' percolate through the audience.

'Following this sale, in about a month's time, we will be able to announce our final total.'

There's some polite clapping, but Rob is on his feet, holding his hand up for silence. He asks Betsi's permission to say something. She nods, as mystified as the rest of us as to what he's going to say.

'Ladies and gentlemen,' he begins, 'I have a message for Mrs Sylvester, which I've been asked to convey to her at the close of this auction.' He hands her an envelope.

People are craning forward, agog to know what's going on. Betsi is startled, too, but opens the envelope, reads it, then looks as though her eyes might pop out. Recovering her composure, she begins, 'The letter is from Sotheby's,' before reading out:

Dear Mrs Sylvester,

I have to inform you that I have received an offer of six thousand pounds for the Oriental bowl you have entered for auction at a forthcoming sale. The offer comes from a benefactor sympathetic to your cause.

I must stress that the sum of six thousand pounds in no way reflects the value of the bowl, which I advised would be in the region of three thousand pounds, but rather it is an indication of the benefactor's generosity. I strongly advise that you accept the offer. The potential purchaser wishes to remain anonymous.

An eerie hush descends, before whistling and clapping break out and the noise reaches crescendo pitch, forcing the more timid to leave the hall.

Then Rob takes over, says that Stanton has risen to the occasion, the people of Stanton have spoken; they are a force to be reckoned with. Full details will be posted on the door of the hall and the local paper will be informed.

Connor's been watching Rob closely and as soon as he's finished speaking, the sound of 'La Bamba' erupts. It's Ritchie Valens's voice, but it's Connor clapping the beat.

Betsi calls me onto the stage, grasping my arm, 'Stella, I need a cup of tea.'

Chapter Twenty

The clock in the market square strikes the half hour, distorting the opening bars of 'The Blue Danube' floating down the High Street.

'Betsi's a marvellous organiser,' Oona enthuses. 'She's really excelled herself; she's even got the town band to play this evening.'

Outside the hall, the band pauses for breath, some taking a drink of water, others loosening their collar studs. Leading the trombones is Harry Evans while Nicholas Rumens is on tuba and the Vernon twins play the drums. At a signal from Ted Phillips, the band leader, they gather themselves together again and break into 'Chantilly lace and a pretty face and a pony tail hangin' down...'

There are fewer cars here now than there were this afternoon.

'It's difficult for some of the farmers to come back this evening, because of milking times,' I remark to my aunt.

'Freddie's car isn't here, either. I don't suppose he'll be long. He's fetching Edna and Hillary.'

'Oona. Stella. Over here.' Betsi wants to show us something.

'What do you think of this?' and she indicates an enormous bouquet of pink-and-white carnations and sprays of asparagus fern, all tied together with a big bow.

'Gorgeous. Who gave those?' Oona asks.

'Mr Littler. They're for Edna. The florist from Gosford delivered them this morning.'

'She'll love them,' and I smell their perfume, like oil of cloves and pepper mixed with something indefinable.

'I'll lend her a vase if she hasn't got one big enough to hold them,' Betsi decides.

Oona's halfway through saying that carnations last for ages when there's an enormous cheer from outside and the band launches into 'For She's a Jolly Good Fellow' and we rush outside to clap as Edna arrives.

Mr Littler presented Edna with the flowers and said, 'The whole town is proud of you.'

And Edna replied, 'My dream has come true.'

Betsi wiped the corners of her eyes and Roy Marsden invited Edna, Hillary and Betsi to tea in the Mayor's Parlour. Then Connor put a record on and grace and a blessing fell over the town as everyone sat down together to eat.

Now that evening glows in my memory for Betsi's triumph, money freely given, the band drumming and blowing their tribute, Hillary's pride and Edna's happiness.

There is another reason, too, why I will not forget that night, entirely different from the one above.

When supper was over, people started to drift outside, some to smoke and others to enjoy the last of the sun.

'Shall we go somewhere?' Connor suggested.

I have to tell him. I remember the mermaid's face.

'If you take me home, you can have the jumper I've made for you.'

Oona's waiting behind to help with the clearing up, so it'd be just us. We leave, two ghosts departing the feast and no one notices we're going until we've gone.

Number One, Beauchamp Terrace has bottled and preserved the warmth of the day, and a heavy oppression descends on me as we enter.

146

'Come in.' I've said it many times before, but tonight it's different because there is no joy in my voice.

The jumper is where I've left it on the console table in the hallway.

'Here it is. Do you like the colour? It's teal blue, the colour of a wild duck.'

Connor takes the garment and holds it up against his chest.

'The size looks about right and the colour's good.'

He kisses the top of my head lightly. I'm ready to tell him, when he says, 'Thanks, Stell, thanks for everything. I'll be needing some clothes, because I've got an eighteen-month scholarship, taking me to New Zealand.'

His lips come down to find my mouth but an unexpected wind slips under the brass draught excluder and swirls around our feet. I jerk my head away and the wind lifts Mamma's needlepoint rug up and down until it makes a flapping noise, like the canvas sails of a yacht. Crystal droplets on the chandelier clink violently, rattling the chains that hold them, like a boat straining at its moorings. Waves, high as the rooftops cover my head. I twist and turn, trying to catch my breath, any breath, just to breathe.

Roses, leaves, broken glass and water crash from the table, tipping and spilling all over the wooden herringbone-patterned floor. I pull back, cover my ears, and when I look again, the storm has subsided and I'm standing alone in the wreckage.

Perhaps I exaggerate. Maybe I mistook a ripple for a tsunami, or perhaps I had no idea how to steer a boat.

Outside a van revs; pulls away. In the silence that he leaves behind, I hear Connor talking about accountants, farm management, only one bite of some apple, Mam telling him opportunity knocks only once, she will be fine, he must go, marriage can wait, he is young, I am young, we've got plenty of time.

147

I mop the floor, put fresh water in the vase, rearrange the flowers and when I've finished, no one would know anything untoward had happened. Only when I walk away do I notice a single rosebud lying on the floor.

Chapter Twenty-one

'Stell, I've left a letter on my dressing table, renewing the house and contents insurance.'

Oona is hurrying through the door, anxious to be in good time for her first day in Gosford County Hospital.

'I'll pop it in the box when I go for the bread.'

'You're an angel. Thanks. Sure you're not going to be bored today?'

'I'll find things to do and I'll have tea ready by the time you're home. That'll keep me busy this afternoon.'

I'm thinking I've all the time in the world now, only trouble is, I don't know what to do with it, when the telephone's ring interrupts my thoughts.

'What do you make of the offer on the bowl?' I recognise Betsi's voice.

'I'd love to know who the mystery donor is. Oona and I have exhausted ourselves puzzling over it, but we've no idea.'

'Saturday evening it was all chicken feathers, garlic skins, everyone making wild and hopeless guesses.'

'So what are we going to do?'

'We'll have a meeting. If you and your aunt, Mr Littler and Edna come to the hall we'll discuss our reply to Mr Berkeley.'

'Yes, best to think things through.'

'Shall we say seven-thirty tonight, then? I haven't contacted the others yet but I'll rearrange things if they can't make it.'

Bread from the Harvest Bun is not ready until ten-thirty in the mornings, so I fill the time with housework, starting by whisking around the house with the vacuum. I'm polishing the brass on the front door when a familiar voice says, 'Need a hand?' It's Edna, whom I hardly recognise.

It's not just the dark-blue cotton trousers or the striped matelot-style top she's wearing, but her hair has been styled to a neat shape with a flattering fringe to soften the effect.

'I almost didn't know you. You look completely different,' I say admiringly. Edna is probably no more than thirty-five, but I had not realised that until now.

'I've been to Miss Bishop for a trim and shampoo.'

'She's done a good job. That style suits you. Clothes are nice, too.'

Edna blushes. 'I went to Gosford on the bus last week. Hillary chose some things for herself, as well.'

'You look super fit.'

'I'm not stopping training now. I'm going to fit a two-mile walk in every day.'

'You're a celebrity. You'll have your photo in the paper soon,' I tease her. 'You'll be famous.'

When Edna's gone, promising to be at this evening's meeting, I peg a neat row of tea towels on the line and go upstairs for Oona's letter.

My aunt sleeps in what used to be Mamma and Dadda's bedroom. The only thing that has changed is the mattress.

'Feather beds are so unhealthy,' she declared in Bamford's one day and on the spur of the moment, because she is impulsive, she ordered a new de luxe mattress, placing an advert in the paper to sell the old feather bed.

Mum screamed with laughter when she heard someone had bought the feather mattress.

'Surely not that old thing,' she hooted.

'There is nothing you cannot sell. It's surprising what people are interested in,' was my aunt's caustic response. No matter how particular Oona was when cleaning, a stray feather always escaped from that mattress.

To Mum, a feather signalled protection. 'An angel must be close. Look, she's left us a feather to show she's guarding us,' she'd tell me.

Oona hasn't got a valance on the bed, because she calls them 'dust traps'. The mattress fabric, patterned with yellow roses, is visible. She could have had a pink mattress, but pink is not Oona's colour.

Of all the rooms in the house, bedrooms are the most revealing. Mum's bedroom, in London, has a bamboo headboard, silk-lined walls and a tailored bedspread in a shade of Cantaloupe melon. 'Sophisticated,' was the word my aunt used to describe it.

Oona is more 'no nonsense', favouring 'hospital corners' on her sheets, which she folds and tucks precisely.

The letter for posting is on the glass tray holding the swansdown puff and the bowl of face powder, the Velouty cream that Oona rarely uses. It's then that I notice a leather folder at the foot of the bed, which appears to have fallen from under the mattress. I used to keep Valentine cards under my mattress in a handkerchief case, the ones I bought but never sent. Perhaps my aunt has a secret admirer who sends her little notes of affection that she hides away, though it seems unlikely.

As I put it back where I found it, a thick cream document slips out, opening as it falls.

Family names, written in a copperplate hand, flow across the page in scarlet ink and prick my eyes.

I know what the writing reveals even before reading it, though I've never seen it before and I cannot explain how this is.

Freud talked of the 'primeval consciousness', the collective memory, ancient knowledge that guards us. I understand his reasoning for, however hot the night, I cannot allow my feet to dangle out of bed, lest a snake bites them, though snakes have not been known to inhabit the bedrooms of Beauchamp Terrace, not during this century, anyway.

Perhaps Freud omitted to mention the 'family consciousness', performing as it does the double function of informing and protecting. Thus vital knowledge can be stored without recourse to retrieval, should it be found unpalatable. The certificate is folded and slipped inside the wallet and left as I found it. Can it be true that things cease to exist when they are not acknowledged?

I tiptoe out of the room, though no one is listening. Downstairs, everything is the same, but at an acute angle, as though the axis of the house has shifted. On the kitchen table my shopping list is puddled with the clear blue-and-red light that strains through the glass kitchen door, candying into clarets, burgundies, peonies, bilberry jam, jelly and fruit tart stains.

I've promised to cook tea tonight and I will. Why should we go hungry merely because I have witnessed something I was not meant to. But as Jung said, everything that happens is the result of intention; there are no coincidences, merely the universe's way of calling our attention to things that need consideration.

To think is both a blessing and a curse, in equal measure.

Sir Robert Walpole, eighteenth-century Prime Minister and supreme pragmatist, who developed to a high degree the art of survival, understood the necessity to tack and veer when conditions required him to do so. No principles were so dear to his heart, or mattered sufficiently enough, that he felt obliged to lay down his life for them. The eye of the storm was best avoided and if one desired a modicum of equilibrium in this world, why then, it was sometimes necessary to avert one's gaze. In the bon mot, 'Let sleeping dogs lie', he found his own truth and, if chance will have it, so may I.

The only butcher in Stanton is closed on a Monday and this tends to restrain the scope of the menu. When I glanced at a copy of *Woman's Own* earlier, Philip Harben recommended scrambled eggs or an omelette as a light savoury dish.

'Dare to be brave and take the eggs off the heat before they are overcooked,' he added, or something like that.

As a person who enjoys pork sausages cooked in goose fat, an egg is not Oona's first choice for the evening meal.

Turning to a *Good Housekeeping* booklet in the hope of inspiration, I come across an Asian speciality, known as 'Goby Aloo Saag'. The cookery editor must be quite a parochial person, never straying far from Soho; otherwise she would have known that, in Stanton, a thousand-and-one exotic spices are just not available.

I flip through some other ideas, 'poached cucumber accompanied by cod mornay, plus Julienne carrots'. No good. Battered cod, chips, salt and vinegar would be my aunt's choice.

'Macaroni Cheese' keeps popping up in these recipes but Oona is more a fried liver and bacon person and she is fond of rabbit, stewed with onions, sage, leeks and carrots.

If I had a rabbit I could make a cake I read about in *The Modern Housewife's Cookbook*, (John Leng & Co. Ltd, London and Dundee, 1936, £2.11/6).

It has a recipe for fleed cakes requiring: 1lb of all-purpose flour, 4 oz butter, 8 oz fleed, fleed being the internal fat of a pig or a rabbit.

There is no mention of sugar in the recipe so the dough might, more accurately, be described as a pastry, and a pastry more suited to making game pie. The recipe recommends eating the rabbit for dinner when all the fleed has been removed.

There are numerous other cake recipes in the book to tempt the soul, including Victoria sandwich, apple gingerbread, honey fingers, oatmeal macaroons, ladies fingers (thick cream and fresh strawberries are needed for these, plus powdered sugar), raspberry rings, carraway drops, cinnamon slices, raisin rounds, vanilla shapes, chocolate eclairs, jam puffs, Bath buns, Primbles and cockle-shell cakes. Cakes enough to sink a battleship, feed a Sunday School party and have a panful over to throw to the chickens the next day.

Even after a tour of the town, the best dish I can think of for tea is corned beef fritters, new potatoes and fried tomatoes.

I would have liked to serve a green side salad of baby lettuce, fresh basil, shallots, cracked pepper, lemon thyme, chopped walnuts with a French dressing of cold-pressed olive oil, red wine, sea salt, cayenne pepper, minced garlic and a smidgeon of demerara sugar, all shaken together and poured over the salad at the very last minute, but could find no lettuce for sale anywhere.

The pudding is easy. I'm using the recipe I learnt in Stanton High for Queen of Puddings. It requires only half a loaf of stale breadcrumbs, four eggs, castor sugar, half a pot of runny raspberry jam (sweet, but acid enough to tingle on the tongue), cream or, failing that, top of the milk, the grated rind of a lemon and two ounces of butter. The meringue can be smoothed over the top, twenty minutes before the end of the cooking time. At this point the oven temperature should be lowered, because you have to watch for scorching. The egg whites can be protected with greaseproof paper, but then you've got to mind the paper doesn't catch light.

When I've prepared the meal I sit in the garden, smelling the tinder-dry earth in the flower borders, the dandelion 'marigolds', the rotting odour coming from the compost. Bees busy themselves in the bush of *rosa rugosa* by the back door while I browse through a magazine. Holidays are featured, the seaside sort, where people take large trunks and wear a different outfit each day. An idea takes root in my mind. Mum wants to see me, my aunt is busy with her new job and I've got nothing to do. Now might be a good time to go to London and I could take Carol's blanket to her as well.

The fritters are crisping to perfection, the tomatoes are fried to succulence, chopped parsley dusts the potatoes and in the oven the pudding drips sweetness, crowned with a chalky tiara of meringue, when I hear Oona coming through the front door.

'How did it go?' I'm eager to hear all about it.

'I'm going to like the job,' she laughs happily. 'It's lovely working in a hospital again. Lots of people asked me about the fundraising.'

I give her my news. 'Edna's had a new hairstyle, courtesy of Miss Bishop and Betsi's asked us to a meeting this evening, seven-thirty. You too tired?'

'No, of course not.'

'Once I've eaten and changed we'll go. What've you cooked? Something smells tasty.'

I put a generous helping of food in front of her and Oona smiles with pleasure.

'You're a good cook. You enjoy preparing food, don't you?'

I brush the compliment aside. 'Did you have canteen lunch today?'

'Beetroot, spam, boiled potatoes. I was ready for this, though. Only food eaten at home truly satisfies me,' my aunt says contentedly.

Holiday Special. Oona's noticed my magazine lying on a chair.

'Have you thought about going to see Mum?'

Occasionally my mind goes into slow motion when it has difficulty processing things, like now. Oona has called Salli 'Mum', as she always does but, really, I know now she is being inaccurate. I concentrate hard on Sir Robert Walpole until I'm able to say.

'I wondered if I should go soon, in case a job comes up later on.'

Oona looks relieved. 'I think that would be a very good idea.'

'As long as it suits you,' I hasten to add.

'I expect Connor is busy with the hay and anyway you need a boost.'

Now is a good time to tell Oona about Connor's scholarship and how he'll be away.

When I've finished she asks, 'So you plan to marry when he comes home?'

'I don't want to commit myself to marriage yet.'

I'm not ready to reveal that I've finished with him.

'That's a wise plan. During the war, people got engaged then didn't see each other for years. When they met again they'd changed, but were tied by a promise.'

My aunt has a knack for being understanding.

Chapter Twenty-two

'Thank you all for coming,' Betsi begins. Oona, Mr Littler, Edna and I are clustered on chairs around a small bamboo table. 'Six thousand pounds is a good offer,' she continues, 'but I'm not sure what the general feeling is about it.'

'If Mr Berkeley estimates its value at three thousand pounds, then six thousand is an excellent return,' Oona agrees.

'There's not much point in allowing the bowl to go to auction, in that case,' I comment.

'A bird in hand is better than two in the bush,' Edna observes.

'And it might not even reach three thousand at auction and have to be withdrawn, leaving us in an awkward position,' my aunt adds.

Until now, Mr Littler has said very little.

'I think it's safe to accept what Mr Berkeley says, because he is a world-ranked expert in his field and, of course, we are dealing with Sotheby's, so we can take it that the advice we're being given is the best.'

This is the response Betsi was hoping for.

'So we're all agreed? We'll take the six thousand pounds on offer.' Betsi looks very satisfied with the decision.

'I'll write a letter and we'll all sign it,' Mr Littler offers.

Afterwards, a restlessness seizes me. Much as I like Betsi, Edna and Mr Littler, I'm bored with them, tired of the fundraising, the bowl, the proposals for the hospital, even the knitting and all that wool stuffed everywhere.

Outside the sky is concave, dusky blue, the colour of dreams, or denim when it's been washed too often. There's another world, somewhere, far away.

Where's Carol tonight? Sitting in some smoky wine bar with people her own age, stiletto heels tapping to the music playing in the background. Outside, taxis will be waiting to whisk revellers to the latest 'in' nightclub.

Wherever she is, she will not be sitting in a community hall with older people, walking home through quiet streets where, sometimes, a snore can be heard coming through an open bedroom window.

'If you want to hear the music, you gotta sing it for yourself.' (Carol.)

'But you need guts for that.'(Me.)

'Like a walk before we go home?' my aunt wonders.

'We could go along the Parrog for a bucketful of sea air.'

The rhododendrons are in full flame, purple and wild, trumpeting down the banks, and birds are skittering around, getting ready for bed.

'Come and sit on this seat for a while.' Oona flops down on a bench. 'I meant to ask you about the knitting classes. What's happening with those?'

'Hillary's tied up with the swimming gala so we've decided to have a break until the autumn.'

'Why not visit Mum this week? How would that suit you?'

I wonder if my aunt senses my dissatisfaction.

'I could do. Tom is away at an antiques fair in Norfolk and she might like some company.'

'Go tomorrow. Stanton will be quiet this week now the fundraising is over.'

'I'll need a day or two to pack,' I begin, before my aunt cuts me short.

'Nonsense. Just throw a few things into a case. You can catch the eight o'clock train from the harbour and be in London by teatime. Ring Mum as soon as we're in.'

Twenty minutes later and I'm on the phone.

'I should be in Paddington by late afternoon.'

'I'll be there. I'm looking forward to having you all to myself for a few days. The shops are full of summery things that you'll love.'

I laugh. This is Mum, avid for any excuse to shop.

'I've a five-hundred pound cheque, so I should have plenty of choice,' I say.

'You don't need money. My treat will be a summer wardrobe for the new you.'

Approaching Paddington station I half expect to see Lizzie Reynolds sitting on the platform waiting to welcome girls from Stanton who are arriving for their first job in the city.

As well as being a secretary in the Diplomatic Corps and treasurer of the 'London/Stanton Society', she acts as an unofficial welfare officer, a task she performs admirably, checking accommodation and conducting a lengthy correspondence with the mothers of her 'protégées'.

As the train slows I feel the old anticipation I always do when I'm going to see Mum.

And then, standing halfway along the platform, different from everyone else, is Mum, wearing a silk dress splashed with orange flowers, nipped in at the waist by a little orange sash and a cream, coolie style hat on her head. In that huge building, which seems like an aviary from which people are trying to escape, Mum is a beautiful bird of paradise.

Spotting me, she cries, 'Darling, darling, over here.'

We bury each other in kisses until a porter appears and carries my small bag to a waiting cab.

'We'll get you home, you can freshen up and, wow! A little supper in a trattoria this evening, perhaps. How's that?'

My mother's laugh is infectious and I wonder why I have not been to see her sooner.

When I've changed into a swirly cotton skirt, patterned with palm trees and old buildings that might be in Morocco or Turkey, for all I know, never having been there, I wash my face and apply fresh foundation and lipstick.

'I've got tea all ready. You must be famished.'

Tying an organdie apron around her, Salli arranges pink and green china on a delicately embroidered cloth.

From the oven she brings a tomato and basil tart.

'I heated this earlier so it's still warm,' she explains.

'Smells gorgeous.'

'I had it from the deli around the corner. A sprinkling of Parmesan cheese and it's ready to eat.'

Although not a good cook, Mum has the knack of producing wonderful meals. Her skill lies in knowing how to source food and her presentation is always immaculate.

When we've finished the tart and are sipping our tea Mum remembers some tiny strawberry tartlets from the fridge.

'These are a treat,' I remark. 'I don't know if I'll be able to eat later.'

'Oh, enjoy them. There's hours to go before we have supper.'

'Did you have a nice time in Rye?' I ask and for reply, Mum wrinkles her nose.

'I was only there for four nights but I seemed to have missed out on a chunk of things that have been happening to you.'

'My job?'

'Have you thought of training in textiles? You're good at colours and you love wools and yarns.'

'I expect that would mean a long college course and I'm not really sure if that's what I want.'

'How would it be to work in Liberty's? All those fabulous Oriental textiles and a lovely old building?'

Not like the timber yard, she means, but avoids saying so. Mum's voice is earnest. I know she wants the best for me and I know she's vexed.

'I wish I knew what I wanted,' I tell her. 'Not knowing is the hard part.'

'Don't rush into anything yet. Look at Nicky,' and she rolls her eyes ruefully. 'Six months in France and she's not bothered about a job, unless you count the bit of waitressing and cleaning she's been doing. She hasn't a clue about what she wants to do, though her language skills are improving, according to Tom.'

I'm beginning to feel some sympathy for Nicky.

Salli rubs the gold and turquoise ring she wears on her little finger, Mamma's ring, and studies it as though seeking guidance.

'Stell. You've worked since you were sixteen and I admire you for it, but what is there for you in Stanton? With Connor away this is your chance to spread your wings.'

I nod, but I don't want to talk about Connor.

'Come and stay with me for a while. Stanton is such a small place, darling, and so inhibiting.'

Last week, through the upstairs bay window in Beauchamp Terrace, I saw a twelve-year-old version of myself walking up the road in a lilac candytuft patterned dress, with a 32AA bra beneath my vest, Dolly Butterbean by my side.

I was thinking about the effect of chance and wondered what would have happened to Dolly's career if we'd walked on the other side of the road?

When Dolly slipped off the kerb and broke her toe, her dreams of becoming a ballerina and dancing the title role in the 'Dying Swan' went down the drain in one moment.

But Dolly was not a girl to be defeated. By the age of sixteen, she was nearly six-feet tall, so could not have been a ballerina, even without a broken toe. Instead she became a 'Bluebell' in Paris and was featured in *Picture Post*, under her stage name of 'Gloria'.

Miss Bishop showed all her clients the magazine for she had once trimmed Dolly's hair. 'I'm so proud of her. I knew all along she was destined for stardom,' she declared, turning to the picture of Dolly in a headdress that might have been designed for a circus horse and a bunch of plumed feathers at the back of her costume. 'So nice when a local girl makes good,' Miss Bishop said and this time I think she meant it.

'I feel everything is tumbling around me. I'm not sure if I've thought things through properly,' I confide to Mum.

'Go with your feelings. When things wear out, something fresh takes their place.'

Mum opens the French windows wide.

'Come out and see the garden,' she beckons, allowing me time to consider what she's said.

Like most town gardens in London, this has a long narrow shape planted with cordylines and the smoke bush, *Rhus cotinus*, which blurs the boundaries, making it appear larger than it is. At the end of the garden is a massive Dutch tulip tree surrounded by hosta lillies.

'If it weren't for the rooftops on either side, we might be in the country,' I remark.

'I couldn't live without a garden. I do miss the country and the sea around Stanton, but I've adapted to London now,' and Mum picks a bunch of French lavender and gives it to me.

Chapter Twenty-three

'Stell, today, I thought we could browse around a little boutique near here. It's got things you won't see elsewhere.'

'Boutique.' The word leads me into a world of exoticism. I spin it through the air a few times, letting it displace words like 'bovine', 'boring', 'boredom', 'borough', stopping only when I come to the word 'born'.

'Nothing like Miss Margaroli's clothes, you mean.'

Today, Mum's in a sludgy-coloured dress with a leather belt and tooled shoes from a shop specialising in Spanish goods. With her coppery-coloured hair she looks slightly Mexican.

'Because you're small, clothes look good on you,' I compliment her.

She considers, before deciding, 'Tall people like you can wear anything, darling. You'll love Kiki's clothes – they're delicious.'

We park at the kerb outside Kiki B's. A bay tree stands guard on the pavement and a pink-and-white candy-stripe awning shades the window from the sun. My mouth waters at the thought of what we'll find inside.

'Come on,' Mum commands. 'Let's get truffling.'

The main room of the shop resembles a French boudoir. Cabbage roses climb the wallpaper and clothes are casually arranged on padded velvet chairs or hang from lacy coat hangers. A floor-to-ceiling mirror dominates one of the walls.

'Salli, halloo, darling.' Kiki appears from the back of the shop to greet Mum, who is obviously a favourite customer.

'I've got Stella today. She's dying for a look around.'

Kiki turns to me, explaining, 'My clothes are mostly continental but I do have one-offs from the graduate shows. Take your time. Try on whatever you like. I'm in the back if you need me,' and she disappears in a cloud of perfume, sooty eyelashes and long, tumbling hair.

'Look, Stell. Aren't these divine?' Mum's holding up some velvet embroidered trousers, tight and low-slung with gold coins around the waistband.

'They'd look just right with this top,' and she indicates a white ruffled blouse with long frilly cuffs.

'Go and try them on,' she urges.

'I'm surprised you like them.'

'Why's that, darling?'

'Tailored and classics are more you.'

'Let's be adventurous. Go and try them, Stell.'

Seeing my reflection in the changing room mirror, I have to admit she has a point.

'I look completely different.'

'In what way?' Mum presses me.

'Casual, up-to-date, young and—' Then it dawns on me, 'more like Carol.'

'You like them?'

'I do,' I say slowly.

'Good. We'll have them,' and Mum waves her cheque book. 'This is London. You're on holiday.'

Kiki packs the clothes in a gold-and-pink-striped carrier bag. Just holding it makes me feel good.

'Stell, I've just remembered some dry cleaning.' Mum takes a ticket from her bag. 'Here's the car keys. I'll only be a second,' and she crosses the road.

A travel agent's window catches my attention. There's a holiday in

Rome, reminding me of the time Auntie Oona and I went to see the film, *Three Coins in a Fountain*, five years ago, when I was fifteen.

'That's exactly what you need. A good holiday.' Mum's returned. 'Where'd you like to go?'

'I was only looking.'

'Italy looks nice or Spain, perhaps. Oh, look at this.' Mum peers closely. 'There's a flight to New York, too.'

'Miss Briggs, the Welsh teacher from Stanton High, travelled to Patagonia when she retired last summer. She did the whole journey by boat and was away for a year,' I mention. 'She sent a regular letter to the *Stanton and Gosford Times* telling them what she'd seen.'

'By air it's possible to be in America in less than a day. Imagine!' Mum's voice is excited.

'Your mum plunges in at the deep end when she's interested in something,' my aunt commented once. 'No half measures with Salli. It's the whole hog, or nothing.'

'Let's go in for a look,' and Mum's already through the door.

'Which country in particular are you thinking of?' asks the travel agent.

'Rome,' Mum answers.

'A good choice. Lovely city, lots of art galleries and museums.'

He puts a pile of leaflets in front of us.

'Would you prefer Spain, darling?'

I'm gazing at a picture of the Chrysler Building. 'Art Deco, 1930s,' I read.

'A very famous landmark,' the salesman murmurs. 'Pan Am flies non-stop to New York, now. That's really something.'

He holds out a brochure. 'Take this with you. You'll find everything you need to know about getting to New York in there.'

I hold the image of the Chrysler building in my mind. It's the most beautiful building I've ever seen. I want to go to New York, I want to see it.

Chapter Twenty-four

'Are you enjoying London? I had to ring to see how you are.'

I tell my aunt about the velvet trousers and blouse and that we're going to shop in Bond Street and Mum's bought tickets for *The Mousetrap* at the Ambassadors Theatre.

'I'm so glad you're having a lovely time. Mum tells me you're thinking of a holiday.'

My aunt's voice rises at the end of the sentence like an unseen question mark. Mum and my aunt are so close that, as soon as one has an idea, the other knows about it.

'We've looked at brochures, nothing's been decided. I should be thinking of a job, not a holiday.'

'I've got your passport tucked away somewhere. I'll send it by registered post, just in case.'

'Thank you.' I'm learning it's easier sometimes not to protest.

'I've been reading the *Stanton and Gosford Times*. There's a photo of Edna on the front page. In the middle they've got Edna with you, Freddie and Hillary. Underneath, there's an article about the hospital, the fundraising and the 'mystery buyer' of the bowl. Stanton is very big news.'

'Keep it for me.'

'I bought two and I'm sending you one, so you should have it in a day or two.'

Next morning I go downstairs in my dressing gown. Mum is already up and dressed in a 'house dress' from Dickens and Jones.

'Sleep all right, darling?'

'I've overslept.' I glance at the clock. It's already eight-thirty.

'There's coffee in the pot, or I'll make some tea.'

'Perhaps I should dress first.'

'Why? You're on holiday. Have some juice,' and Mum pours orange juice into a blue glass.

'Papers?'

'It's luxury to have the papers delivered.'

'I know,' Mum says, 'and I can't do anything in the morning until I've drunk a few cups of coffee and skipped through the headlines.'

The papers are spread out in a fan shape on a low table.

'Any one?' I ask, reaching for the nearest.

I've always liked the stories on pages four or five and today it's a slimming tale: 'How I ate my way through pounds of butter and lard and grew thin.'

Then I flick the page over and a headline leaps out: 'The woman who was afraid to go out.' I can't believe it, it's Edna. The national press has got wind of the story. There's a picture of the old, overweight Edna, and there's the new, slim Edna.

Mum looks at me enquiringly, 'Something interesting?'

'Edna. The one who did the walk on Saturday. She's in a national newspaper, telling her story.'

'They say there's always two stories, the one you tell and the one you don't.'

I begin reading, *My True Story by Edna Gibbons.*

I was born in the north, in a terrace house, small as a thimble. My mam was a widow and I left school early, to work in Woolies.

Leonard was a sailor, home on shore leave when I met him. I had gone to the Rialto cinema with my friend, Pam Venables. He walked us home and a few weeks later he sent a postcard from Malta. I wrote back and that's how it started.

167

After the Navy, he became a carpenter and we married. Len liked amateur dramatics and when our daughter, Hillary, was born he appeared in The Pirates of Penzance.

I suppose it was all the actresses he was mixing with but he started criticising me. Why didn't I wear more make-up like Cassie Simms or do my hair like Eileen Benson? Small things but they wore me down.

If his meal was not on the table the minute he entered the house there'd be a scene. I was a plain cook, but not as good as his mother, who never made stew without adding suet dumplings.

On the outside things looked all right, me bathing Hilly, reading her a story at night, but I knew explosions were never far away when he was around.

When the drinking started I had to take in washing and ironing. With all the worry, I lost weight. Leonard laughed and called me 'skin and bones'. He had no sympathy.

'You should see Val Connolly,' he'd say. 'Now she's eggs and bacon.'

The day he got himself a small part in Much Binding in the Marsh and went to London was a blessing. We'd see a few pounds now and then, but in the end, nothing.

A wedding photograph came in the post one day of Leonard and a young girl smiling up at him. This was the final straw. I had to get right away from everyone who knew me.

I'd seen a holiday caravan advertised in Stanton and could just manage the rent. Later on, we were allocated a council house and it felt like a palace. I was still afraid that Leonard might find us and eating all day kept the fear down, but I was afraid to go out.

The turning point came when Hilly and I joined a knitting class. The group decided to raise money to keep the local hospital open. Now I had friends and could face Leonard if he turned up. I decided my challenge would be to leave the house and walk the coastal path, donating money to the fund if I could do it.

I have a job and Hillary and I are here to stay in Stanton.

At the foot of the article it says: *Edna has asked that her fee for this story be given to the Stanton fund for the local hospital.*

The morning is warm and Mum opens the French doors.

'Ready for something to eat? How about an omelette?'

She gives me a curious glance when I don't answer immediately.

'Do you know her well?'

'I thought I did.'

Chapter Twenty-five

I've been in London for only a short time and I've acquired a new wardrobe, courtesy of Mum.

'I don't see you often so I can spoil you when I do.'

Mum understands that clothes function beyond the basic necessity of warmth and covering, existing as the expression of a mood, or feeling. In Harvey Nichols, she guides me to a velvet windcheater, lined in patterned silk.

'Slip it on,' she urges. 'How do you feel in it?'

'I'm ready for a walk in the park or a boat ride across an enchanted lake.'

Mum laughs delightedly. 'Wonderful. That jacket is fulfilling its purpose.'

After we've chosen three-quarter-length trousers and a daisy-printed blouse to pull the outfit together, we're ready to go to the restaurant.

'Come on. We can have sandwiches and Kunzle cakes. I'm dying for a pot of tea.'

Mum's kicked her shoes off and we're sitting at a window table.

'Enjoying?'

'Stanton seems a long time ago now.'

'It's good to get away. Things look different from a distance.'

When the tea arrives, for no particular reason, I remember that coffee is the national drink of America.

'Have you thought any more about a holiday abroad? I'm ready for Rome, the Trevi Fountain, Vatican city. How's about it?' Mum's looking hopefully at me.

Last night, in the large front bedroom with its wicker furniture and flowery curtains, I turned the five hundred pounds that the Perkins had sent me over and over in my mind, like a silver globe of opportunity. I'd use it to go to New York.

'I'm not sure about Italy.'

'Spain? San Sebastian. Flamenco, guitars, paella.'

'I'd like to go to New York.'

'New York? That's a bit far. I'm not sure. Next year perhaps—'

'I was thinking of going alone.'

'By yourself? Not alone, darling.'

'Why not? The travel agent sees to all the details. I've only got to get on the plane.'

Mum's looking slightly distraught, as though it's her fault that this has come about.

'There's more tea in the pot,' I say, nudging it gently towards her.

Chapter Twenty-six

Things happened quickly after that. Mum tried hard to dissuade me from going to the States and Auntie Oona arrived on the train.

'I can't stay long. I had to talk to you. I'm not sure you should be going alone to America.' A deep frown follows.

I suspect Mum and Auntie Oona of being in collusion and I have prepared my ammunition accordingly.

'Mrs Bayliss didn't stop Carol from working in Milan,' I counter slyly.

A chink of silence slips between us. We both understand that Mrs Bayliss could not have stopped Carol from doing anything she wanted.

'I don't want to stop you—' Auntie Oona falters as Mum joins us.

'We've been talking about Stella's holiday. There were no trips to New York when we were young, Salli, were there?'

'No. It was Aberystwyth and the Cliff Hotel for us. Remember the time my hair got tangled in my ice cream cone? Mamma had to take me straight back to the hotel to wash it.'

Mum gets it. She's talking a little too quickly. She's nervous. She knows it's too late. They can't stop me. I'm off to New York. They've retreated to long ago land. It's a safe place to be at times like these.

Auntie Oona remembers boat trips in the bay, Punch and Judy shows, Constitution Hill, lobster for lunch at the hotel in Devil's Bridge.

In a while, my aunt asks if I've any dates in mind for New York.

'I think there may be a flight leaving at the end of next week.' I know for sure there's a flight next week. 'I'll see if I can find the details.' (They're under my pillow.)

The three of us pore over the departure and return times, the available hotels, the cabs, the trains, the trams. We see pictures of Times Square and Central Park.

'Oh, look, Salli, horse-and-carriage rides through the Park,' remarks my aunt.

When we're dizzy with information, Auntie Oona says, 'Mum and I are paying for the flight.' She and my mother smile delightedly at each other.

I wake early. An ice candle crackles against the sleep-warm flesh of my thighs, claws at my belly, scrapes its way to the polished tin knocker guarding the quiet chambers of my heart and rattles hard.

'Wake up, little kiddie. Today you're off to find your own "Great American Dream" and you're going, frit-frightened or not.'

The sky is a tinted-spectacle-blue shade this morning. I check for messages, but there's nothing there.

Descendants of an extinct native North American tribe would get my meaning. They're sent messages all the time. Someone might be walking along the street, going for a loaf of bread, maybe a haircut, when a bunch of leaves falls at his feet. You or I might kick the leaves into the gutter, wondering which day the road sweeper comes by, but not if we're native North Americans. These people understand that nothing happens by chance.

The age or number of the leaves, which direction they're pointing, any blemishes or holes they may have, how far from the kerb they land, all have a meaning.

Sometimes the breeze is the messenger, other times it could be the clouds.

I'm thinking, now, of an old man I heard of. One night he went to his garden shed for a cigarette (his wife was the fussy sort. 'Wipe those cobwebs from your EYES', 'NO Smoking', 'Only DEAD rabbits indoors'). You get the drift.

By the time the Rizlas ran out, he knew he'd better get back fast or she'd bolt the door on him.

Halfway up the cockle-shell path, he happens to glance at the sky and, lo and behold, he sees some dark clouds piling up. Straightaway, he says: 'That's World War II rolling towards us, that is.'

Perhaps it's my veins, Welsh blood, *caws* and *bara menyn*, all that, and a load more. Other tribes can see things because of their blood. Could have been different if I'd been born on a reservation, or if I didn't like *cawl potch*.

I check the sky once more before dressing but it's blank, blank like the unknowable rune.

'Make sure you've got everything.' (Mum when I'm buckling my case.)

'Packed enough sanitary towels?' (Auntie Oona.) I'm not answering that.

I'm ready. I can't wait. It's been all fuss and *ffwdanu*, take care, make sure your clothes are aired.

Anyone would think I was on a one-way ticket to the blinkin' moon.

Mum's by the front door, in a navy-and-white polka-dot dress with a red belt and shoes. My aunt is her equal in a blue-and-black hydrangea-patterned dress, white shoes and handbag, Queen Mum style. They'd look good at a garden party.

Auntie Oona casts an approving eye over my dress. 'The boat-shaped neckline suits you. Dark blue is a sensible colour for travelling. D'you need a cardigan to slip over your shoulders?'

'They give you a blanket on the plane if you're chilly. The travel agent said.'

Her lips twitch. She doesn't like the reply.

'The car's ready, boot's open, Stell,' Mum calls.

I pick up my bag. 'Let's go.' A few steps ahead, freedom awaits.

'I'll avoid Central London and head west for Hillingdon.'

'I couldn't drive in this traffic, Salli. There are cars everywhere. It's nothing like Stanton.'

'Oh, you'd get used to it.'

Their voices rise and fall, their words stroking the air. Soon, I will leave this world created for me by my aunt and my mother.

'We're nearly there.'

'Oh look, Stella, can you see?' My aunt points to the sky.

I peer out. How has she managed to spot a message when her blood can't be that different from mine? 'There's a plane coming in to land.'

'Yeah.' My voice is flat. I'm disappointed. It's only a plane.

A plane. Coming in to land. To land and then take off. Take off FOR AMERICA. A jitterbug flip starts up inside me. (I'm edgy, but I can keep it down.)

What's that poem about parting being a sorrow? The guy's got it wrong. An ending is a new beginning. (I can't help it. This is what stress does to me, puts me on double overtime at short notice then scrambles it.)

After parking the car we make it to the main building.

Two Pan Am air hostesses throw us a smile. (*Mam annwyl*, they must enjoy their jobs to do that. I mean, smile at the passengers; come back the next day; smile at the passengers; fly off again). I'm feeling lots better now.

'Those blue suits and little white gloves look smart.' Mum delves into her bag. 'Barley sugar. Suck one when the plane takes off. They'll stop your ears popping.'

Auntie Oona returns from the news-stand and waves a *Harper's Bazaar* magazine my way.

When I've checked in my suitcase, shown my passport and received the boarding pass, it's time to say goodbye and have a final hug. I try not to show I'm relieved they're going.

'Ring just as soon as you can,' Auntie Oona says. 'And send us cards,' laughs Mum.

I wave until they disappear, two small figures floating through the crowd. There's an invisible space between them, the gap that they're keeping warm for me but I'm not sure I'll fit in there when I get back.

A quick flick over the other passengers in the departure lounge and I see they're mainly men who, I'm guessing, are going to New York on business. There are about five couples and just a few people travelling alone.

I sit down, hoping that if I smile enough someone will think I'm one of those air hostesses, off for a jaunt on my day off.

My gaze strays to the Pan Am Boeing 707, waiting outside for us to board.

An older woman, who's been standing near the window, comes over.

'Mind if I join you? It shouldn't be too long now before we're allowed to go on board.'

Her accent is American. Dressed simply in a loose-fitting jacket and matching skirt with tanned skin, her appearance is athletic, as though she plays a lot of tennis or golf.

'Are you going home?' I ask.

She nods. 'I came over for a vacation, always wanted to see London and I've not been disappointed, not at all. How about you?'

'This is a holiday for me. I just happened to go into a travel agent's, saw a poster of the Chrysler building and decided I was coming.'

'A whim? Wow! Powerful magic is released when you act on the spur of the moment.'

'My aunt and mum took some convincing but they came round, eventually.'

'You won't regret coming. By the way, I'm Lalla Shalalla.' (I had to listen carefully for that.)

'And I'm Stella.'

'Well, nice to meet you, Stella.'

We're chatting comfortably, when an announcement comes over the tannoy, 'All passengers for New York, Pan Am flight—'

This is definitely grown-up time now.

'Come on, Stella. We've got to move. I'll see if I can sit by you.'

Outside, as I follow my new friend up the steps, a jumble shop rummage of ideas bursts through my mind.

I'm 'International'. I'll be in the *Stanton and Gosford Times's* local news section, courtesy of Miss Bishop, the 'Jot on the Spot' correspondent.

It will go something like this (she's got a formula): 'Miss Stella Randall, Beauchamp Terrace, is enjoying a holiday in New York.' *Bois bach,* I've shaken off the timber yard at last.

When we're settled in our seats, Lalla takes her shoes off. 'We've quite a few hours ahead of us. Might as well make myself comfortable.'

'Is this the first time you've been in England?'

'My first time out of the States. Never been to Europe at all. Thought I'd better come before I'm too old to want to.'

Then we concentrate on fastening our belts and listening to the emergency procedures.

With the first roar of the engines as the plane begins to move, I remember the barley sugars. I like the taste. I've eaten three before we're even in the air and Lalla's still got hers in her hand.

A roar like a tormented beast rushes through the cabin and a few moments later the plane surges forward. The engines' thrust carries us upwards until London is far below somewhere, and I don't need to crunch another barley sugar.

'Next stop, New York,' says Lalla.

We're an hour into the flight. I've flicked through the pictures in *Harper's* and Lalla's folded her copy of the *New York Times*.

'So. What's your line of work, Stella?'

She's frank and direct and I like her. I tell her about the timber yard.

'Sometimes it's not one thing that triggers change, but small things clustering together can stack up. A holiday's good to sort your brain out.'

After a while Lalla dozes and my mind drifts to Stanton. Auntie Oona said that Betsi has banked a six thousand pound cheque from Sotheby's plus the two thousand pounds profit from the auction and the other events. Next month a public meeting will be held, attended by our MP Nick Appleby, county councillors and townspeople, to discuss local feeling about the hospital.

We're flying through a tessellation of clouds when the drinks trolley arrives and Lalla comes back from the dead. We each have a juice and she wants to know about Stanton.

'How big a town is it?'

'About five thousand people or so. It's got a market in the town hall every Thursday, with faggots, cheese, salty butter, bacon, aprons, tea towels.'

'Markets are the same wherever you go, from Tallahassee to the North Pole,' Lalla decides.

'I never thought I'd tire of the place, but I have now.'

'Too much balance can mean stalemate. Maybe this is your time to tackle things.'

I think back to the voice of Mr Berkeley, the Oriental porcelain expert from Sotheby's.

'The artist painted with passion, love, from his soul and with his whole being. This is what gives the bowl its integrity, a palpable vibrancy.'

I want to remember those words 'passion, love, soul,' and take them with me wherever I may go.

Lalla's talking about Sayville now, the town where she lives.

'It's on the South Shore of Long Island, very popular with New Yorkers, especially when the temperature rockets in the summer. We've got wonderful beaches and gracious old homes. If you've read *The Great Gatsby* you'll know of the "Gold Coast" mansions on the north side.'

'The heat will make a change for me. In Stanton our summers can be cool, even cold.'

'Whereabouts are you staying?' Lalla wonders.

'Midtown Manhattan, West 55th Street, near Central Park. The Hotel Martinez.'

'Central Park, did you say? West 55th is between Central Park and Times Square. Good choice. You'll be slap bang in the middle of things. There's loads of places to eat, with onion rolls, cream cheese bagels, salt beef sandwiches on rye bread and the like.'

From her bag she brings out a little card.

'Here. Take this. Put it somewhere safe.'

I read, *Mrs Lalla Shalalla, drama and voice teacher, Old Bakery Cottage, 43 Green Avenue, Sayville, Suffolk County, Long Island. Tel 215-625-015.*

'Sayville's about twelve miles out of Queen's County, where we'll be landing. You look for a bus heading for Suffolk County. It will take the Montauk Highway route.

'Sayville is a hamlet on the edge of the town of Islip. It's not hard to find. Once you arrive, you can ask someone to direct you to Green Avenue. We're a friendly community and people like helping each other.' She puts her hand on my arm.

'Look me up. I mean it. Please, don't go back to England without coming to see me.'

'I'd love to, and I'd like to see Sayville, too.'

'This is your captain. We'll be landing at Idlewild Airport soon. They'll let us in because I'm a native New Yorker and speak the language.'

Laughter ripples through the cabin.

'The weather ahead's about 80 fahrenheit, so I'd call it hot. The New York skyline is just coming into view.'

I know how he's feeling. Good. He's brought a Boeing 707, plus passengers, across the Atlantic. He's elated, like me. I'm elated and awed, as well. A miracle has occurred. I didn't fly the plane over, but I've made it to New York, by myself.

Lalla looks out of the window. 'Queen's County is at the western end of Long Island. I expect you know that it's named after the wife of Charles II?'

'No, I didn't,' I admit.

'Never mind. History is such a vast subject that we've all got chunks of it missing here and there,' and she taps the side of her head, as we prepare for touchdown.

When we've landed and found our bags, Lalla has some time to spare before her bus is due.

'I'll see you into a cab,' she offers, but when we go over to the ranks most of them have been taken.

'Oh look, there's one over there,' I say.

'Leave that. It's a gypsy cab, it's not licensed. Don't go near it.'

Lalla grabs my arm, 'I've an idea. Start your holiday with me. I've plenty of room. I live by myself. Come to Sayville.'

'I can't. It's imposing,' I protest.

'I've asked you. You'll see places you might otherwise have missed. South Shore is at its best this time of year. Stay for a few days, or longer, and move on just as soon as you feel ready.'

'I'm supposed to be at the Martinez.'

'Have you paid a reservation fee?'

'No. I was told single rooms are always available.'

'That's decided it. You're coming with me.'

Perhaps I should have protested more. Carol would have headed straight into Manhattan.

Once we're in the bus, heading for Suffolk County, I sit back in my seat, allowing the different accents to percolate around me, enjoying their variety.

'Although Sayville is small, there's lots going on. We've cake-bake competitions, art clubs, pumpkin festivals, quilting groups. When he was in high school, Ethan, that's my son, used to spend most of his summer breaks on the beach, boating, fishing, beach barbecues. He belonged to the Bugle Corps and the Scouts too.'

After half an hour, the bus slows and comes to a halt by a cluster of houses.

'Journey's end, Stella. Green Avenue, Sayville.'

When the bus has gone, I take in my surrounding. The houses are old, seasidey, in pastel colours.

'Told you it was pretty, didn't I?'

'It's like Toytown. I'll have to take photographs before I leave.'

Lalla laughs. 'I guess it is a bit doll. We're a proper village though. There's schools, doctors, shops. You can get anything you want here. You all right with that case? Nearly there now.'

A few steps on and Lalla stops by a wooden gate leading to a white-painted house.

'Here we are. Old Bakery Cottage, otherwise known as home.'

The front door opens into a large square hall with dark polished floorboards, a hallstand and a wicker chair.

'Leave your bags here. I need to go out for bread, milk, a few things till tomorrow. There's a shop that's open almost round the clock at the top of the road, in Edwards Street. Want to come?'

Chapter Twenty-seven

I rang Auntie Oona and Mum the day after I arrived. They seemed surprised I was still alive, though didn't say so.

This afternoon, Lalla's in the garden and I'm sitting under the veranda, the coolest place I can find. Bakery Cottage is a clapboard house and it creaks most of the time, especially in this afternoon's heat.

Last week I wrote a letter to my aunt and mother, to explain about Lalla's invitation to Sayville.

It's postcards this week to save time and I've written the same on both of them.

'I am staying for a few more days with Lalla. Wish you could see the little villages around here. So glad I came. Lots and lots of love, Stella xxx.'

You could say the postcard is the coward's way of keeping in touch, a form of communication too severely restricted by the lack of space on the card for any meaningful information to be imparted.

When Lalla asked me to stay, I thought she might be lonely but she teaches for a few hours each week and belongs to a quilting bee and to the bridge club. She's a keen gardener too.

Putting the cards aside, I join Lalla, picking my way carefully between the long stems of phlox, velvety rudbeckia and flat heads of orange yarrow. The purple and blue delphiniums are my favourites, especially when interplanted with the acid lime of *Alchemilla mollis* or 'My Lady's Mantle'.

'Shall I get you a drink?' I ask.

She straightens up, adjusting her raffia sun hat, the dark pink valerian, tall hollyhocks and giant angelica dwarfing her.

'Where's your hat, girl? You'll be brown as a griddled chicken if you don't watch the sun. Put this on.' She reaches into her apron pocket and throws me a cotton sunhat.

'The plants are running riot since I've been away. Just look at those lupins and fennel fronds.'

I glance over at the meadow of wild flowers adjoining the garden. Sensing my interest, she beckons me to follow her.

'This field gets a late mowing, after the plants have seeded. The colours change throughout the year. In summer there are blue bonnets, wild pink roses, Indian blanket, yellow corn tick that the North American Indians used for dye, lemon mint, basket flower, Jamaican primrose, prickly poppy, Mexican hat, Indian paintbrush.' She pauses. 'That enough names for you? I'm running out of puff just saying them.

'Come on.' Lalla tips the hat over her face. 'Let's get away from this heat. It's not good.'

Although I've been with Lalla for a week already, each time I mention leaving she changes the subject. Only occasionally does the birth certificate cross my mind.

Tonight, I'm cooking supper for Lalla and her friends from the bridge club.

I've left my order in Ferny Hollow Stores, requesting a large chicken, heavy cream, limes, tea, potatoes, spring onions, oranges and tomatoes. I want this to be a special meal.

'Everything's ready,' says Marvin Whicher, the owner of the store, when I call to collect the goods. 'The Earl Grey was not so easy to track down, but we got it.

'The chicken is corn fed, plump as a pumpkin. Hope it suits you.'

Rushing back to the house, I begin preparing the food. Lalla is out at her 'sewing bee' so I have the house to myself.

While the tea brews for five minutes, allowing the flavour to develop, I whisk olive oil, coarse salt, powdered mustard and white pepper together, then rub the oily mixture into the skin.

Lalla's got a heavy iron casserole and the chicken fits neatly inside it. I pour the tea into the container until it covers the bird. With the lid tightly in place it can be left to simmer for three hours, when the flesh should be tender, falling off the bone.

The cream for the mayonnaise is heated to just under boiling point, the egg yolks are added, and the mixture beaten furiously, to prevent curdling. I'll let it cool before adding the juice of the lime, Dijon mustard for bite, vinegar, some oil, then beat all over again.

When the sauce is ready, it should be thick and 'the colour of butter when the cows have been feeding on sweet, young grass', according to the book.

By late afternoon the chicken is cooling, the potato and green salads are ready. I've got black olives glistening in oil, feta cheese, bread rolls and salted butter.

I throw sliced kiwi fruit, seeded grapes and raspberries into a glass bowl and drench them in Muscadet wine. Later, I'll float blue borage flowers on the top.

A vehicle pulls up outside and through the window I see a dark-haired man helping a small boy jump from the truck. I've an idea it's Lalla's son and grandson and as I'm reaching for a towel to wipe my hands, the kitchen door bursts open.

'Grandma, Grandma,' calls the child. He pulls up short when he sees me and hesitates.

'Hallo,' I say. 'Are you Taylor?'

'How do you know my name?'

And then Ethan arrives, Lalla's son.

'Don't tell me, you're Stella, yes?'

I nod. 'And you're just like your photograph. Your mother won't be long. She's in her sewing class.'

His brow puckers slightly and I notice his eyes are dark, almost navy blue.

'I didn't mean to barge in on you, but I did ring Mom to say we'd be around.'

'You're not barging in. I'm only a visitor.'

Taylor's hopping from one foot to the other.

I whisper in his ear, 'Like some juice and cookies?' (I've picked the language up quickly.)

'Can I have two cookies and two straws in my glass?'

He climbs onto a high chair. 'Dad, Dad where's Grandma?'

'She'll be a little while.'

'I'll make us some coffee,' I offer.

'What did you say your name was? Stella?'

I nod.

'Stella, Estelle or Star,' Ethan says. 'That's a really pretty name.'

For some unknown reason, I feel myself blushing.

Taylor drinks the juice noisily while Ethan surveys the food.

'Someone around here is a pretty good cook,' he remarks. I like his air of self-assurance and relaxed confidence.

'Do you and Mom feast like this every day?'

'I've made a surprise supper for your mother and her friends.'

'Are you a professional chef?'

'It's just a hobby.'

He scrutinises the chicken. 'I doubt there'll be leftovers, but if there are, I'll have them.'

'I'll try to keep you something.'

I kneel down. 'How old are you, Taylor?'

The child holds up four fingers. 'This is how old I am now. Do you know what I'm having for my next birthday?'

'A bike? A two wheel bike?' I venture.

He laughs delightedly, shaking his head. 'No. I'm having a tree house. Daddy is making it and I'm helping, aren't I, Dad?'

Sneaking a glance at Ethan, I see him nodding.

Grinning at his father, Taylor drains his glass and runs into the garden, with a cookie in his hand.

'So, how long are you here for?'

Chatting, we move outside to the veranda and watch Taylor climbing an apple tree.

After a while I glance at my watch and realise I must hurry.

Ethan stands up and I try not to look at him. 'We'd better be moving too,' he says. 'I'm taking Taylor for a burger and a milkshake. You need time to get ready for Mom's supper.'

When they've left, the phone rings. It's Lalla.

'Has Ethan arrived?'

'Yes and he's gone for a drive-through with Taylor.'

'I forgot to mention he was coming. If he gets back before me tell him to take his things to the loft. The bed's made up and everything is ready.'

I replace the receiver, staring out at the purple-flowering sage, catmint, bronze rudbeckia and hibiscus. It is probably a trick of the light but I see the garden and field behind in Beauchamp Terrace, like a slide from a magic lantern, and then the scene vanishes.

Rummaging through a drawer I find a crochet cloth to fling over the metal table outside. When I've piled the Mexican pottery plates high at one end, together with some assorted napkins, it's beginning to look good. Later, when the guests arrive, I'll bring chilled wine for them to sip before serving the food.

I had planned to wrap myself in one of Lalla's flowered pinafores but decide to wear a Peter Pan collared dress with short sleeves and a full skirt. The dress is in cream broderie anglaise over a layer of red tulle and I've not worn it before, so that makes it extra special. I pull my hair back with a black velvet ribbon.

When Lalla arrives with her guests I am complimented on the wine and the food, which soon vanishes. I'm relieved I made enough for generous helpings.

Afterwards, Lalla helps me load the dishwasher and says she has a proposition.

'Can you bake cakes for a church fete we're having next week? It's the town's annual flower show. There'll be competitions for the best wild flower posy, the best roses, the best arrangement. Oh! I'm sure you know the sort of thing I mean. We always lay a tea on afterwards – I'm on the committee.'

Sensing my hesitation, Lalla encourages me by saying, 'Bake whatever takes your fancy. Even Norah Ferguson, who's picky, raved about your food.'

'I'll give it a go, if you're sure.'

'We've a food fund and we take the cost of the ingredients out of it, so there's no problem there.'

Lalla suddenly stretches her arms above her head and yawns.

'I'm tired. Where is that son of mine and Taylor?'

As if on cue, the door opens and Ethan and Taylor appear.

'I'd about given up on you,' Lalla admonishes.

'Sorry, Grandma,' says Taylor. 'It's Daddy's fault.'

We all laugh. 'We met some people we knew and talked too long,' Ethan explains.

'Come and see your room,' Lalla says. 'You all right for tonight, Stell?'

'Of course,' I reply.

'Have a good night, then and thank you again,' she says disappearing with Taylor and Ethan following her.

Half an hour later, I'm still in the kitchen, studying one of Lalla's recipe books when the door opens.

'Mind if I join you?'

Startled, I look around to see Ethan.

'I gather the evening was a great success?'

'Well, all the food went. I managed to keep you a slice of cake. Do you like cream?'

Ethan settles himself on a high stool and watches me as I place the cake and cream in front of him.

'Delicious,' he pronounces when he's put a large chunk in his mouth. 'You must do a lot of baking.'

I feel my cheeks glowing but I'm glad he is too busy with the cake to notice.

As he finishes the cake, he surprises me by saying, 'You never told me what your job was.'

'I'd like to say I was a tightrope walker,' I joke.

He raises his eyes quizzically.

'I worked in the office of a timber yard as an accounts clerk.'

He watches me carefully.

'Not the world's most exciting job but at the time I liked it. I had some money when it closed and I decided I was not going back. Time for something different I suppose.'

'What ideas have you come up with?'

'I'm not trained for anything and this all happened quite suddenly. I know this sounds lame but there's no other way of putting it.'

'Go for something different.'

He walks to the fridge, pouring himself a glass of milk. 'Want some?' he asks, holding the carton up. I shake my head.

'I suppose Mom told you I'm a dentist but that's not to say that, given the opportunity, I wouldn't like to do something else.'

'What's stopping you?'

'I studied for years, invested time and money in my career. I'm beginning to reap the rewards, so now is not the time to walk away, I guess.'

He gets up, takes his plate to the sink. 'I'm off to cuddle up with Taylor. The cake was lovely. Thanks again.'

I'm folding a cloth, when he puts his head around the door again, winks and says, 'Night night, Estelle.'

Chapter Twenty-eight

The next day Lalla is up before me.

'I've brewed the coffee. Have some with me, Stella.'

'Where are Taylor and Ethan?'

'Gone to see friends. They'll be back later.'

This kitchen has so much chrome I can almost see my face in it and the fridge is pink and Italian.

'We don't have anything like this at home. Our gas cooker is from the thirties.'

Lalla shoots me a look. 'Bet your food tastes good, though.'

She brings the coffee to the table in steel cups.

'My ancestors were Welsh. I think I mentioned it?'

'Tell me about them.'

'My grandfather was a preacher. He came over in the mid-nineteenth century. I'll show you his photo.'

Lalla hurries into the front room and is soon back, bearing a sepia photograph in a crude wooden frame. I can just make out the lettering 'Rev. Mr Brown', beneath a sombre picture of a man with mutton chop whiskers.

Lalla's finger underlines the fading script, broken in places, tracing a family line. 'He bred corgis which he brought over with him. Do you know the kind of dog I mean?'

'The Queen likes corgis,' I reply.

Lalla's face lights up.

'My grandfather was the only person in these parts who bred them, which was a godsend for the family income.'

'Why did your relatives come over here?' I prompt.

'They had no choice, really. Life was hard in the old country and opportunity scarce. Still, he settled and so did my grandmother, Esther Mary. They had five children and all lived to a very old age.'

She puts the photograph down and stirs a heaped teaspoon of brown sugar into the coffee. 'This is my country and I think of myself as American but I know where my roots are.'

'That's important,' I agree. 'A sense of belonging gives you balance, I suppose.'

She nods.

'Ethan. Did I tell you about him?'

Her voice dropped. 'He lost his wife, Debra, in childbirth and he's brought Taylor up alone.'

It's my turn to look surprised now.

'That first year they lived with me, then Ethan took some time off and they moved back to their own place. Ethan wanted to get to know his boy properly, prove he could cope alone I suppose.'

'Taylor's happy, Ethan's happy.'

'I tell myself it's going to be OK and I hope it is.'

I pat her hand.

'Don't want to talk about myself all the time,' Lalla says. 'What about your family?'

I stir in my chair.

'I didn't mean to pry.'

'You're not. Salli, my mother, was widowed just before I was born. We lived with her sister, Oona, until Mum remarried.' My tongue becomes swollen with lies, as though it doesn't belong in my mouth.

'Families are not always how you expect them to be,' Lalla responds, rising briskly to her feet.

'Those pots outside need watering. Coming to help me?'

That night my bedroom with the rag rug, the cushions worked with pineapple motifs and the Polish cupboard with peeling hearts painted on the drawers, is beginning to look familiar.

I take out a writing pad. There are things that need to be said. I begin Salli's letter first.

Dear Mum,

Hope you are well. I am still in Long Island with Lalla. I'm baking a (Californian) raisin cake later and I've been trying out new recipes. Baking is a very homely activity, connected with warmth and love, I suppose. Lalla has Welsh ancestry, perhaps that's why we get on so well. She says that knowing your roots gives you balance. Perhaps we should talk about roots and I mean secrets, too. Why did you and Auntie Oona conceal the truth from me? I had a right to know.

I abandon Mum's letter, finding it hard to write more. Was I going to sign off 'Lots and lots of love, Stella xxx', when I felt confused and angry? What did I hope the letter would achieve, anyway?

On a fresh sheet, I begin Oona's letter.

Dear Auntie Oona,

I've written to Mum about hidden things in this family. Why all the secrecy? Why didn't you tell me you were my mother?

I shut the writing pad. I have a feeling the two of them would catch the next flight to New York if I posted the letters.

Next morning I wake early scanning the horizon, the space where land and sky don't quite meet, and there is a luminous glow.

I read the letters I wrote last night, then take them to the wash basin in the corner of the room and run the cold water tap over them until the ink stains my fingers and trickles in brown and purple dribbles down the side of the sink, like the dregs from a stale bottle of wine.

There is only the slightest of stains left on the pages, which I rip into little pieces and throw in a soggy mass into the bin.

Perhaps I need to answer some questions. Why am I here in America? What do I hope to find?

Chapter Twenty-nine

'Marvin Whicher wants to rent out the back room of the store,' Lalla announces over breakfast, fixing me with her steady gaze. 'He needs the extra income.'

'I thought he had a good business?'

'Sure, but he's getting older and needs to put something by for when he'll not be able to work.'

She pulls on her cigarette. 'He's come up with the idea of a coffee bar.'

Lalla spreads a spoonful of apricot jam over her croissant.

'Grocery sales drop off after the summer. Older folk don't come out so often.'

'Does he deliver?'

'He does, but it cuts into his profit. The building could bring in more money without requiring too much effort on his part.'

She licks her finger and runs it round her plate, gathering stray crumbs.

'How about it, Stella? You'd be ideal. You've got loads of recipes and ideas. You're someone different, new to Sayville. People would drop by for coffee and cake and order extra groceries with Marvin. It could be good all round.'

'But I'll be flying back to London in a few weeks.'

Lalla inclines her head.

'Why not wait here a while – three months, say?'

'I've never cooked professionally, it's only been a hobby with me;

something I've done for family and a few friends.'

I think of Betsi and Carol.

'I was a waitress once, during the school holidays, in a tea room called The Sampler.'

Lalla sits up sharply. 'That's it. I love it. "The Sampler". D'you see?'

She's excited but I'm puzzled.

'You love the name?'

'The Sampler suggests a little tea room, one of those places where they serve tinned sardines on buttered toast, Welsh Rarebit and poached eggs.' Lalla reaches for a pencil and scrap of paper.

'You could have coffee and cookies in the morning, savouries midday then English tea and little pastries in the afternoon. It would be so different. We've nothing quite like it in Sayville.'

'Even if I say "Yes" what about a work permit?'

'Let's fill in the broad picture before you fuss about details.'

A thought occurs to me. Nicky has been in France for six months.

'Take the room for a month. See how it goes. If you don't like it, just say so.'

I pour us both some more coffee.

As if reading my thoughts, Lalla says, 'Now, if you're worrying about start-up costs, it can be done on a shoestring.'

'I have some money. Enough to start a coffee shop, I think.'

'I can fix you up with china, that kind of thing,' Lalla continues.

'You've been more than generous, already. I think I can manage. If I can't, I'll tell you.'

'Promise?'

'Of course.'

'Good. That's all settled then? I can tell Marvin you are going ahead?'

Butterflies don't take long to arrive, zooming around inside me, but I ignore them and nod. I could manage tea, coffee and cake. No one was asking for much more.

'When can I say you'll start? Marvin's anxious to get the project running as soon as possible.'

'I'll need a few days. I'll distribute leaflets, posters, that sort of thing.'

'How about local radio? That's free publicity,' suggests Lalla. 'Come on, let's get down there and see what it's like.'

When we enter Marvin's store, he's making up an order.

'Go right in,' he says, indicating the back of the shop.

My heart sinks when I see the gloomy room. Lalla's face is expressionless.

'Needs a bit of work,' she comments wryly.

The walls, though free of cobwebs, have not seen fresh paint for many years. 'It'll take some work to get ready,' I venture.

A cunning look crosses Lalla's face.

'Marvin, Marvin, can you spare us a moment?' she calls.

Grumbling, Marvin appears. In the gloom his eyes remind me of black-eyed beans.

'I've got orders to make up. I'm in a rush.'

'This won't take a minute. Now listen here. Stella's not going to pay full rental for a room in this condition.'

She watches for his reaction.

'Needs a little spit and polish, that's all.'

'It's just not appealing,' Lalla retorts. 'You agreeable to negotiation?'

'Drop the rental, you mean? Can't do it,' Marvin declares with an air of finality.

'And Stella's not starting a tea room if you don't ease up on it, Marvin,' Lalla says firmly.

'I'd be giving it away if I dropped the rent,' Marvin mumbles.

'OK, if that's your final word.' Lalla, gathers up her bag and turns to go.

'No, wait.' Forlornly, Marvin moves his bald head from side to side. 'What if I come down by ten dollars a month? How's that?'

Lalla considers. 'Stella?'

'I'll take it for a month and see how it works out.'

Marvin grins. 'Good. You'll do all right, young lady, I can tell. You'll be fine.'

We shake hands and before leaving I buy a tender Camembert cheese, a jar of black olives and freshly baked sourdough bread for our lunch.

'"Challenging" is the word I'd use to describe that room,' Lalla says, as we walk back to her house. 'But I've an idea how to get around it.'

That very afternoon she draws up a plan.

'Frankly, the place is drab. Marvin's dead lucky you're prepared to take it on.'

'I'm not sure I know how to improve it.'

'I'll help you fix it up.'

I look enquiringly at Lalla.

'Say if you don't agree, but we could make it look a little bit different.'

'How?' I wonder.

'Well, it's poky and whatever you do you're not going to change that. Play up the darkness. Make it look cosy, like a parlour. How does that strike you?'

Lalla has hoarded some newspapers which she thinks might look good plastered on the walls of the tea room.

'They're no good to me now but they'll be a novelty in the tea room, that's if you like them,' she hastily added.

'It'll be something different,' I agree.

'We'll make a flour and water paste and spread it on the walls before sticking the pages on and praying they don't come down again,' she laughs.

The following day, after arranging a time with Marvin, we begin our preparations.

196

We've not been working for more than half an hour before Marvin puts his head around the door.

'How're you getting on?' His glance takes in the disarray.

'We'll call you for your opinion when we're ready.' Lalla shoos him back into the shop.

'Best not to let fools and babies see half-finished things,' she comments when he's gone, leaving me wondering which category Marvin falls into.

It helps that the newspaper pages are large and thin. Another hour and we've finished the walls and opened the back door to let the breeze in.

'Any tears, just patch them up with more newspaper,' advises Lalla cheerfully when I stand back to examine our work.

'Last job of the day coming up,' she declares, rummaging in her shopping bag for a bottle of disinfectant and some old rags.

'All that's left to do now is wipe these tables down and then we're finished.'

The next morning presents a jewel of a day, one of those you'd like to capture and keep for ever.

My destination is a thrift store I've noticed on the outskirts of Sayville. When I arrive the window display includes cups and saucers with hand-painted crocuses and linen cloths, a little frayed perhaps, but embroidered with chain-stitch lazy daisies. Soon I've selected cups, saucers, bowls, jugs, plates and an assortment of cutlery.

'Interested in a trolley?' Gus Ivory, the owner, shows me a faux marble-topped brass trolley. 'And I've some pottery coffee cups, as well. If you want them, I can drop everything off for you. I know Marvin Whicher's shop. I pass there every evening.'

A small surge of happiness bubbles inside me. Things are taking shape.

On my way home, recipes pound in my head. I will bake two or three elaborate gateaux each week. Every day I'll cook fresh buttermilk scones, Boston cream pie, shortbread biscuits, syrupy flapjacks and cherry cobbler with fresh cream.

Later, passing Marvin's store, a poster in the window announces the opening of The Sampler tea room, on Monday of the following week.

On the following Saturday afternoon, when I'm putting the finishing touches to the tea room, Marvin taps the door.

'Stella, Eva-Lisa would like a word.'

Standing behind Marvin is a woman, in her late twenties, perhaps. Her face has a raw-boned look, as though she has led a hard life.

She appears shy and Marvin does the talking for her.

'Eva-Lisa here, is wondering if you'll be needing help clearing up, that kind of thing?'

I hesitate, unsure how busy I will be, but perhaps an extra pair of hands might be useful. I nod my thanks to Marvin as he retreats, and pull a chair out for Eva-Lisa. 'Come and sit down,' I invite. 'What hours are you able to work?'

'All day if you like or part-time. Whenever you need help.'

'Do you have experience of working somewhere like this?'

She looks at me doubtfully. 'I've washed dishes in the motel.'

'How about if you come in for two hours at lunchtime each day, helping me serve and wash up, that kind of thing. I can't promise too much until I know how things will work out.'

I ask her what she was paid in the motel and we agree she will start work the following week.

'I might have to close if I don't have enough customers,' I explain.

She smiles. 'A tea room is quite something in Sayville. People are going to like it.'

After Eva-Lisa has gone I hope that employing someone local will boost trade.

Chapter Thirty

Lalla flushes with excitement and waves a letter in front of me. 'Stella, I hope you don't think I'm being very boastful, but I have had a letter from Bingham Dawes, that's my old alma mater. They want to present me with an honorary degree for the work I've been doing with the youngsters of Sayville.'

She flops into the big seat by the window.

'That's wonderful news. Congratulations.'

'There's only one snag. It's in just over a week's time.'

'Oh?'

'I'm planning on being away for a few days, staying with my sister. How're you going to manage without me?'

'I'll manage just fine. Don't you go worrying about me now.'

'I'm thinking of the tea room.'

'Honestly, you go and enjoy yourself. Make the most of your big day.'

'Do you mind seeing that the house ticks over?'

'Of course not. I'm glad to be of some help to you.'

Her face clears. 'Good. That's decided then. I'll leave phone numbers, but I'm more than sorry it's happening just when you're setting up shop.'

'It's marvellous for you,' I reply.

Ethan and Taylor are hoping to come with me,' she finishes happily.

A few days later, Lindsey Gilham, a member of the bridge club rings to ask if I can cater for a small supper at her home in three days time. Something simple, nothing complicated, she says.

I suggest a chilled orange and tomato soup to start, accompanied by hot onion bread; a baked ham and waxy potatoes with salad, and nectarine and orange liqueur tart with almond pastry.

Lindsey sounds warm and friendly on the phone. She explains where she lives and asks if I would like to drop by later to talk about my ideas and see her kitchen.

In only a few short weeks I am beginning to feel a part of this friendly community and it shows in the clothes I'm wearing, things I'd never have dreamt of in Stanton.

I might wear a paisley-patterned skirt and drawstring blouse with espadrilles when I visit Lindsey, I decide.

Lalla took me shopping to 'Bardhams' the other day.

'The clothes are expensive, but they've got a good sale on now, so it's worth looking.'

'As good an excuse as any for going shopping,' I'd agreed.

A pair of espadrilles with a cord sole and blue-and-white gingham uppers had caught my eye. Lalla watched me examining them before putting them back again.

'Try them on,' she'd urged. 'They've been marked down, too.'

'They're not the type of thing I wear,' I'd said.

'Why not?'

'They'll look scruffy and untidy in no time.'

'Not planning on wearing them for ever are you? They're just a bit of fun.'

'They feel comfortable.'

'Wear them for a few weeks and then throw them away. Come on, I'm getting them for you.'

Lalla brushed away my protests with, 'What's a few dollars?'

Before we leave the store, I catch some of Lalla's enthusiasm and buy some skirts and blouses, all at discount. Later, I remembered about needing a uniform for The Sampler.

'Uniform?' shrieks Lalla when I mention it. 'For goodness sakes, girl, you are the proprietress of the tea room. The people around here will want to see an English lady not a waitress.'

'Mmm. That's true. I hadn't thought of it like that.'

'Wait till we reach home. I might come up with something,' and she smiles secretly to herself.

That evening, true to her word, Lalla presents me with a bolt of material.

'That uniform you were talking about. How's about this?'

Together we unroll the cotton sateen fabric, white with a pale-pink outline of roses.

'Now, a tightly cinched waist and a full skirt puffed with layers of net. What do you say to that?'

'Wonderful, but—'

'But what?'

'Do I have the time to make it up?'

'I'll run up a few skirts in no time. All you need is a linen blouse or two and we're away.'

I hug her, but she brushes away my thanks.

'I haven't sewn for years and I'm going to enjoy this.'

The local paper carries an announcement.

An English tea room called 'The Sampler', situated at the back of Marvin Whicher's grocery store, is to open shortly. Miss Stella Randall is running it, specialising in morning coffee, pastries, afternoon teas, sandwiches and home-made cakes.

Lalla brandishes the paper. 'Well, you sure don't want for publicity. You're in the *Sayville Weekly Star*, plus I've told everyone I can think of.'

*

A few frantic days later, on Monday morning, dressed in a skirt Lalla has whizzed up on her Singer sewing machine, I arrive at the tea room at six-thirty. Three hours after that, scones cool on a rack, a queen-sized Victoria sandwich trembles on a shelf and flapjacks, shortbread biscuits, gingerbread with slices of crystallised ginger, fondant fancies, some iced in pink and others in green, all decorated with sugared violets, jostle for space across the worktops. A Dundee fruit cake sings quietly in the oven, mopping up the left-over heat.

Marvin is at the door.

'Someone just called to ask what do you have for lunch, Stella?'

'Baked potatoes, salad and rolls, corn chowder. If things get busy during the week, I'll have more of a selection, maybe.'

Then, unexpectedly, Eva-Lisa arrived.

'I thought I'd come early in case there's a rush on.' She hangs her coat up. 'Don't worry about paying me for this morning; I need time to see how you're going to run things.'

'I'm glad you came. We might get busy,' I welcome her.

By ten-thirty the water urn gurgles and teapots and cafetières are lined up. Each table has a tiny vase of flowers. The crocheted and embroidered cloths, though a little worn here and there, have been expertly mended by Lalla.

Marvin comes to the door again.

'There's a few Cadillacs around the square. Got me wondering if they were heading here. Come and see.'

I follow him to the front window of the shop.

'There's Dora Goldstein.' He points out a woman in her early sixties with a stiff hairdo and thick make-up. 'Harvey, her husband, was in banking. She's a good customer of mine. Entertains a lot and buys most of her food here. Whoa! She's coming this way. I better get behind the counter.'

I retreat to the tea room, peeping into the shop through the glass panel in the door.

'D'you have sweet potatoes this week?' I hear Dora ask.

'I can order them by tomorrow, if that suits you, Mrs Goldstein.'

'And jalapeño peppers?'

'How many would you like?'

'I've jotted it down somewhere.'

Dora reaches into a crocodile-skin bag and brings out a list as long as a skein of yarn. Anyone would think she ran a hotel.

Eagerly, Marvin scrutinises the order.

'If you have other errands in town I'll have it ready within half an hour. If you bring the car round I'll bring your goods out.'

Dora turns. Her head inclines.

'I can smell coffee. Is that from the tea room?'

'Yes, Ma'am. You come with me and I'll introduce you to Stella, who's running it. Her cakes are home-made, quite something. She uses the best ingredients, supplied by myself, of course.' He chuckles.

I take up my position behind the counter and smile a greeting.

'Stella. Mrs Goldstein would like some coffee.'

'Actually, I think I'll try tea.'

'With lemon or milk?' I enquire.

'I'll have lemon, please.'

Dora eyes the Victoria sponge for a moment, then the scones, the flapjacks, the macaroons and the Richmond Maids of Honour.

'And a slice of chocolate cake would be nice.'

While Eva-Lisa prepares the order, Marvin accompanies Dora to the table, holds the chair for her and gives me a knowing nod as he returns to the shop.

Lalla has lent me a gramophone. I switch it on and Ivor Novello's 'We'll Gather Lilacs in The Spring Again' plays softly, breaking the silence.

When I place the tray in front of her Dora is appreciative.

'Oh my! It does look pretty. I love the shady lady,' she says, referring to the embroidered Crinoline lady and the mother-of-pearl handles on the cutlery. I watch Dora unfolding the lacy napkin and spreading it on her lap.

'You're my first customer,' I say.

'I hope I bring you luck,' she smiles.

Busying myself behind the counter, I see Lalla arriving with a trail of friends behind her.

'No need to rush with our orders, we'll study the menu first and enjoy the music.'

Soon, a buzz of conversation warms the air. The chocolate cake goes quickly and the coffee walnut sponge has proved popular, too.

After the morning customers have left, Eva-Lisa clears away while I check the potatoes and we begin laying the tables for lunch. When I look at my watch I cannot believe how quickly the time has gone. I am really pleased Eva-Lisa came in early. Without her I would have felt rushed.

We have fifteen customers at midday and by two o'clock, Eva-Lisa has washed the dishes and left and I'm finishing the last of the soup and wiping my bowl with the roll, when Marvin comes in.

'Any leftovers?' he asks, hopefully.

'There's a potato in the oven. Help yourself. I'm afraid there's no soup left.'

My feet feel like balloons, ready to take off by themselves.

'I've been real busy for a Monday,' Marvin says, settling himself on a stool. I push the butter dish in his direction.

'Thanks, Stella, Let's hope this keeps up. This place could be a real hit,' he says, taking in the nearly empty cake stands.

'It's been a novelty today, but we might do all right. There's coffee in the pot when you're ready.'

He grunts his appreciation.

After the shop has closed, I weigh the ingredients for the next day, count the takings, wash the cloths. I can see stars in the sky when I walk back to Lalla's home.

'How did it go? Are you pleased?' she wants to know.

'It was far better than I had hoped and thank you. You and all your friends made a difference. Set the pot boiling, sort of thing. Tomorrow, though, I might have to drag people in for a coffee.'

'Wait and see. Everyone raved about your cakes. One thing though,' said Lalla, frowning.

'Yes?'

'Don't overtire yourself. Making a go of things is fine but its hard work. Sure you want to be a success, but if it gets tough you'll have to cut back somewhere, profits or not.'

I agree.

'Come on,' says Lalla, going to the fridge. 'We're celebrating the opening of The Sampler, the best thing to happen in this town for years.'

Lalla places a bottle of Sauternes, two glasses and a bowl of figs on the table.

'Look! I've even brought a bowl of honey to dip the figs in. I'm getting like you, now, Stella, thinking of the little touches.' She pours us a glass of wine each and holds hers up.

'I want to propose a toast, Stella, to you and The Sampler.'

'Thank you. But it was your idea initially.'

'But you ran with it and put in the work.'

We sip the wine and I take a fig.

'What is happening with Ethan and Taylor?' I ask.

Lalla sits back in her chair, looking thoughtful.

'Ethan has accepted a job in Caersalem University, teaching dentistry. It'll give him more holidays and shorter hours than he works now. They're moving house so they'll be closer to me, and I'm hoping to see more of them, but with families, you sometimes have to stand back…'

Chapter Thirty-one

Dora Goldstein stirs a cube of sugar into her coffee. 'This tea room reminds me of my Grandma's kitchen in the west, where nothing went to waste. Remember those blue-and-white cotton flour bags? Grandma cut them up and used them as dish rags. Grandad's woollen shirts were turned into rag rugs for the floors. I can see her now, a candle burning at her side, bending over the fabric squares, stitching them onto sacks.

All the sheets were darned and patched but they smelt lovely, because dry lavender heads from the garden were sprinkled between them in the airing cupboard.'

Dora's nails were manicured and a large diamond ring nestled alongside her gold wedding band. She was clad in a shantung silk suit which had a pleated skirt and a nipped-in jacket in a shade of cream. No one could have guessed from her appearance that she had been brought up on a poor farm.

Bending her head to cut her cake, her diamond earrings flashed, sparkling like the diamond flower spray in her lapel.

'Grease from the goose was saved for winter, in case a poultice would be needed for a bad chest. Other times Grandma used it for shortening in a pie crust, or instead of butter in a molasses cake.'

Dora takes a small sip of coffee. 'I guess that sort of thing would not appeal to people nowadays but it sure tasted good when you were hungry.

'Soap was precious, too, and Grandma saved every sliver of soap, boiling it up in Grandpa's old sock to make a new ball. Times were worse than hard, especially with the wind blowing in under the door at night.

'Old sacks were pushed in the gaps to keep out the weather and the mice. Of course, everything is different now, so much easier.'

'Funny that Dora Goldstein,' muses Lalla when I tell her that Dora had been in The Sampler again, recalling her childhood. 'I would never have thought her the type to admit to a poor upbringing. Always so fine but I never saw the other side to her. You think you know people but they can always surprise you.'

The next day Eva-Lisa arrives early again. I don't think I could manage without her now and she refuses payment for the extra hours she is putting in. 'I want to give you a good start,' she explains.

Today her skin is chapped and red.

'Something's irritating my skin,' she mentions, when she catches me staring at her face.

'Come by the window,' I instruct. Eva-Lisa's skin appears tender on her cheeks, her chin and her forehead. When I put my hands close to her face I can feel the heat pulsating.

'Tried any creams?' I enquire.

'All sorts but nothing works and some creams make it worse.'

'Sit there a moment,' and I indicate a chair.

Mashing a ripe avocado into a clean bowl I stir a few drops of olive oil into the mixture.

Freddie Littler often advised olive oil to soothe sore skin and I read in one of Lalla's magazines that avocado was an effective treatment for irritated skin. This simple concoction might help it.

I explain the ingredients to Eva-Lisa before asking, 'Do you trust me to try it on your skin?'

'I'll try anything,' Eva-Lisa says wearily. 'It's bothered me for years, flaring up now and then.'

Pushing her hair off her face, I apply the cream liberally.

'Rest there while I make you some fresh orange juice and say to yourself, quietly, "My skin is healing."'

When I return, Eva-Lisa looks relaxed.

'How's it feeling?'

'It seems cooler already,' she replies gratefully.

'You'll have to do this a few times each day until there's an improvement. Sip this juice while I simmer some sage leaves. We'll wipe the cream from your face with the sage liquid. Whatever's left over you can take home to use tonight.'

'Sage leaves?' grins Eva-Lisa.

'My grandmother in Wales always did this, so my aunt says, and we make some up in the winter, now and then.'

'You shouldn't bother, Stella, really.'

'There's nothing worse than sore skin. Anyway, I love using ordinary kitchen ingredients for the face. Marvin's selling watercress today and that's good for the skin, too. My aunt boils parsley and drinks the liquid to cleanse the blood, which is supposed to help the skin.'

I thought of Oona, sowing parsley seeds when there was a full moon, which meant the seeds were sure to germinate.

'You're really funny,' Eva laughs. 'I've never had drinks like this before. No one has taken any interest in my skin, either.'

'All you need do is simmer things like onion, garlic, chicken stock and young nettle tips until they're tender. Cool the liquid and drink a cupful three times a day. But it's not a quick cure. You have to be patient.

'Sit there a while now. I'll scramble some eggs for us.'

Eva-Lisa starts to protest but I quieten her.

'I've been up since six. I've had breakfast once, but I could eat again. Come on, I'll join you.'

While the eggs are cooking, I slip slices of brown bread into the toaster.

'You need some sunshine in your life. You've drained your strength,' I diagnose.

'Whew! I'm beginning to feel better already,' Eva-Lisa says when we begin eating. 'It's this new farmstead we've taken on. Nothing large, but we're at it all hours. The bank owns everything but our souls,' she says ruefully.

'Eggs taste good,' she continues, through a full mouth. 'It's a treat to have food put in front of me.'

'What did you do before you were a farmer's wife?' I ask.

'I trained as a hairdresser though you may not believe it,' she says patting her unruly mop of hair.

Eva-Lisa did not take long finishing the eggs. The way she ate reminded me of Oona, swiftly and quickly, enjoying everything.

I butter a scone.

'If that's for me, I'm full,' Eva-Lisa protests.

'Let's share it. Do you like quince jam?'

'Quince? I haven't had any in years. Where did you get that jelly?'

When Eva-Lisa said 'jelly' I remembered Lalla referring to jam as 'jelly' the other night.

'I made it from the quinces in Lalla's garden. There's lemon juice in it to help it set and give it bite.'

I cut a half for Eva-Lisa then pour us some coffee, noticing how much more relaxed she is now.

'I didn't know how hungry I was,' she remarks.

'Farm work is tiring and so is working in a tea room.'

'I enjoy coming here. It's something different so it doesn't seem like work somehow. How long you planning on waiting?' she wonders, as the last crumbs of scone disappear from her plate.

'I'm giving it until Christmas, if I have enough trade.'

She nods. 'It's sure unusual, a tea room here. I can't get used to it in a small place like this. Nice, though.'

'No?'

'Nothing much happens around here. People aren't very imaginative.'

I think of the card I had sent the previous evening to Salli and Oona.

Sorry I've no time to send a long letter. The tea room is going down well. Wish you could see it. Looking forward to seeing you but can't say when.

It was past six o'clock on that first Saturday night when I saw Digger Blackwood's figure coming over the square. Marvin had gone home. He was singing with a glee club and they had an engagement.

Digger had a loping gait, like a lurcher: head down, ears back, eyes watchful. He peered through the window then tried the door. I was going to ignore him but decided to unlock the door. 'I'm sorry Marvin's gone. He closes five-thirty on a Saturday,' I said.

'Sure, I know, but I'd hoped to catch him.'

'Anything I can do. What did you want?'

'No, no. Don't trouble yourself, Miss. It was only some bread and a smidgin of butter, perhaps.'

I pulled the door wider.

'Come in. Marvin's cleared the shelves but I've half a loaf I was going to feed to the crows. You can have it and I can spare you some butter.'

'That's more than kind.'

'You're welcome.'

'Wife's broken her ankle,' he explained. 'Can't get out. I'd done the shopping but clean forgot the butter and bread. Now, how much am I owing you?' And he pulled out a fistful of money.

210

'On the house.'

'That's very good of you. Leave it to me, Miss. I'll be telling everyone about The Sampler.'

Chapter Thirty-two

Crisp leaves form pagodas of red, yellow and fairy gold in the garden and spiders twist silver-chained webs, linking together the scarlet hips of the rose bushes.

Oona writes…

Stella, my love,

Beauchamp Terrace is not the same without you and I miss you every day.

For a moment, I see Oona and myself sitting on the settee, near the table lamp, my aunt frowning over the crossword and the knitting on my lap. The knitting on my lap? I have not knitted for weeks and I have not given it a thought.

There's a little surprise for you when you come home. I'm not giving anything away yet though!

Edna comes once a week to help with the cleaning. Miss Bishop has had a nasty fall and has fractured her hip. She is nearly seventy and is giving up the business. I can have my hair done in Gosford now! Freddie Littler has bought the Old Drill Hall and is applying for permission to open a cinema. Eddie Simms has worked miracles in the garden and has a vegetable patch. We share the pickings each week. I hope you are not doing too much in the café but I think it is a lovely idea. I have taken up golf.

Longing to see you,

Auntie Oona xx

PS Mum will write soon.

I fold the letter away. If Oona had begged, I might have returned home immediately, but with no job, to what? But I could not wait in America indefinitely, even if the tea room proved a success.

As I count the money to pay Eva-Lisa the following week, she ventures a question.

'How is the business doing?'

'Everything gets eaten and there are plenty of customers.'

'Yes, but is it worthwhile?'

'It's a whole lot of work for little money, so far.'

I've come to rely on Eva-Lisa, not only for her enthusiasm but for her shrewdness, too, and I want to be honest with her.

'There are two things you could do to increase income, you know?' She looks at me through her heavy lashes and I notice her skin is improving.

'Yes?'

'Putting your prices up is one of them.'

'That would mean fewer customers, though.'

'Maybe, but profits might not be any lower. Fewer customers paying more could be the answer. Your cakes draw people in but take ages to make. Toast and sandwiches would be quicker and could bring in as much money.'

She watches my reaction nervously. 'I hope I've not said the wrong thing but you're working real hard. We could do a "lunch-time special" – omelettes or pasta, so people come in to see what's different.'

'You've really thought it through, haven't you,' I say, impressed.

Rising early to get the cakes in the oven was proving a strain. I decided Eva-Lisa's suggestions were worth trying.

At the end of the day Digger Blackwood arrived, a parcel under his arm.

'Got some presents for you, Miss,' he announces, revealing two woodblock pictures of bees and a canvas painted with a bowl of cherries, a loaf and a pitcher.

He watches for my reactions to see if I like them.

'They're lovely. Where did you get them?'

'My hobby. I paint,' he says, shyly.

'You painted them?' I'm surprised. His hands look rough with broken nails, as though he spent his days clawing rocks from hard ground.

'I went to art school but couldn't make a living. I just knock out the odd thing now and then.'

'You should do more.'

He shrugs.

'These are to repay you for what you gave the other Saturday. I thought they'd decorate your walls and I've signed them. I might get some orders if people see them.'

Before leaving, Digger hangs the paintings on the wall and I tell him they've cheered the place up no end.

Lalla's been gone a few days but I've not had time to miss her.

The sandwiches and rolls are proving a big hit and I'm making simpler cakes, like bara brith, a Welsh fruited tea loaf, and Welsh cakes with currants and spice, cooked on a bakestone.

'How about a Thanksgiving Dinner?' Eva-Lisa springs on me one morning.

'I've never cooked that in my life,' I protest.

'I'll do the cooking. Turkey, cranberry and orange stuffing, corn bread, pumpkin pie, mince pies. And I can supply the turkeys at a very good price; they're the finest birds for miles.'

'But this place is too small.'

'No. Not here. Let's get the hall where the bridge club meets.'

'I think it's going to be too much on top of the tea room,' I say dubiously.

'I'll worry about the supper. We'll think of it as a community get-together. Leave it all to me.'

It seems a tall order but if Eva-Lisa says she can, I'm one hundred per cent sure she can.

Marvin's mind appears to be in a constant whirr. Today, he asks how would it be if I took over the little flat he has at the top of the shop?

Perhaps he's hoping he'll catch me on my back foot with Lalla away.

'I can't give you an answer right now,' remembering Lalla had called him 'a cunning little fox'.

'Wait until Lalla returns, is it?' he asks hopefully and I agree.

Lalla rings to tell me the degree ceremony has gone well and she's met old friends. 'Are you managing all right, Stell?' she asks, worried.

I remember to mention Marvin's ideas for a flat.

'A little flat?' Lalla sounds puzzled.

'Since when has Marvin Whicher had a little flat at the top of the shop, I'd like to know?'

'He says I could have all of the top floor.'

'Mmm. Well he doesn't use it, I suppose. But, why would you need a flat? You're staying with me.'

'Lalla,' I said, 'I've stayed too long.'

'I like having you here.'

'Thank you. But when I came it was for a few days and now it's stretching into weeks and maybe months. Besides—'

'Yes?' she asks sharply.

'There's the question of Ethan and Taylor…Ethan works some evenings and if he and Taylor lived here you would be a ready-made babysitter. And it is Ethan's home.'

'Ethan's buying a house close by. He's too independent to live with me, so don't go worrying about him. If you want to see what Marvin's offering, I'll look at it with you when I come back. Don't make any decision yet, though.

215

'How do you feel about that?'

'If it's suitable I've made up my mind. I'm taking it,' I say firmly. 'You've got to have your home to yourself again.'

'We'll talk later. I'll have to be going now. I've a supper invitation and I don't want to keep anyone waiting.'

Chapter Thirty-three

'Don't get carried away by Marvin. Watch him. The man's a bloodsucker.'

Lalla and I are waiting for Marvin to lock the shop and show us the flat.

'Don't look too keen on the idea, even if you like it. Remember, you can back out at any time,' is Lalla's advice.

The upstairs of the shop is accessed by an outside staircase and we follow Marvin.

'The rails are rusty, but at least the steps are in good condition,' comments Lalla.

'Here we are, ladies,' says Marvin, pretending not to hear her and pushing open the door. Evening sunlight brightens the sparsely furnished room we step into. It has a faded three-piece suite, a coffee table and a corner cupboard. I like the feel of the place immediately.

'Only partly furnished,' Lalla says, inspecting the chenille three-piece suite. 'The place needs some rugs on the floor to cosy it up and where are the drapes for the windows?'

Marvin lifts his shoulders in an ambiguous fashion.

'Tenant to supply her own is it?' Lalla's enjoying herself.

'Let's see the kitchen next,' she commands.

A narrow passageway leads into a tiny kitchen, where there are some pine storage cupboards, a porcelain sink, a cooker which, though elderly, looks clean and unused, and a stool.

Behind Marvin's back, Lalla cast me a quizzical glance.

In the bedroom, there is a wooden bed minus a mattress, a bedside table and a wardrobe. A shelf, with a mirror above, serves as a dressing table.

'No one can sleep on that bed without a mattress.' Lalla shoots a glance at Marvin, who nods meekly.

'I can get a mattress easily enough. But, d'you like the flat? Does it pass inspection?' enquires Marvin.

'Stella hasn't made her mind up yet. She needs more time to think it out.'

'How long?' ventures Marvin.

'We'll let you know tomorrow.'

When we're alone, Lalla asks, 'What did you make of it?'

'I'd like to try it. It's convenient for the tea room.'

'Best to sleep on it first. I must admit it's better than I thought it would be.'

When we've exhausted the subject of the flat, I remember some newspaper cuttings Salli has sent.

'Come into the sitting room,' Lalla invites. 'I've got some musical scores to sort for an evening we're planning.'

Settling myself in a comfortable armchair, I look at Mum's letter again.

Thought you might like a gossipy read. There's lots of tittle-tattle about Princess Margaret in the papers at the moment and I know how you love royalty. Margaret is rumoured to be seeing society photographer Anthony Armstrong-Jones. Although he has no title, he is quite posh, 'crachach' *in fact.* (Mum uses the Welsh word *crachach* when she wants to say someone is upper class).

In the photographs, Margaret wears full-skirted dresses, showing off her tiny waist and enormous bosom. Her platform, peep-toed shoes are a size three, diamonds sparkle in her earlobes and her eyes are large and so innocent.

The accompanying article says that Rita Tushingham, the actress, is very similar in looks to the Princess and shows a photograph of Rita. Try as I might, I see no similarity between the two. Apparently, Tony's previous girlfriend was named Jacqui Chann, and she has dark, exotic looks, completely different from Margaret's.

Queen Elizabeth, Margaret's sister, is in some of the pictures, too. Elizabeth's face is the stronger of the two, but Margaret's jawline gives her a very determined appearance.

I imagine Margaret spending her days choosing beautiful clothes for all the overseas tours and official functions she attends. Then, over the page, there's a picture of Margaret seated at a grand piano, with a cigarette in a long holder in one hand. 'The Princess is an excellent pianist,' says the caption and underneath there's an article about Margaret's fine ear for mimicry and how she's the life and soul of any party and sparkles in the right company. After the trauma she had suffered following her decision not to marry the dashing Group Captain Peter Townsend I thought it nice that Margaret was enjoying herself. I was halfway down the page when Lalla straightened up from the music she'd been studying.

'It's getting chilly in here. I'm going to put a match to the fire. You cold?'

'I'm fine. Don't bother for me.'

'I've been longing to light a fire for a while. It brightens the room as well as being cosy,' Lalla says, watching the silver birch logs in the grate igniting.

'Like some coffee?' she asks.

When Lalla returns with the coffee I'm still engrossed in the royals.

'You reading about Margaret and her new beau?'

'Yes. I hope she's found someone at last.'

Lalla is peering at the back of my paper.

'Is that the Queen Mum, waving her arm again? Always does it. And those teeth of hers look like they could do with a good scrub. I can see the long kid gloves and the massive brooch. Might have come from a dime store by the size of it.'

I look up, surprised.

'You don't like them?'

'Oh. I don't particularly dislike them but they are so predictable. Part of their fascination, I suppose. The Queen Mum is always dressed in something flowery and pastel; white shoes on her feet that look as if they've been cleaned with that stuff you paint on tennis shoes. Then there's those heavy strings of pearls around her neck which are getting a teensy bit boring, don't you think? She seems so smug, as though she's doing everyone a favour by smiling and waving to them.'

'It says she buys most of her clothes with Norman Hartnell.'

'She should try a different dressmaker,' says Lalla acerbically, passing me a cup of coffee. 'And Princess Margaret's hair looks as if her sister has taken a Toni perm and kirby grips to it.'

Lalla sighs. 'I shouldn't be nasty. I'm getting bitter. That's what age does.'

'Nonsense. You're not old.'

'I'm older than the Queen Mum. She's fifty-nine, as old as the century, but I'm sixty-five.'

'Everything about you, the clothes you wear, the fact your hair is not permed, make you look much livelier than the Queen Mother. That cerise jumper and trousers is far more flattering than some fussy, draped dress with a matching hat and massive brooch. And besides, you're not overweight.

'Anthony Armstrong-Jones is good-looking. I hope Princess Margaret has found love again.'

I give Lalla the article.

She studies the pictures for a while. 'I wonder how her child is?'

'Prince Charles or Princess Anne?' I ask, assuming she is referring to the Queen's children.

Lalla gives me a knowing look. 'No. Princess Margaret's child.'

'But she hasn't got one,' I say. 'She's never married.'

'Since when do you have to be married to have a child?'

Sensing my confusion, Lalla is amused.

'Princess Margaret Rose, is supposed to have had a child by her Group Captain.'

'A child by Peter Townsend?'

'Didn't you know that?'

'We always have the *News of the World* and the *Sunday Times*. My aunt says she likes to see the two sides of things, but I didn't hear anything about Princess Margaret's baby.'

Whilst my mind is whirring, I remember magazine articles saying the Queen ate sparingly but Princess Margaret needed to watch her diet.

I mention this to Lalla who exclaims, 'Oh, it was a form of shorthand. Journalists are always being fed gossip. When they're afraid to come straight out with things they use a form of code.'

'Where is the child now?' I've started to assume Lalla knows everything about the royals.

Lalla tops up her coffee cup.

'First, he – it was a boy, you know – was taken to Wales, before being adopted by a couple in Kenya. I expect that's far enough away for safety. I did read that when Margaret visits Kenya the child and his adoptive mother are given a prominent position in which to stand, so Meg can see her son.'

'Really? This is all news to me.'

'Well, not so many people know about it, apparently, but it isn't something you can hide for ever. The truth always escapes, however clever people think they are at disguising it. Queen Elizabeth and her mum will probably be relieved if Margaret does marry her photographer.'

'Your newspapers are probably freer to publish things about the royals than our papers are,' I decide.

'We're not so reverent over here because we see people as human beings rather than pantomime characters. You've always got to read between the lines if you want to get to the interesting bits. Newspapers have to be sold and scandal goes down well anywhere in the world.

'I've some chocolate somewhere,' says Lalla rising to her feet.

'Oh, not for me, thank you,' I say.

When Lalla returns from the kitchen she brings two glasses of wine and some Valrhona chocolate.

I protest, but Lalla presses a glass into my hands. 'Wine is good for you. And chocolate. Let's have a treat.'

'Lovely,' I say, raising my glass. I thought we'd exhausted the topic of the royal family but Lalla soon returns to them.

'George VI, Elizabeth and Margaret's father, wore make-up in the evening.'

I took a mouthful of the wine and swallowed it without tasting.

Lalla was getting into the swing of things now, I could see.

'They say the Queen was a result of artificial insemination, if you know what I mean. Apparently, George VI was not too keen on that type of thing, so the rumour goes. Now, the Queen Mum, there's a deceptive little lady, who looks as though apple pie wouldn't melt in her mouth.'

'Why. What has she been up to?' This conversation was becoming stranger and stranger.

'Lessons in the potting shed with Sir Kenneth Clark.' There is a note of triumph in Lalla's voice.

'What type of lessons?'

'Art History.'

I try hard not to laugh. 'Is that so?'

'Who knows? But, apparently, when Sir Ken learnt that Lizzie and

George did not get up until mid-morning after a night on the tiles, he decreed that, whatever time they rolled home to Buckie Palace, they must be up, dressed and seated at the breakfast table by nine o'clock the next morning.'

'And were they?'

'Well when Lizzie told George this, he exploded. "No more lessons in the garden shed," he said, putting an end to that relationship. It got them out of bed in the mornings, though.'

Lalla was beginning to sound like a Palace insider.

'It would be nice for Margaret to marry, though,' I conclude.

'Have you ever—' begins Lalla, before cutting into her own sentence. 'I'm sorry. That's prying. Don't answer.'

'Ever what? Ever had a boyfriend? Ever been in love?'

Lalla twists the stem of the wine glass between her fingers until the liquid swirls round and around in a dark vortex.

'I've had a boyfriend and I sort of loved him once.'

'What changed things?'

This is a really difficult question. I think hard before answering. 'It was partly my job coming to an end. Everything looked different after that. I'd been discontented for a while, tired of small-town life, but afraid to change things. I compared my life to my friend, Carol's. I wanted to be more adventurous, like her.'

Lalla nods, interested in what I'm saying.

'Connor, the boy I was seeing, is a farmer. He wanted to marry me but I would never have left Stanton if I had. I suppose I didn't love him enough.'

Lalla throws another log onto the fire.

'I loved someone once.' I detect a wistfulness in Lalla's voice.

'Ethan's father?' I speak carefully, for she has said she's divorced.

'I don't mean him.'

'After you parted you fell in love again?'

Lalla stares at me, defiantly.

'I was married when I met someone else.'

The log rolls to the front of the fire and she pushes it to the back of the grate with the toe of her shoe.

'I'd been married ten years to Ted, my husband, when a new consultant came to the hospital where I was theatre nurse.'

Little flames flicker in the fire, green, like Indian emeralds and blue, like sapphires.

'Most consultants were pretty good but this one was excellent. I admired his skills but, more than that, there was something about him that drew me. Some of the doctors barely acknowledged you but Al always greeted me and explained what he was going to do during an operation. I'd have the instruments ready for him, second guessing what he needed. Afterwards, when I got him a coffee, he'd talk about how he thought the operation had gone. He made me feel valued, I suppose.'

She shifts in her chair, a small figure in the lamplight. Her head is bent but she glances my way.

'One thing led to another – always does. You like someone; you find it hard to stop yourself. In the end you want to own them.'

She studies her hands for a moment, allowing memories to surface.

'I'd watch for his car. The minute it was in the parking lot I'd feel better. It was just knowing he was close by. I loved everything about that man. Yes, OK, women fall for doctors like they fall for Divines or military men in uniform. Something of the saviour element about them, I guess. But I'd worked with doctors for years and most of them left me cold. And I was married, not meant to be looking.'

The table lamp softened Lalla's face and she appeared as a younger, more vibrant version of herself.

'I knew things weren't right in my marriage. There was no more I could do to fix it. I found it hard to draw away from Al. Each time he came into a room I'd try not to look, not to give the game away. I wanted to keep my passion a secret. I never discussed him with any of the other nurses; I tried to keep everything strictly professional in the hospital.'

She gave a helpless little sigh. 'He had everything you'd look for in a man. They say love is blind but that is a lie. I could have traced his outline, everything about him, in my sleep. When I closed my eyes, he was there. His was the image I saw first thing in the morning, not Ted's.'

Looking directly at me, she says, 'I've experienced true love,' but in the cadence of her speech I hear the sadness of loss.

'Your husband, Ted? Did he find out?'

'Ted might have been dead for all I cared. The relationship had long been over.'

I felt like an intruder, as though Lalla had been lulled into telling me more than she had meant to.

'I had an affair,' Lalla says simply.

She picks up a cigarette from the packet she keeps on the little table by the arm of her chair and slips it in her mouth, lights it and inhales deeply.

'I thought I loved Ted when I married him. I was already thirty, which was late for a woman and I felt he was my last chance. There was no grand passion on my side but I think he really was in love with me. He was a careful man, thought twice before he did things, the sort of man who never let anything go to waste. I remember telling my mother he could take a shower and dry himself on a facecloth to save wetting a towel. At first, that sort of things is amusing but, as time go by, it becomes annoying.

'I wanted someone who could drink the last drops of brandy and enjoy it, without caring if he left some for the next time but that was not Ted. He was incapable of the grand gesture, but that wasn't his fault.'

225

She takes a deep breath, as though something is impelling her to go on. I don't want her to regret tomorrow what she tells me tonight.

'We had Ethan and did all the expected things. Settled down, bought a house. I did fancy things with tomatoes, filled them with fresh peas, collected finger bowls, water jugs, heavy vases to serve celery in with Graham Crackers and cheeses on a Friday night. "Fair Isle" food, but I was pleased with myself.

'My interest in home life faded after meeting Al. He was twenty years older than me and did not have many years to go before he would be due for retirement. One summer, he took his wife for a cruise to Europe, but in the first few days of the voyage, what do you think? He had a massive heart attack and died.'

She stubs her cigarette out.

'How did I know? News came back to the hospital. Everyone was stunned.

'All the time I had been seeing Al I said not a word to Ted but, as soon as Al died, I told him and moved out. I could have buried the affair but I could no longer go on living with him, because he could never have understood a grand passion. To stay with him would have belittled what Al and I had shared.

'And Ted's feelings? I think he got over it eventually, but it hurt him. He was shocked. I had been the pastor's wife but never fitted into the role easily.' Lalla stops abruptly to ask, 'Why am I telling you all this?'

'Because you've never told anyone before?'

'I've not talked about it; people knew, but I wasn't bothered, because what I had with Al was a kind of madness.'

She gulped down the last of the wine in her glass.

One of the logs rolled out of the fire onto the hearth and I moved to scrape the charred pieces back into the fire.

'Leave it,' Lalla says, almost fiercely. 'Don't fuss.'

I pat her arm.

226

'No need to pity me, Stella. I knew love and passion.' She looks at me, almost wearily. 'Some people don't get to experience it, but I did.'

Abruptly, her mood lifts.

'Come on.' She gets up quickly. 'I said I'd find that recipe for angel cake and I will.'

Chapter Thirty-four

Angel kiss cake

One cup sugar, pinch salt, two stiffly beaten egg whites, one-and-a-half cups all-purpose flour, three tsps baking powder, small cup scalded milk, one tsp vanilla essence, apricot jam. Thick cream and fresh grated coconut to decorate.

The last weeks of October are dazzling, with all the signs that the earth must bunker down a while to give itself renewal, another beginning.

I'm ready for my first customer of the day, when Digger Blackwood arrives.

'Kira's been busy. She's sending you these. Wants to know if you can make use of them.' He swings the rucksack off his back and brings out a pile of linen napkins.

'We had a clean-out over the weekend and she found these at the back of a cupboard. Right away, she says, "Go and ask Stella if she wants them."'

'All washed and pressed,' he says, lifting one up for my inspection.

Cream with a braided red edging, they were just what I needed and told him so.

'They'll be more than useful. Thank her from me.'

'No need for thanks. We're glad of the cupboard room. We'd never use them, no; not once in a paper moon, we wouldn't.'

'How's Kira's ankle?'

'Oh, getting better, but can't put much weight on that foot of hers, not even if a tram came heading her way.'

When Digger has gone I ponder what might help Kira. Mamma Catherine had a recipe, known as 'kill or cure' to Salli, but Oona swore by it. I knew it off by heart.

Take six new laid eggs, warm from the hen (if you've got one), otherwise you'll have to use the freshest eggs you can get hold of. Wash the eggs carefully then place them in an earthenware crock. Douse them in a pound of coarse brown sugar, four silver thimbles of ground ginger, the juice of three lemons and half a bottle of smugglers' brandy (a hard one, that). Cover the bowl with a plate and store for three weeks in a cool dark place, like a pantry, at the end of which time the eggshells should have melted. Beat the resulting dark, treacly mixture with a wooden spoon, then strain through a muslin cloth into a basin. Next, stir in a pint of pouring cream and bottle until required. A tablespoon should be taken three times a day until the patient has recovered or the eggnog has finished.

The only snag with this recipe is the three weeks you have to wait for it to mature.

Auntie Oona has her own way of thinking about these things. For a nurse, she can be very unscientific. Oona believes, like Mamma did, that the body functions best when it is regularly purged. She likes to soak senna pods in water overnight and drink the liquid in the morning.

I was given syrup of figs and, much to Salli's annoyance, would ask for more because I liked the taste.

'All these emetics,' Salli would say when Oona was out of earshot, because she hated to argue with her, 'are entirely unnecessary. All that is needed is plenty of fresh fruit and vegetables and nature will do the rest.'

Oona maintained that a bodily purge produced a corresponding mental lift.

I decide to give Kira some cakes which, though not as effective as the purges, would be a whole lot more socially acceptable.

A few minutes later, Lalla arrives and marvels at the light-as-a-feather cake that sits on a glass stand in front of her.

'I've never made an angel kiss cake as good as that, even when I've held my breath whisking it together,' she says admiringly. 'It just goes to prove my theory that cake makers are born, not made.'

'I was concerned about the oven temperature but I must have got it right, because it's quite pale.'

'The coconut is lovely and moist and smells delicious,' Lalla notices.

Then I tell her about Kira's napkins.

'You haven't met her, have you? My,' and Lalla looks around furtively in case she's being overheard, 'that woman has teeth like a horse, a great big cart horse. I couldn't say this to her face, but her teeth are like granite slabs. How she could be attractive with teeth like that beats me,' and she rolls her eyes before adding, 'but she is attractive, though.'

I look enquiringly.

'Once the bridge club hired a coach for a day's outing. We had some spare seats so Digger and Kira came along. Men like Tom Layton, the old fool, and Bennie Jarvis, both widowers, buzzed around her. There were other women there, unattached, but it was Kira who was getting all the attention. As for Digger, I've never seen a man so frightened. He clung to her like shit to a blanket.'

Lalla grabs my arm.

'Sorry, darling. I know you're not used to that sort of language.' She muses. 'I think her attraction lies in a warm personality and a sort of flair that draws men to her.'

I was surprised how interested Lalla was in Kira.

'Take her dress sense, if that's the expression I'm looking for. Always looks as though she's heading for somewhere exotic. Maybe it's to do with her mind. Y'know, she wants to escape to a tropical island, can't, but gets the dress out anyway.' She shakes her head in wonderment.

'The other day it was a sleeveless dress in a big check, more suitable for a horse blanket than a frock. On the coach she ate brown sugar and condensed milk sandwiches. No wonder her ankle is slow to heal. It's to do with poor nutrition, I guess.'

As we got busy Dora Goldstein arrived and ordered Spanish Cortado, an espresso cut through with hot milk. I left Eva-Lisa in to make it, because it was new to me.

When Dora came to pay the bill she commented, 'That was good. Is it worth asking for the recipe for that angel cake?'

'Did you like it?'

'It was divine. "Angel kiss cake?" It's the only kiss I'm likely to get,' she smiles. 'Tell me, what's the secret? How come it's so light?'

'There's no shortening for a start.'

'No butter?'

'No. Just egg whites and hot milk to hold it together.'

'That's some recipe, Stella. I tell you what. You show me how to make that cake some time and I'll look out some unusual recipes for you.'

'Thank you. I didn't know you were a keen cook?'

'Used to be when we travelled a bit and lived here and there. I always collected local recipes, different things, you know.'

'I'll tell you when I'm making it again and I'll write all the instructions down.'

'Thanks,' she says, giving me a wink.

Chapter Thirty-five

This is my last week as Lalla's guest. I'm renting Marvin's flat and moving at the end of the week.

On Sunday Lalla asks if I would like to join her and Taylor for a picnic. She'll take the car two miles down the road to Staceyland Park and we'll feed the ducks and play ball. 'Ethan has paperwork to sort so I am taking Taylor off his hands. Forget about cooking anything. We can have rolls and fruit and there's a vendor selling paper cup coffee in the park. In the fresh air, the coffee doesn't taste so bad.'

Despite what Lalla said I've brought chocolate cornflake cakes and lardy scones. A picnic without something sweet never seems right. I wrap apples and some chocolate for Taylor.

We've arranged to pick Taylor up on the way to the park but before we leave, Ethan rings to say he is on his way over with Taylor.

Ten minutes later, Ethan's car comes up the drive.

Taylor runs in and whoops, 'My dad's coming too.'

'What happened to the paperwork?' inquires Lalla, when Ethan appears at the door.

I look at Ethan in his beige linen trousers and light-coloured shirt. His hair is thick, quite short on the sides, long on top.

'I ditched it. The weather's too good to miss. I'll catch up on it later.'

The days are cooler now, but still warm. In Staceyland Park, Lalla sits and watches Ethan throw balls to Taylor who bats them as hard as he can and I run to field them.

When Lalla calls us to eat, I'm feeling hungrier than I have in a long time.

At the end of the afternoon, before leaving the park, Taylor has a request.

'Please Dad can we stay with Grandma tonight?' he pleads

'Not tonight. Next week, maybe. You need a good hot shower. Just look at your knees.'

'Can Stella come home with us if we can't stay with Grandma?'

I pat his head. I don't want this day to end either.

'I have to get up early tomorrow. I have cakes to bake.'

'How early?'

'Oh, just as the birds are waking up?'

He thinks about this for a moment.

'You'll be needing supper and a story before you go to sleep,' says Ethan.

'But, Dad, I'm not tired,' protests Taylor.

When Ethan and Taylor drive away, I feel an unexpected sadness. Ethan is thirty-five. To stop my thoughts from going any further, I riffle through my recipe file and check the ingredients for velvet cake which I'm planning on making soon.

The next morning I'm about to put a homity pie into the oven when Marvin calls me. There's a transatlantic call from Wales waiting for me. Holding the pie dish, I hurry to the phone.

It's Salli. She rang Lalla's number but I'd left for the tea room.

'Nothing to worry about, darling, but Auntie Oona has been taken to hospital.'

The dish slithers from my hand, spins then shatters into tiny pieces: crushed shells, pearls, broken worlds.

'She's had a slight heart attack but is doing fine. She's out of danger and should be home in a few days' time.'

Mashed potatoes, pastry, herbs, garlic, onions, cheese form a mountain ridge on the floor.

Marvin has been standing in the shadows, watching closely and he comes forward now and puts his arm around my shoulders.

It's difficult to speak but I manage to tell Mum I will ring back within the hour.

'Don't worry, don't worry, don't worry,' rings in my ears, Mum's voice over and over again.

Then Lalla arrives. Salli has explained everything to her about Oona.

'I've made a reservation for you on a later flight today; I hope that's all right, honey?'

I nod gratefully.

Eva-Lisa arrives then.

'I'll just have to close. Take whatever you want from the tea room and then perhaps you can tidy up.'

Eva-Lisa hugs me.

'Let me run it for you, just until you come back.'

'Thanks,' I say, my thoughts swirling like Catherine wheels in my head.

'We better leave,' urges Lalla.

Once in the car Lalla says, 'I'll drive you to the airport when you've packed a bag.'

I feel kindness showering on me, like a sparkling fountain. Lalla waits with me until my flight number is called and I have to board.

'I'll ring you as soon as I can,' I promise. We hug each other.

'Take care and lots and lots of love to everyone in Stanton,' calls Lalla as I give a final wave.

Chapter Thirty-six

On the flight home I doze, light from the cabin bobbling my face, strange voices serrating my dreams.

From out of the velvet darkness, Marvin Whicher appears. I know it's him because there are black-eyed beans in the sockets where his eyes used to be. 'Stella, honey, why did you leave me? Don't you love me? I'm lonely, just got the bugs to keep me company now.'

There's no one sitting by me and I'm alone with my thoughts. A peaceful atmosphere descends on the cabin. On the flight over, I was excited, wondering what I'd find in the States. Now, I know that endings can be swifter than beginnings.

Hours into the flight the captain's voice breaks the silence.

'The wind that held the plane up on the way over is blowing us back quickly. We should make Heathrow on scheduled time. The weather in London is warm for the time of the year. Enjoy the rest of your flight.'

The flight is due in Heathrow at one o'clock in the morning and it arrives at five minutes past one.

When the plane has touched down and I'm through customs I realise that although I've hardly had any sleep for hours, I have an energy that overrides tiredness.

Then, as I'm looking for a taxi to Paddington, I hear someone calling my name, 'Stella, Stella. Over here.'

It's Tom.

'Oh, you shouldn't have bothered to come,' I exclaim, 'but it's lovely to see you.' And I mean it.

He gives me a kiss and this is the first time I've ever felt any connection to him.

'I've got a tankful of petrol and I'll drive you back to Stanton.'

But I prefer to go by train. 'I'd like to be alone a while longer.'

He nods. 'I understand. It's all been so sudden. Come on, I'll drive you to Paddington.'

Fortunately, we do not have long to wait.

'At least, this train goes straight through. It means you won't have to change at Swansea. Try to relax for a few hours,' Tom advises. 'I'll ring later.'

We leave the station and are swallowed into the deep blackness of the night. When I've dozed, I wake to a yellow dawn. We've left England behind and it's Welsh countryside all the way now. Nearer Stanton, rivers, tidal estuaries, mud flats, marshland, gleam in the early morning light. It's still the same coastline, but so different now I've been away.

As the train slows for Stanton, I gather my belongings. I almost cry with relief when I notice a familiar grey-and-white car parked under some pine trees. As I step from the train, Mum and Freddie Littler come to meet me.

'Stella, I can't believe it, darling, you're back.' Mum's thrown a turquoise cashmere wrap over black trousers. She pulls me to her. 'Auntie Oona will be so pleased to see you, too.'

Mr Littler comes forward to shake my hand. 'How was America? It seems no time since you've been gone. June was it?'

He picks up my case and nods at the station clock, which shows eight-thirty. 'Train's on time, too.'

'How did you know I'd be on this train?'

'Tom rang first thing this morning,' Mum says.

Freddie drives quickly over the Parrog, up the hill, slowing for the steep bend at the top.

'Auntie Oona's much better. They think it was only a mild attack. She just needs some rest before she'll be able to come home.'

'I'd like to see her. Could we go now?' I wonder.

Mum looks doubtful. 'Perhaps they'd allow a few minutes, we could try.'

'Aren't you tired?' Freddie asks.

'I'd just like Auntie Oona to know I'm here.'

'They may let you in for a few minutes,' Freddie thinks, turning into the hospital.

There's a ward sister near the main reception and I ask to see my aunt.

'Just ten minutes, then,' she says.

As I follow the nurse to my aunt's room I catch a glimpse of my dishevelled appearance in a mirror. A bath and clean clothes will be my first priority this morning, I decide.

I'm feeling nervous, wondering if Auntie Oona will look very ill, which might upset me, but she's sitting up in bed wearing a white jersey nightdress and a blue bedjacket with a pie-crust frill around the neckline when I see her.

'Stella, Stella,' she cries, holding out her arms.

Tiredness makes me dizzy. A little girl in a cotton dress and crocheted bolero runs to her mother. I know those two. It's Oona and me.

There's another scene now. It's a young Oona holding a baby Stella. We're both wrapped in a shell-pink shawl, spinning through the darkness in a peapod to stop at Number One, Beauchamp Terrace.

I remember the sky, even now, even though twenty years have gone by. It was brilliant black with a powdering of salt-blue stars.

My aunt's arms pull me close, and the words '*Cariad fach Mammie*' are whispered so softly I scarcely hear them, but I do. My mother has uttered them, for her own comfort, perhaps, but I catch them.

A tear, bright as a faceted diamond, glistens on Oona's cheek. She pretends to sneeze and wipes it away with a fine lawn handkerchief.

'Your mum brought the flowers,' she says, indicating the vase of bronze chrysanthemums on the windowsill. 'Their perfume is lovely but it does get up my nose sometimes.'

Then I place my cheek next to Oona's, enjoying the softness of her skin, the closeness of mother and daughter.

The nurse comes in with pills and a jug of water. It's time to go.

'I'll be back later,' I tell her.

Chapter Thirty-seven

Waves of relief and a sense of completeness sweep over me as Freddie's car pulls up in Beauchamp Terrace. Mum – I've always called Salli 'Mum' and really there is no point changing now – invites him in.

'I'll call later,' Freddie promises. 'You need to get to bed, Stella, you've been travelling for hours.'

'Freddie's so good to have around,' Mum says, when he's gone. 'He's very fond of Auntie Oona, too.'

Mum hugs me again, examining me closely.

'You're not worrying, now are you? Auntie Oona's much better. She'll be home soon. You must be starving. I'll make an omelette and toast, with plenty of tea. How's that?'

'I'll just change into a dressing gown. My clothes are sticking to me.'

'It'll all be ready when you come down.'

I'm pleased everything is just as it was when I left. Nothing has changed. Today, the squeaky floorboards on the landing are creaking with happiness because I'm back.

Entering the bedroom, nothing prepares me for what awaits.

I gasp and laugh out loud. Reds and golds glow like a room from an Eastern Palace, just a little smaller.

There's a red glass chandelier, a padded silk bedhead, big white pillows and a painting on the wall of cherry blossom, white curtains at the window. The room is vibrant without being cloying. A huge mirror dominates one wall. It is more beautiful than I could have

239

imagined. I'm reeling with wonder when I hear Mum's footsteps approaching.

'Do you like it, Stell? Is it how you imagined it would be?'

'I love it. Adore it. How did this happen?'

'Auntie Oona knew you liked Penelope's ideas, so she asked her to decorate the room so you'd have a surprise.

'Auntie Oona would have loved to have seen your face, but she'll be home in a few days.'

'I can't wait for visiting to tell her how lovely it is.'

During breakfast Mum insists I go to bed as soon as we've eaten.

'It's getting on for ten-thirty, darling,' she laughs. 'Sleep for as long as you like.'

'It's lovely, just lovely, to be home again.'

'And you've got a new bedroom.'

'It's just what I wanted. So different from my old one.'

I didn't make it for afternoon visiting. When I awoke it was four-thirty by the clock and I was still tired. The house was quiet and there was no sign of Mum, so I guessed she had gone to the hospital.

After a quick bath I slipped into a pair of last winter's trousers with the silk blouse that Mum had given me and Maggie Hibbert had so admired.

I'd got used to coffee in Sayville but now I'm home I want tea. Heading to the kitchen to put the kettle on a knock on the door stops me. It's Freddie Littler.

'I hope I haven't disturbed you,' he says. 'Could you give these chocolates to your aunt? I won't be visiting tonight. You and she need time alone.'

'You've been so kind,' I reply, taking the gift. 'Come inside. It's your Thursday half-day, so I'm not keeping you from the shop, am I?'

'How was America? I might go there some day. You surprised quite a lot of people when you went, but not me. I always knew you had a bit of spirit in you.'

240

I smile weakly at the compliment.

'I expect Stanton's not big enough for you now you've been away?' he asks, his eyes twinkling.

'It's lovely being back. I didn't realise until yesterday how much I'd missed everybody.'

'Oona will be glad you're back.'

Outside, some leaves tap at the window in a splurge of orange.

'I've always admired Oona, Salli too, of course. Years ago, I was a pharmacist in Queen Charlotte's, where your aunt was nursing. She had an energy that was so attractive but I knew she had someone special at the time.'

'I admired', 'she had': a conjugation of verbs, the unravelling of something buried. I had a falling sensation. Everything slows, like when you're falling and you wonder where the pain will get you.

My breath becomes shallow and I study the lozenge pattern on Freddie's woollen Argyle socks, the punched pattern in his leather shoes; the creases of his trousers.

'I never married. I suppose I held the image of Oona in my mind. After her fiancé was killed in a car crash in Ireland, I lost touch with her for a while.'

Freddie looks at me gravely. 'Over the last few weeks, she and I have spent a lot of time together. It stirs memories.'

He glances at his watch. 'I'm just an old bore and I have to get back to the shop.' He rises to his feet. 'If you want me, you know where I am. Call me any time. And if you don't mind taking the chocolates—'

'I've brought a few different shades of nail varnish. Which one would you like, Oona?'

My aunt came home from hospital this afternoon and the three of us are on the settee.

Oona looks at the nail polish but is more interested in what happened to me in America. 'Tell me about The Sampler, Stell, and you'll have to write to Lalla or ring her soon. She'll want to know what's happening here.'

After we've been talking for a while the room becomes warm and I start to drift in and out of sleep. I hear my aunt talking, saying the time has come when they really must explain everything. 'I know you and Dadda said it didn't matter what other people thought, but I couldn't face the gossip there would have been in a small place like this.'

'Say nothing yet. Wait until you're stronger and we'll think about the best way to do it. I'll go to see to the tea.'

I don't move for a long while, pretending to be asleep.

Next day, Mum goes to have her hair done in Gosford and Auntie Oona and I are alone.

Now my aunt is home from hospital, her fingers glow with Mamma's turquoise rings and Mamma's wedding ring is on her little finger.

I hold her hands. 'I love the pink in old gold.'

'Stella,' I know the tone of my aunt's voice and I have an idea a difficult topic might arise. 'Stella, there are some things I should have told you a long time ago.'

Her eyes search my face. I don't want anything spoiling this day.

'There's no need. I heard you and Mum yesterday when I was half asleep on the settee.'

'You did?'

My aunt looks relieved.

I nod. 'There's no need to say anything. I think I always knew I belonged to you. It's something I can't explain, but I did know you were my mother.'

My mother's been listening intensely.

'It was a difficult situation for me. I just didn't know what to do. If

242

people thought Salli was your mother, it simplified things, or so I thought at the time.'

'Sometimes talking too much about things spoils what is,' I say.

'And what is?'

'It's you and me and Mum. It's all I ever wanted and needed. You are my mother and I am your daughter.' I hug her tightly.

I twist Mamma's ring around Oona's finger and realise the ring is slack.

'You've lost weight. I'll do some baking. I'll make Boston cream pie. That'll tempt your appetite.'

'Thank you, Stell. Thank you for the baking and thank you for understanding.'

'Freddie Littler is keen on you, I think.'

'We're fond of each other: that's all.'

'I think he is in love with you.'

My aunt's face assumes a serious expression. 'He may be in love with me, but I'm not in love with him, not in the least.'

'No?'

'No. I don't believe in romantic love.'

'No? Why's that?'

Oona smiles. 'I know about the love between a mother and child. It's the lasting kind, but romantic love… And as for Freddie, he's just a friend. Besides, I like my life as it is.'

That night I dream of Oona bathing me, Salli putting me to bed. Sometime's I am Oona's daughter, other times I belong to Salli.

Next day Mum and I discuss the arrangements for Auntie Oona's convalescence.

'Edna is willing to do extra hours for us, she told me last week,' my aunt explains.

'I can always come on the train, any time I'm needed,' Mum offers.

Then Mum pats the seat beside her. 'Come and sit by me for a moment, Stell. There are things I think I should tell you. Auntie Oona

243

is wonderful but sometimes she's hopeless at saying things,' and she laughs ruefully.

'D'you mean the fiancé who was killed?'

Mum seems surprised.

'You know, do you?'

'I think I've finally pieced it together.'

And before we can say more the telephone rings. It's the international operator and it's a call for me. While I wait to be connected, I study the photo of Dadda riding Dysart that hangs on wall above a picture of Mum, Auntie Oona and myself.

Then I look at the rug Mamma sewed, the colours alive and bright like liquorice, mulberry, rose adder, spindrift, bottle green. The pattern is intricate, fresh and intense, sewn with her heart and her soul and with all the love and passion of this family.

A few clicks down the line and it's Ethan's voice.

'Stella, I had to ring. How're things that end? Did you get back all right?'

Then Taylor butts in, 'Ask Stella when she's coming to see us, Dad.'

'When are you coming back? Taylor misses you.'

'Don't you miss me?' I ask but before he can answer, I can hear Lalla's voice in background and Ethan explains he's on the phone to me. 'It's Stella, Mom. Stella.'

'Stella, have a word with Mom.'

'Stella. I've put a letter in the post. I didn't like to ring in case you were busy seeing to your aunt.'

'She's fine now, much better and out of hospital.'

'You've got to come back, Stella.'

'What's happening with The Sampler?'

'Eva-Lisa is running it and Dora Goldstein is helping her bake the fancy cakes. My goodness, who would have thought it of Dora but she's turned out to be a real trouper. The cakes are not as good as yours, mind. I'll call you next week but I'm putting you back to Ethan, it's his call, after all.'

'Stella, you've got to come back. Taylor wants us to take him to see the Chrysler building, go skating in Central Park. Now, tell me when are you coming back? Give me a date to look forward to, Stella.'

After a long while, I put the phone down. An ocean and fifteen years difference in our ages separate Ethan and me, but Taylor wants me to take him skating.

I go to my bedroom, and in the silence Ethan's voice calls my name.

'Stella. Stella.' My name floats through the sky, like white light condensing on leaves, on flowers, like oil floating on water.